Yeats is Dead!

Yeats Is Dead! is a novel written by fifteen Irish writers, a fundraising project intitiated and developed by the Amnesty Education Trust. In recent years founder members of the Trust organised two large-scale comedy shows in Dublin, which were later televised by ITV. This novel is the third in an ongoing series of fundraising events involving Irish artists in support of Amnesty. All of the authors' royalties from *Yeats Is Dead!* will be used to support Human Rights education, particularly for children and teenagers. Among the projects the book will fund is the provision of Human Rights educational materials and discussion opportunities for primary school children in both parts of the island of Ireland.

Thank you for your support.

YEATS IS DEAD!

A NOVEL BY FIFTEEN IRISH WRITERS

Edited by Joseph O'Connor

JONATHAN CAPE
LONDON

Published by Jonathan Cape 2001

2 4 6 8 10 9 7 5 3 1

First published in Great Britain in 2001 by
Jonathan Cape
Random House, 20 Vauxhall Bridge Road,
London SW1V 2SA

The Random House Group Limited Reg. No. 954009
www.randomhouse.co.uk

Yeats is Dead! is a work of comic fiction. No similarity with any actual person is intended, nor should any be inferred.

A CIP catalogue record for this book
is available from the British Library

ISBN 0-224-06175-5

Papers used by The Random House Group Limited are natural, recyclable products made from wood grown in sustainable forests; the manufacturing processes conform to the environmental regulations of the country of origin

Typeset by Palimpsest Book Production Limited,
Polmont, Stirlingshire

Printed and bound in Great Britain by
Mackays of Chatham PLC, Chatham, Kent

They left St Gerand on 14 December 1940 at 3 o'clock in the morning, and made their way slowly but without incident to Zurich, where they arrived on 17 December.

In Zurich Joyce stayed at a pension and lived quietly. He walked about with his grandson and told him stories; he made a few notes which unfortunately do not indicate with what sort of book he would next have boarded English literature.

On 13 January 1941, at 2.15 in the morning, Joyce died.

Richard Ellmann, from the introductory notes to the final chapter of his *Selected Letters of James Joyce*, 1975

Yeats is Dead!

Chapter One: by Roddy Doyle

'I think he was dead before I shot him.'

'I beg your pardon?' said Roberts.

'I think he was dead,' said Nestor. 'Already. Before . . . you know.'

Roberts looked down at the dead man.

'He was *talking* to me,' Roberts said. 'He was right in the middle of a fucking sentence.'

'But.'

'"Tell her I'll have it by . . ." if I recall it correctly.'

'But.'

'And now,' said Roberts, 'we'll never know what he was going to say. Tonight? Christmas? The light of the silvery moon? Holy *Jesus*, what a mess.'

'But,' said Nestor.

'Yes?' snapped Roberts.

'He went really pale, like, and he' – Nestor grabbed his left tit – 'Well, he . . .'

'Clutched?' Roberts offered.

'Yeah,' said Nestor. 'He clutched his chest.'

'He had a heart attack. Is that what you're telling me?'

'Yeah,' said Nestor. 'He looked terrible. His face. I've seen it before. I've a cousin.'

'Who had a heart attack.'

'Yeah.'

'And he looked just like that.'

'Yeah.'

'And he's still alive.'

'Yeah.'

'Oh good,' said Roberts. 'Maybe our friend here will stand up in a minute and shake himself. But hang on, though. You didn't shoot your cousin, sure you didn't?'

'Well no.'

'And why would you have?' said Roberts. 'Sure, he's your cousin.'

'. . . I,' said Nestor.

And then Roberts hit him. Hard.

'What'll I do with you?' Roberts said.

And he hit him again, another almost friendly whack across the ear, harmless but for the car keys clasped between his fingers.

Nestor ducked away to a corner. He knocked over a pouffe and the mug of tea perched on it, placed there by the dead man four, five minutes before, just as Roberts had knocked on his door and walked in with Nestor.

'That'll stain,' said Roberts.

The rug, the shaggy fleece of a synthetic sheep, was already soaking up the tea. Roberts took the centre pages from the *Daily Mirror* beside the pouffe and placed then gently over the stain. He patted the paper.

'So,' he said.

Nestor was examining his ear. His right hand was still holding the gun. He drew back his head and nutted the wall. It clanged.

The dead man's home was made of tin. In a field near Courtown or Skerries it would have been a mobile home. Here, in the filthy backyard of a ruined cottage on the edge of the very edge of Dublin, it was a shack.

Four tin walls; a tin roof that was snowing rust. The caravan was lopsided, up on assorted bricks and one flat wheel, surrounded, almost invaded by nettles and weeds that swayed and stank. Hardly a thing inside, only a few stacks of mouldy old newspapers, a grimy crumpled poster of James Joyce on the wall.

Roberts owned a house in Rathmines. With the help of his sister's husband, he'd converted it into thirteen bedsits. He looked around him now; a few bits of chipboard, a couple of extra beds and he could have squeezed in four students, even six, no problem – the dead body wouldn't have been noticed in the middle of their filth and parties. The place had potential. He'd find out who owned it.

He felt it wobble when he stood upright.

'So,' he said.

Nestor had a handkerchief to his ear.

'She won't be happy,' said Roberts. 'She won't be happy at all at all.' He was talking about Mrs Bloom.

'She told us to worry him,' said Roberts. 'Does he look worried to you?'

'No,' said Nestor.

'No,' Roberts agreed. 'I don't think I've ever seen a less worried-looking man.'

'He had a heart attack,' said Nestor.

'That would account for the hole in his chest,' said Roberts.

'It was an accident.'

'You really think I'm gonna go back and tell her that, do you?'

'He clutched his chest.'

'I'll clutch your bollocks with a pliers if you ever mention his chest or his heart again. Say after me: I shot him.'

'But I didn't mean to.'

'Say it.'

'I shot him.'

'Good. Fine. Now we're getting somewhere. You shot him. He had something she wanted. We were to worry him. A few slaps, a little glimpse at the gun there. A straightforward enough job of work. But you went and shot the poor chap. Didn't you?'

'It went off.'

'Yes,' said Roberts. 'I noticed.'

'It was the gloves.'

'*What?*'

'They're new.'

'They're nice.'

'They're a bit . . .'

'Stiff?'

'Yeah,' said Nestor.

'I know the way,' said Roberts.

He toed the dead man's foot.

'It was the gloves did it, mister,' he told the body. Then he looked at Nestor again.

'What am I going to say to her?'

Nestor said nothing.

'Well?'

'I don't know.'

'And does that worry you at all?'

'Yeah.'

'Good,' said Roberts. 'Because it worries me too. It worries me a lot. And I need the company.'

Mrs Bloom wasn't exactly their boss. Neither of them was financially dependent on her. They both had day jobs, permanent and pensionable, well away from Mrs Bloom. In addition Roberts had his bedsits, and two or three other pots on the Baby Belling. He had a share in a kissogram service. He owned the '87 Lancia that ferried the French maids and naughty nurses and television continuity announcers – a Roberts invention, and a hit – out and around the city, from sad to sadder bastard, seven days a week. He held the croissant and baguette franchise in a twenty-four-hour shop around the corner from his bedsits.

'If you gave shite a nice smell you'd find plenty of people willing to buy it at four in the morning,' he told Dymphna (the nun, schoolgirl and continuity announcer).

'I know,' said Dymphna, as she cleared the steam off the passenger window and looked out for the right address.

'Talk dirty to me,' said Roberts.

'Again?'

'Go on.'

'The Flood Tribunal.'

He had a bit of set-aside near his brother's farm, down home. He had a team of twenty-three boys and girls on the road throughout the year, selling guaranteed Irish Christmas cards, made in the Philippines, for spina bifida, Bosnian hospitals and Roberts. And he had one or two other things going as well. This and that. He saw possibilities everywhere. He clicked awake at five every morning, ideas already pinging around him before he had his feet in his slippers. An entrepreneur. That was what Roberts was. 'You have to be born one,' a woman sitting beside him at a Department of Industry training seminar had once said. And Roberts had agreed with her. He had been born one.

'That bollocks still has his communion money,' it was often said of Roberts. About most people that was never meant literally, but in Roberts's case it was true, literally. Roberts's communion money, all £3 13s. 8d. of it in shiny old coins he had lovingly polished, was in a tobacco tin one foot under the sod, five paces – adult paces; ten on his communion day – to the right of the hinged gate of the field that was now his set-aside. Now the EU paid him money for doing nothing with the field. He wasn't even allowed to walk into it. There was a satellite keeping an eye on all the empty fields in Ireland, making sure that they stayed empty. But one of these cloudy nights he was going to sneak into his field, dig up the tobacco tin – Condor – and bring the gleaming contents to a coin dealer on Aughrim Street, a member of the International Association of Professional Numismatists and a subscriber to a Latvian porn magazine that Roberts distributed by hand to thirteen Dublin addresses on the first Friday of the month, between half-five and seven in the morning, before going to work. He would do it just to find out how much the coins were worth. Then he'd bury them again. In a new place.

Entrepreneur. He loved the word.

'What's that French word that means businessman?' he'd once asked his wife as he sat up to the fire pretending to do the *Independent* crossword.

'Entrepreneur,' said Patsy.

'What?' said Roberts.

'Entrepreneur.'

'Spell it for me,' said Roberts.

Nestor wasn't an entrepreneur. Along with leprosy and a ride against a train station wall, an idea was something that Nestor had never had. But still he made a reasonable living. He had the day job, of course, not that it brought in much. So four nights a week, in black bomber jacket and wired for sound, he stood at the entrance of Major Disaster's, a pub in the basement of Little Los Angeles, a carpark and total shopping experience at the top of Grafton Street, Europe's sexiest retail sewer. He let young couples and gangs of girls go past him but stopped lone men and British stag parties, if they were wearing either kilts or co-ordinated T-shirts.

'It's the national costume of Scawtland!'

'It's a dress,' said Nestor's colleague, Rattigan.

Nestor rarely spoke. He was never violent, always polite; he went to the toilet only during his breaks. He never drank, didn't smoke, never pawed drunk women. He stood in front or stood aside and, when called upon to do so by the voice in his ear, went inside and escorted people out. Rattigan, who drank, smoked and often went to the toilet against the Telecom building across the street, hated him.

'You're perfect, aren't you?'

'No,' said Nestor.

'You are, yeh cunt.'

'I'm not,' said Nestor.

'Look at you,' said Rattigan. 'Mister Perfect. This one coming up now. In the red. Would you ride her? Would you?'

Nestor didn't answer him.

'No, you wouldn't. You wouldn't even dream of it, sure you wouldn't? She's dripping for it, look at her. Look. *Look.* And the other one with her. The two of them together. The arse on the other one, lookit.'

Nestor suffered in silence. He was, in fact, gay. He admitted the women of Rattigan's crumby dreams while his heart went quietly pitter-patter for the men they kept out, the stag lads and loners, the men in kilts and co-ordinated T-shirts.

Roberts kicked the dead man's foot again.

'You're a terrible man,' he said to Nestor.

'Sorry,' said Nestor. 'Will I clean it up?'

'It?' said Roberts.

The gun was an Israeli Desert Eagle, a large and powerful pistol designed for long-range shooting. Nestor had fired it three feet away from the dead man's chest.

'It?' said Roberts. 'Have you a week?'

The back wall was drenched with bloody globules of the dead man's interior.

'"Good boys, O yes,"' Roberts said. He was imitating Mrs Bloom's voice now. '"You cleaned up after you, did you? Good boys." I don't think we'll be hearing *that* when we go back to her, do you? So I don't think we'll fucking bother!'

He moved two careful steps to the left and pushed the dead man's Superser gas heater. As he'd expected, it refused to move. Roberts owned thirteen Supersers, one in each bedsit, and not one of them moved freely on its castors.

'Will this fit in the boot, d'you think?'

'No,' said Nestor.

'On its side?'

'Maybe.'

'We might take it with us. Come here and help me.'

This was the type of thing Roberts and Nestor often did for Mrs Bloom, walking in on people they'd never met and pointing guns or fingers at them. Four times out of five when she summoned Roberts on the batphone, it was to give him a name and address and a brief instruction. 'Worry him, O yes.' Or 'Hit him, yes, twice, and tell him I was asking for him.' A simple message – sometimes a simple action – was usually all that was required. They never had to wait around for answers or merchandise. Someone else, Roberts supposed, came along later to do that; he didn't know and he didn't care. What he did know was that he was a small cog in Mrs Bloom's machinery. A tiny, minor, insignificant cog that could be whipped out and replaced any time she felt the inclination. Just like that. In a flash. He knew it. The knowledge frightened him and made him love her even more.

'We better get out of here,' said Roberts. 'You'll have to take your top off.'

'Why?' said Nestor.

He was wearing Manchester United's latest away jersey.

'It'll be remembered if we're seen leaving,' said Roberts.

'Half the men and boys in Dublin wear Man United jerseys,' said Nestor.

'Yes,' said Roberts. 'But not with their names on the back.'

'Oh,' said Nestor.

'Oh,' said Roberts. 'Is there a Batty Nestor playing at number 10 for Manchester United?'

'No,' said Nestor sheepishly. 'Teddy Sheringham.'

'Good for Teddy.'

'What'll I wear instead?'

'Something of his,' said Roberts, nodding at the dead man.

'But . . . it's covered in blood,' said Nestor.

'Not that particular shirt,' said Roberts. 'It's not your colour. Something else.'

He nodded at the door behind the dead man's head.

'In there.'

Nestor planned a route around the shattered corpse.

'Chop chop,' said Roberts.

Nestor pushed open the door and walked in. Roberts, alone now except for the dead man, really started to dread facing Mrs Bloom.

She was an extraordinary woman. She lived in a small, terraced house on the northside.

'It's handy for the airport.'

But she'd never travelled in a plane herself, had never been further from her home than Dollymount Strand. She didn't even have a passport. The first time Roberts saw her, after he'd been led through the house from the front door by Mrs Blixen, she'd been sitting in the back garden, on a papal throne, with a copybook in her lap and a biro in her hand. As he'd walked across the little patio he'd heard the roar of a plane flying low over them, a noise that increased, then slowly receded and faded away to silence as he watched her. She took a strapless watch from the pocket of her mauve duffel coat – it was a wild, cold day, a very odd day to be sitting out in the garden – and she looked at it. Then he heard her speak for the first time; to herself, or so he thought.

'EI 603 from Schiphol, O yes.'

She opened the copybook and wrote something down. Roberts knew immediately: he was in the presence of a genius. She controlled a global empire from the back garden of a corporation house, bang in the middle of the Celtic Tiger's litter tray. She made a red mark beside a column of numbers, closed the copybook, put it away.

'You come to me recommended,' she said, without looking at him.

'Can I ask by who?'

'That doesn't matter.'

He looked at her profile. Her eyes were fixed on the back wall and the three scrawny rosebushes that lined it. But he could tell that her ears were still trained on the sky. And what ears. The lug he could see had the curve and almost the size of a baby's arse. The wind pushed great healthy folds of grey hair in front of her face. She hooked the hair back behind the arse. Still staring at the wall, she spoke again.

'You are greedy, O cruel and discreet. Is that right?'

'Yes,' said Roberts.

'We'll see,' said Mrs Bloom. 'O yes.'

That was three years ago. Since then, two or three times a week, Roberts and Nestor had delivered messages for Mrs Bloom, worried and hounded for Mrs Bloom. They'd kicked down doors, broken windows, pulled hair, shoved gun barrels into mouths, held throats, spat in faces, set fire to pets for Mrs Bloom. All plain, undemanding stuff.

'She's some woman,' Roberts once said to Nestor, as they got back into the car after collecting a name and address from Mrs Bloom. 'Isn't she?'

Nestor concentrated on his seat belt.

'Isn't she?'

'She's all right,' said Nestor.

'All right? *All right?*'

'She's nice.'

'Nice!'

'Leave me alone, will you. She's old.'

'Ah,' said Roberts. 'It's the mother thing, is it?'

Nestor wanted to close down the conversation.

'Yeah,' said Nestor.

'You don't want to admit that you'd like to ride your mother. Is that it?'

'Yeah,' said Nestor.

'Fair enough,' said Roberts. And gave him a knowing wink.

Actually, it was hard to put an age on Mrs Bloom. Her hair was grey, but fantastically so; it was alive and full. It was hair to dive into and roll around in, hair to hibernate in, even die in.

Roberts picked up the empty box: Loving Care. His wife was bent over the side of the bath, wearing plastic bags on her hands and squirting black goo into the clumps of wet hair at the back of her head.

'Why do you use this awful stuff?' he said.

'To hide the grey,' said Patsy.

'You don't have to do that,' said Roberts. 'I like it.'

'Shut the door on your way out,' said Patsy.

Mrs Bloom's face was lived-in but unlined, the face of

a woman who'd rolled with life's knocks. And she had the eyes of a woman who'd become used to handing out the knocks. When she turned them on Roberts the first time, he'd wanted to run. To run at her and to run far away. They were deep, blue and fierce. They drew him in and repelled him, ordered him to come here and warned him to stay well clear.

'We'll see, O yes.'

And he'd fallen in love, as helplessly as an entrepreneur could let himself fall. He'd wanted to get down and sit at her feet. Three years later, he still had to tell his knees to hold him up when he was standing beside Mrs Bloom.

She was some woman; she really was. She had the whole word in her bag; there was no stopping her. As a teenager she'd made her money robbing shoplifters. Before that, she'd forced the other boys and girls in Mixed Infants to buy their own lunches off her. As the woman at the Department of Industry seminar had said to Roberts, you had to be born one, and as far as Roberts was concerned, Mrs Bloom had been born the biggest one of the lot.

Entrepreneur.

She'd tried her hand at most things, but drew the line at honesty. She robbed everything, as a matter of principle. Every mouthful she ate, every stitch she possessed, every one of the thousands of books that walled and shrank every room in the house, everything that wasn't already free she had stolen or ordered stolen on her behalf. Even the way she breathed made it look like she was stealing the air, gulping it down before someone else could use it. Security and technological improvements were puffing along behind her; she could crack any code or system. She'd discovered that you could open Fiats with Mini wipers, that you could decode car stereos by putting them overnight in the freezer. She owned chunks of the Cayman Islands before she stole the atlas to find out where they were. She was selling stolen heroin in Leitrim before it was ever heard of in Dublin. All without budging from the papal throne in her back garden (stolen O yes, during the Offertory of the Pope's mass in the Phoenix Park in 1979).

Roberts was mad about her.

'It suits you,' he told Dymphna, as she tried to keep the wig from sliding over her face.

'It's horrible,' said Dymphna. 'Who'd want grey hair?'

'Shush,' said Roberts. 'Keep it on. For me.'

'It's makin' me head sweat.'

'Go on. I'll get you a Magnum at the next garage.'

'A cone?'

'Okay, okay,' said Roberts. 'O yes.'

There was no Mr Bloom, as far as Roberts knew; he was dead or eaten, he presumed. Maybe buried under the rosebushes. As for kiddy Blooms, there were none of those either; no photographs in the hall or kitchen, no toys or evidence of grandchildren. There was just her magnificent self. And Mrs Blixen.

Roberts couldn't figure out Mrs Blixen. At first, he'd thought she must be the maid. The first time he had visited, Mrs Blixen had brought him through the house and out to the garden and left himself and Mrs Bloom alone. But a maid in a corporation house? Roberts had never seen a maid in any sort of house, except once in a brothel in Kinnegad. Then he decided that they might be sisters. It made more sense, except for the facts that they weren't at all alike to look at and they called each other by their surnames.

'And yes Mrs Blixen has brought O the tea.'

And there was Mrs Blixen's accent. It was funny, foreignish. On the second visit, on the way through the kitchen, Roberts had asked her where she'd lived before she came to Ireland.

'I had a farm in Aw-frica,' she'd said.

'Very nice.'

'At the foot of the Ngong hills.'

'Lovely,' said Roberts. 'And how much of that was set-aside?'

Then he'd thought that they might be lovers.

'What d'you think?' he'd asked Nestor.

'No,' said Nestor.

'What makes you so sure?' said Roberts.

'They wear cardigans,' said Nestor.

'Good point,' said Roberts. 'But does that mean that all women who don't wear cardigans *are* lesbians?'

Nestor didn't answer.

'Am I confusing you?' said Roberts.

'Yes,' said Nestor.

'Can you imagine them doing it together?'

'No,' said Nestor.

'I want you to try,' said Roberts. 'Close your eyes.'

'No.'

'Go on,' said Roberts. 'Close them.'

Nestor did what he was told.

'Now,' said Roberts. 'Can you imagine them?'

'No,' said Nestor.

'No,' Roberts agreed. 'I can't either. You can open them now.'

Which pleased Nestor; he was driving.

There was nothing going on between Mrs Bloom and Mrs Blixen. There *was* something odd about them, though. He couldn't put his finger on it. Something to do with all those books lying around the house, but he wasn't sure. He sometimes thought they were playing with him. But it didn't matter. The idea of being the plaything of those two broads kept Roberts awake and giddy, right up to getting-up time, and he didn't mind even one little bit.

Nestor was taking his time choosing a shirt.

'Hurry up,' said Roberts.

'I'm looking for something that fits me.'

'Hurry up!'

'Can I not just wear the jersey inside out?'

'*No!*'

Roberts was trying to hold back his anxiety, but it wasn't easy. He'd never messed up before. He'd always done a good job and, to be fair, so had Nestor. He really didn't know what was going to happen when he walked through Mrs Bloom's house and told her they'd shot the dead man. He'd blame Nestor, of course, and reasonably so; it'd been his finger on the trigger, after all. But he didn't know if that would be enough. And he didn't particularly want Nestor to suffer. He liked Nestor. He was a decent kid. A bit thick, granted, but very reliable. And good to his mammy.

He looked at the dead man again. He knew damn-all about him. His name: Reynolds. His address: behind the derelict cottage, O yes. The message: you have something and Mrs Bloom wants it.

That was the lot. What it was that Mrs Bloom had wanted, he had no idea; money, drugs, information – it could have been anything. Heroin, advice, his wife, shoes – there was no point searching the caravan. Whatever it was, Roberts knew it wasn't there.

You have something and Mrs Bloom wants it.

Worry the man.

Look him sternly in the eye.

Grab his lapel, if he has one.

Push his face against the wall.

Give him a dig.

Let him see the gun.

The usual.

He couldn't say what was going to happen now. He knew nothing about the dead man. Nothing at all. And he suddenly realised that he knew nothing about Mrs Bloom either, nothing that was going to be useful to him. He knew no one else in her organisation. 'You come to me recommended,' she'd said, but to this day he didn't know by whom. He wished now that he'd been more curious.

Another thought crept up behind Roberts and whacked him. He almost dropped on to the rug beside the dead man. What if Mrs Bloom was just *another cog in the machine*? What if she was simply another deliverer of messages? As ignorant and as unimportant as Roberts? And just as expendable.

He couldn't believe he'd never considered that before. The stupidity, the laziness. God almighty, he'd let himself down.

Roberts had great faith in the power of his personality. He was a good-looking man; he'd been told that quite frequently, more often than not, by women he hadn't paid to say it. But it wasn't just about being handsome; what hushed a room when he walked into it was his personality. He'd become sure of that over the years.

'It's not just my looks, sure it's not?'

'No,' said Dymphna.

'No,' Roberts agreed. 'It's something more, isn't it? And I'll tell you, Dympers. If you could bottle it you'd make a fortune.'

It probably came from the same place as his entrepreneurial stuff; he'd been born with it, whatever it was. And, whatever it was, he had it in spades.

'Strong personality. Eight letters. Begins with C.'

'Charisma,' said Patsy.

'Thanks.'

Roberts had been opening doors and legs with charisma for years. It had very rarely let him down. In the soft, cosy place at the back of his head had rested the belief that, if the worst ever came to the worst, he could always charm his way out of any trouble with Mrs Bloom; it would be hard work, granted, prising her ears and eyes from the flight-paths, but he was sure he could do it. But what if it didn't matter? What if he was lassoing the wrong pony?

'Hurry up!'

'I'm coming!'

Roberts kicked the dead man.

'Could you not have ducked?' he hissed at him.

He drew his foot back to kick again, but changed his mind. The first kick had calmed him, and he was wearing his good shoes. And anyway, his faith in Mrs Bloom had come back. She had no boss but herself. He was certain of it.

Nestor came out from behind the curtain, wearing a once-white T-shirt, CHOOSE LIFE in black, across the chest.

'Very nice,' said Roberts.

He was feeling a bit better.

Nestor had his jersey rolled up in his hand.

'Tuck that into your trousers and give me a hand with this thing,' said Roberts as he gave the Superser another experimental push.

Nestor grabbed a handful of old newspaper from the stack in the corner and went to wrap up his jersey in it. But then he stopped. Looking startled. And began reefing through the pile of newsprint.

'This paper's blank,' he said. 'All of it. All the paper in this pile is completely blank.'

'So is your brain,' said Roberts.

'Should we not go before the police come?' said Nestor.

'We are the police,' said Garda Sergeant Roberts. 'But I know what you mean. The good guys. Come on.'

He opened the door.

'Cheerio,' he said to the dead man. 'Keep in touch.'

The caravan wobbled as they stepped down from it. Garda Nestor shut the door after them.

Chapter Two: by Conor McPherson

On the surface Gary Reynolds was being very decent.

The first day off work he had ever taken and here he was mowing the lawn. What's more, the lawnmower would hardly move. It was an old push-mower he'd found in the shed when they moved in. It needed oil and general maintenance but Gary was useless at anything remotely practical. Of course he could have bought a new mower. He could have gone out right there and then, like an adult permitted to spend money and buy things in the real world, and bought a new mower. But men in hardware shops frightened him. Most people frightened him. Bank clerks, builders, doctors and nurses, barmen. They knew what they were talking about. They had his number. They were grown up and organised whereas Gary felt about nine or ten.

He was in fact thirty-two and five stone overweight. Weighing yourself was something grown-ups did. If you knew how much you weighed you might have to diet, and such decisions meant you were in charge of circumstances. You'd taken hold of your life by the scruff. And the prospect of doing that frightened Gary.

Nothing is wrong. That was his attitude. If it's not broken don't give it a belt of a hammer. Pondering your shortcomings was the type of reflection that could unsettle you. Something might *really* turn out to be wrong. And you'd have to do a right load of worrying then.

So here he was pushing a blunt mower for all he was worth. He'd been at it for about twenty minutes by now. At this rate it'd take another hour and three-quarters to finish. Not that it was a big garden: it wasn't. But it seemed like every bit he did he had to redo. The grass was all . . . tangled or something. Every so often the sun came out and baked him. He stopped and wheezed a bit. He was sweating very hard. But he was thinking about what Madelene would say when she saw that he'd done it.

He wasn't doing it for her. He was doing it so she'd have to say thanks. Force a response out of her. They were fighting again. These little wars Gary could handle. They were safe enough; he knew the territory.

They were fighting about one of the usual subjects. The way he'd spoken to her mother, at Madelene's sister's wedding on Saturday. He never really meant to be mean, but increasingly he was beginning to snap at Madelene's relations. A few pints, and the niggling insecurities he felt talking to people – waitresses, telephone operators, staff at the cash-and-carry – these would all vanish and he'd take the opportunity to assert himself. A couple of drinks and he even began not to mind his appearance. He'd be giving himself the eye in mirrors in pubs. The other night he'd mimed playing guitar to an Eagles song, checking himself out in the glass door of the china cabinet, until Madelene banged on the bedroom floor with a slipper or something and he sheepishly lowered the music.

He often sang along with whatever Larry Gogan was playing on the radio as he drove around the country.

Sometimes he'd bang the steering wheel too. At moments like that he reminded himself of Harrison Ford, banging the roof of the car in *Witness* when the Sam Cooke song comes on.

His business was providing toilet blocks for the gents' urinals in pubs. They stank up the van. They stank up his clothes. People always knew that Gary had arrived without having to look around.

He also had an undefined supportive role at the local Spar supermarket which Madelene ran. He paid visits to the cash-and-carry for Madelene, but never for perishables – everything that had a ride in the van ended up smelling of cheap air freshener. The toilet business had been passed on to Gary by his Uncle Peter. Starting a business on his own would have been far too adult. His clients were the same ones his uncle had had. He had never tried expanding or taking on help. If a business dropped off, he let it go.

There was one pub on the outskirts of Clonmel he hated going into. It was a big barn of a place with nothing doing in the daytime, just video games chirping and grunting in the desolation. The barman and regulars were Gary's classic fear. People who might – just might – be talking about him. Whenever he came in, the same four beefy old guys would be sitting at the counter and mumbling, sometimes breaking into a cackle. Gary had simply stopped going there. He was driving along one day and he just went right on past. Kept going. Didn't even look back. He felt guilty and ashamed but not for long. '*Everything's just fine*' was hammering away in his head, getting faster and faster until it was like a shrieking alarm and he had to stop the van and have a cigarette.

Thus his life revolved around the safety of soup and sandwiches in provincial hotels, and trips to the cash-and-carry in sprawling suburbia. And to Gary these held all the dark nervousness of a terrible adventure.

Sometimes the Clonmel thing still bothered him. Made him feel like less of a man. Whenever that happened he drank himself into a state where his anger was directed at absolutely everything. At Madelene's sister's wedding, Madelene's mother had watched him collapse slowly into a table during an elaborate guitar solo in 'Sweet Home Alabama'.

'Garret Reynolds, you're drunk,' she said with triumphant satisfaction as guests rallied round, heaving him out of the piles of roast beef and potatoes.

'Mrs Fenit,' he managed to blurt, 'I don't give a flying shite what you think. I'm a . . .' – he tried to think of something profound and perhaps a touch heroic – 'I'm a man! I'm a *person*! I'm a sad man and *I need some respect*!'

But he continued to lurch sideways into the back of a bridesmaid until he landed on his formidable backside with a loud fart. Of course, he did give a flying shite what Mrs Fenit thought. He gave several flying shites what everybody thought. Most of the time he wished he was invisible.

Still, he had no intention of apologising to Madelene, never mind her mother, or anyone else. Saying sorry would mean there was something wrong. And how can something be wrong when everything's fine all the time?

So here he was, leaning into an old mower, sweat pouring down his back. Making it all okay again. In truth he had taken the day off as part of a campaign to confuse Madelene. He wanted her to say, 'Why aren't you getting up?' And when she said that, he'd be unresponsive and mysterious. She'd be unsettled and go, 'Gary? Are you all right?' And he'd say yes, and that'd be it. He'd be all right and she'd be all right and it would be as though the row had never happened. But to his annoyance it hadn't gone like that. It hadn't gone like that at all.

She'd got up. He'd lain there. He listened to her potter about for half an hour. And then he heard the front door. He bounded to the window to see her pull away in her Opel Kadett. He'd considered banging on the window but instead he sat on the edge of the bed with his hands on his knees.

Now that he'd taken the day off – and there was nothing wrong with that – there was no point in hitting the road. He sat in the kitchen eating a bowl of Frosties and watching Sky News. As the hour progressed and the news was repeated, he idly scratched himself for a bit, then sighed, got dressed and wandered into the garden where he'd had the idea about cutting the grass.

All the houses around him. All empty because everybody had something to do. But he had something to do as well. He was tending his garden. What could be nicer? *I am a man in my garden mowing my lawn*. Safe and serene. Busy. Useful.

He was about to take a break and have a Cup-a-Soup when he heard the distant sound of the doorbell. He immediately assumed it was somebody selling something and he wasn't in the mood (ever) to feel like someone wanted something from him. He strolled in through the patio doors, the anticipation of a human encounter troubling his stomach. He put one knee on the couch in the front lounge and leaned forward into the window for a peek. He got such a fright he actually belched.

It was two cops! A man and a woman. Their Ford Sierra was outside his gate.

His head felt as though it was filling up with air.

The dead man on the slab was definitely his father. He was smaller than Gary remembered and his mouth looked funny.

They hadn't seen each other since Gary's mother Betty's funeral eight years before. Gary had tried for a while to stay in touch, but whenever he'd taken him out for a drink, his father seemed withdrawn and uneasy, bewildered by the events of his own life.

Tommy had taken voluntary redundancy when Gary was ten and his sister, Margaret, was seven, saying he wanted to set up his own company. He'd risen in the pharmaceutical industry as the public became aware of vitamin and mineral supplements, as the local pharmacy became a shop like any other. There was a commercial boom in the medicine market and Tommy was there at the very beginning. He'd been part of a highly successful research team providing ever more attractive dietary aids and wonder tonics.

Gary wasn't sure just what Tommy had hit upon that made him want to strike out on his own, but in the dim corners of his memory he thought it was something to do with anti-ageing – stopping people getting old. He left the company with a nice wad of money, some of which Gary's mother made him invest in a safe venture. That venture was Peter's detergent-supplying business, Gary's little inheritance from his uncle.

Gary remembered his father as a man in control. He wasn't a headcase; he seemed at peace in those days. A bit like Val Doonican with his sweaters and his slippers. A man who stood proudly, feet apart, smoking a cigar on Christmas morning as Gary and Margaret opened the mound of presents they always got.

He had approached several companies with his business idea, even going over to England a few times. But whatever it was, no one wanted to develop it. He was treated like a bit of a hare-brain, a quack. People told him he should cop himself on, go back to the lucrative and steady employment he'd always enjoyed until now.

But instead he brooded. Those were dark days. Gary remembered his father mooching around the house, going for long walks up on Howth Head, sometimes getting snappy at Betty. He'd taken a knock. That much was clear. And he might have felt like a bit of a moron. Ironically the investment he'd made in Peter's company had added to the mess. Cheques were coming in, money wasn't a problem, so Tommy didn't really have to get up off his arse and get a job. He'd always liked a drink and was considered good fun on a night out – but now he began to spend almost every waking hour in a local pub, the Blind Beggar.

Gary could guess at the comfort Tommy found there; the same faces, no one entitled to judge the other because most had given up trying to achieve anything. And it was there on the rainy afternoons of that winter that he'd met Patricia Purefoy, a separated woman in her forties, who had just returned to Ireland from Zurich or France or somewhere. Belgium maybe. And in the murky underwater of a three-day drunk he had kissed her on the lips. He had given up.

They'd staggered together, hand in hand, to Tommy's house where Margaret was playing Lego in the hall. Patricia had accidentally stood on a little Lego house while Tommy slurred his last belligerent apology to Betty. They had walked out into the rain and Betty had wiped her hands over and over, before running down the street after them, pulling at Tommy and begging him to come home and sober up. Tommy had wrenched himself out of her grip and Betty had slipped on a grass verge, spraining her ankle.

She'd limped home, gone upstairs and cried for three days. Her next-door neighbour had brought food in for Gary and Margaret. They'd watched telly all day long. At night Gary could hear his mother crying. He'd get down under the bed and press his forehead against the cool skirting board. One morning it was getting bright when he felt Margaret crawl in behind him, her chest gasping. The first dawn he could remember.

In time Betty had recovered a little. They had great neighbours and her family supported her. But Tommy Reynolds never came back. The longer he left it, the more shameful the local scandal was and the harder it must have been to return. He moved into a holiday cottage Patricia had been left by her parents. It was in a desolate spot outside Kiltiernan, on the Dublin-Wicklow border. Tommy wandered in the woods, scraping specimens of moss, bark and stone. He spent time in the local library and the pub. Anyone who spoke to him remembered strange conversations about standing stones, burial mounds, things in the country-side that were organic, natural, ancient. Everybody felt a bit sorry for him. He lived with Patricia until her liver gave way. After her death, her family took pity on Tommy and gave him the rusty caravan out the back so they could sell the cottage. But no one had ever bought it. He lived in a caravan behind a derelict shack. And now someone had come and shot him and he was dead.

'Is it definitely your father?' asked the pretty woman cop. Gary nodded. He felt sorry for his dad, but at the same time, typically, he found all this deeply embarrassing. He was mortified. He went to phone Margaret.

Gary sat in the front, Margaret in the back. The pretty woman copper drove. She'd told Gary her name but he couldn't remember it. Nobody said anything.

Margaret had been even more distant from Tommy than Gary. He was surprised to see her actually touch the body. And when she turned to him her glasses were misted up with hot tears. She embraced Gary. He looked at the floor.

They were driving up through Carrickmines now. The radio crackled occasionally; the woman cop ignored it. Gary turned and gave Margaret a sad little smile, raising his eyebrows as if to say 'Mad! This is the real thing! Janey mac!' Margaret smiled weakly back at him. She was married to a lorry driver. He was always on the Continent. She had two young children at primary school. She tended to ring Gary more than he rang her. One time they hadn't seen each other for almost a year. Occasionally her kids had stayed at Gary's. They were quiet, well-behaved children. Gary took them to the pictures once. Only when he was buying them burgers and chips afterwards did he discover they'd already seen the film.

They drove up a winding country road. Gary could see Dublin sprawling away to the right. The woman cop had fair hair pulled tightly back into a short pony tail. She reached up to check her bobbin and Gary glanced up her short sleeve. White lacy bra, a little bit of underarm stubble. He wondered if she had a boyfriend. He wondered if he was a cop too. Probably was. Pair of smug bastards. Probably had a barbecue in the summer, all full of cops in their garden. All in their rugby tops, holding their little paper plates and their bottles of Bud. Bastards. Gary found himself feeling superior to the police. He saw them getting sauce on their jeans, getting sick in the flower beds, while his dad was being terrorised in a caravan.

They turned up a narrow lane and arrived at a tiny cottage with broken windows.

'For fuck's sake!'

The scene was fairly disgusting. The battered caravan had once been white. Now it was grey and orange and black. They stepped up into it via an old milk crate and stood together in its smelly warmth. There was a small unmade sofabed, a leather pouffe, a stove with a roasting dish full of cold grease in it, some cupboards, and a newspaper spread over the odds and ends of carpet. Margaret stepped back outside.

One wall was covered in dried brown goo, as was half the floor.

'A barman from the local pub called in to see if he was all right. They hadn't seen him in a couple of days,' said the policewoman. 'I don't know if there's anything you want.'

Gary looked around for a while. The detectives had already taken anything that might help them. They'd found lots of notebooks, full of endless scribbles and scientific jottings, all almost illegible. The books had been sent off to the heads of physics and maths departments at different universities to see just what discipline they explored, if any. Tommy was, after all, an educated man. But so far they'd had no results.

'There was something heavy here.' The policewoman was pointing at four small imprints on a piece of rug. 'It might have been a cabinet or perhaps a safe.'

'A safe?'

'Well, probably not a safe. It was on wheels or castors. Whatever it was, it looks like they took it.'

There was a small saucepan on the stove with congealed baked beans and a tomato chopped up into it. Wedged into the side of a little clock above the stove, Gary saw the edge of a black and white photograph. He pulled it out.

There was Tommy leaning on the bonnet of the new Hillman Hunter he'd bought back in 1973, arms folded, pipe jutting proudly out above his square jaw. An eight-year-old Gary stood beside him in an almost identical pose, beaming shyly up at the camera. Betty stood slightly to the side with Margaret in her arms, cool black sunglasses and a wry, tolerant smile.

He looked at the back of the photograph. There was a date on it. June 1948. He nearly laughed. It was completely wrong. His father hadn't even been married in 1948. He wondered had his father lost his memory, maybe? Had he gone a bit mad or something, out here all on his own?

Gary put it in his pocket and they went back out. Margaret was smoking, gazing off at the woods and the rolling hills. Gary stood beside her for a moment. The policewoman closed the trailer door and they moved off.

'Found this,' said Margaret. 'In a milk bottle over there, by the nettles.'

She held out a jotter page full of strange meaningless words, multi-digit numbers, mathematical symbols – all done out in neat black writing. One line, reading 'Y8S=+!' had a thick circle drawn around it in red biro. It was underlined several times.

'What is it?' Gary asked.

'I dunno. Do you?'

'No.'

'Should we hand it in to the cops maybe?'

'Nah,' said Gary, putting it in his pocket. 'Nice to have something personal from him. Even if we don't know what it is.'

'You're gas,' she said, but she let him keep it.

Crossing the field towards the cottage, Gary saw a yellow gas canister against a wall.

'It . . . wouldn't have been a Superser, would it?'

'What?'

Gary pointed. 'A gas heater. That they nicked.'

The policewoman snorted. 'Right.'

Gary and Margaret sat in the North Star Hotel. Gary was drinking whiskey, Margaret was on tomato juice. Gary hadn't phoned Madelene yet. Your dad dying was very real and grown up. You had to deal with it, face it boldly. So naturally, Gary was paralysed. The whiskey was inducing him to stare at a beermat.

'Who'd want to shoot an old man in a caravan?' said Margaret.

'Mad people.'

'You'd have to be very mad.'

'There's loads of mad people. People living up there in the mountains.'

'What are you talking about?'

'Mad kind of . . . brothers on their own up there.'

'Up where?'

'In the woods.'

'This is Ireland, Gary.'

'Someone looking for money.'

'How much money would he have had?'

'I don't know. Maybe he was a miser.'

She laughed. 'What? With a pot of gold or something?'

'Just, we don't know. That's all I'm saying.'

'Who would?'

'Uncle Peter?'

'Yeah, he might.'

'Mmm. Maybe he saw something in the woods.'

Margaret sighed. 'Like what? Treasure?'

He took out the piece of paper she had found and peered at it. 'Maybe this has something to do with it. What do you think?'

'I doubt it,' she said. 'That's only gobbledegook. Look at it.'

Gary looked at it.

$$Y8S=+!\ E = MC^2 \quad -b\pm\sqrt{\frac{b^2}{4ac}}$$

It didn't make any sense to him. It was all Greek to him, really.

Gary found the funeral arrangements quite nice to do. It was all above board and obvious. It was about money.

It was about what time suited the priest. It was about organising the plot, buying flowers. It wasn't about looking at dead people and thinking you might die yourself. It was about being alive and organising sandwiches in pubs.

Considering Tommy had dropped out of a normal life to begin a shite one, there was a pretty good turnout. Margaret's in-laws, Madelene's family. Madelene's mother put on a sad face but Gary knew she was secretly delighted with how embarrassing Tommy's situation turned out to be. There were lots of Tommy's old pals from work, and it struck Gary that he himself had no pals. He wondered why he'd never noticed it before, and what the hell he did in his free time. He realised he spent a lot of it just sort of fretting. Slightly worrying in some bar before going home for his tea.

In the pub after the burial Gary sat with his Uncle Peter.

'Typical. Couldn't do a fucking thing right. Couldn't even die like a normal person. Had to be assassinated by a hitman. In a caravan.'

'Who'd want to do it, Pete?'

'With Tommy it could've been anyone. Card game. Prossies.'

'Prostitutes?'

'Lonely man and all that. It could've been, couldn't it?'

'I don't know.'

Peter sighed. 'Who does? I'm like you, Gary. It's been years.'

He took a drink, and a long thoughtful pull on his cigarette.

'He was a good person, Gary, at the root of it all. Whatever he did. However stupid it was. It was only because he became confused. He wasn't a bad man . . . Just a bit of an eejit.'

'We found a bit of paper covered in his writing, Pete. All these strange diagrams and stuff. Funny numbers.'

'You still have it?'

Gary slipped it out of his pocket and handed it over. Again the underlined phrase in the rough red circle caught his eye. *Y8S=+!* What did that *mean*?

'I keep thinking this has something to do with it, Pete. I don't know why. But Margaret thinks I'm wrong.'

Peter looked at the paper for a minute. Then, slowly, he shook his head.

'I think Margaret's right, son,' he softly laughed.

'Why's that?'

'Because that's not your dad's handwriting.'

'Oh.'

'Would you not even recognise your own aulfella's writing, no?'

'He didn't write to me much.'

'And what about you, Gary? Did you ever write to him?'

Gary said nothing.

'No,' said Peter. 'Neither did I, kid. But I'd recognise his handwriting anywhere, and that definitely isn't it. He had awful writing. Like a spider gone mad or something.'

The autopsy results showed that Thomas Stanislaus Francis Reynolds had died as a result of a single high-calibre pistol shot which effectively emptied him all over a wall. Death was instant. Gary was surprised to learn that his father had been hospitalised a number of times with heart attack scares. He thought about Tommy lying in some ward with nobody coming to visit him. And for the first time in a long time, Gary cried.

Chapter Three: by Gene Kerrigan

Garda Sergeant Joe Roberts looked Detective Superintendent Andrew Andrews straight in the eye and said, 'Fuck off, sir, and find some other patsy to do your shitwork.'

That was what he said in his mind. In the corridor of the Police Station, just outside Interrogation Room number 2, what he said was, 'Yes, sir, of course, sir. Just give me a minute, sir.'

Andrew Andrews's parents had a sense of humour, which was one of the many things they didn't pass on to Andrew Andrews. He went through his early schooldays thumping people who were stupid enough to make jokes about his name. After a while he got very good at it. Behind his back the kids called him Andy Pandy. One kid, in a mad flush of courage, called him Andy Pandy to his face and got his left arm broken. Andrew told the kid two things: 'Shut up screaming and listen to me,' was the first. 'Tell anyone who did this and I'll break the other one,' was the second. The kid told no one about it until he was twenty-six and still occasionally wetting his bed and his GP sent him to see Professor Anthony Clare and after a few hours' gentle probing the name of Andy Pandy came out.

In his teenage years, Andrew Andrews was for a short time known among his contemporaries, in the Munster town where he grew up, as Randy-Andy-Soft-As-A-

Shandy, the nickname originating in the vengeful spite of a former girlfriend. One of those contemporaries, a chap named Padraig, went out with the former girlfriend a couple of times and she told him the nickname and he had a giggle about it with his sister, and she told her best friend, who told her fiancé, a young man who had neglected to inform her that he was in the throes of a passionate, covert and destined-to-be-shortlived affair with Andrew Andrews' younger sister, Andrea. One thing led to another and a couple of weeks later three girls from the local Presentation Convent paid a lunchtime visit to Our Lady's grotto in the grounds of their school and found Padraig bollock naked and strapped to the grotto's statue. When asked who had done this, Padraig just twitched. After that, no one ever called Andrew Andrews Randy-Andy-Soft-As-A-Shandy again, not even in private, not even among close friends. What they called him instead was 'That mad bastard'.

By the time of this incident Andrew Andrews had left school and joined the police force. Tall and wide, well muscled from rugby, he had never wanted to be anything other than a policeman. His progress through the ranks was rapid and striking. From time to time there were quiet remarks about the regularity with which suspects who had spent time in his presence were reported to have fallen down stairs or bumped into doors. In a safe at the offices of the Irish Council for Civil Liberties there was a modest-sized file devoted entirely to Andrews' activities. The two citizens who dared to make formal allegations to the Police Complaints Board had their moaning dismissed for 'lack of evidence'. Unfortunately for the citizens, when Andrew

Andrews was dealing with them he neglected to do so within the sight of independent witnesses. One of the complainants, a software analyst, was subsequently stopped seventeen times in six weeks while driving to work and was eventually charged with dangerous driving after he allegedly pulled out of a supermarket parking space without checking his rearview mirror. (The charge was dismissed.) The other complainant, the younger brother of a prominent member of the Progressive Democrats, was subsequently found with the makings of two joints in his pocket and was charged with possession of cannabis for sale or supply, after he was picked up in a raid on a party in Ranelagh. It was, curiously enough, the third party in a row which the young man had attended since his complaint and the third in a row to be vigorously raided. His social life contracted somewhat, as people stopped inviting him to their parties. He was fined £10 and lost his job with the National Irish Bank, where for two years he had been quietly and efficiently arranging offshore tax scams for favoured customers.

Andrew Andrews got results. He was regarded in certain official circles as the kind of solid copper who was badly needed to sweep up the criminal droppings of the Celtic Tiger. The plainclothes detectives called him Renko. But the uniformed guards – the likes of Sergeant Joe Roberts – what they called Andrew Andrews was 'Sir'.

'Do you have your notebook?' Andrew Andrews asked Sergeant Roberts.

'Yes, sir,' said Roberts, reaching for the flap of his breast pocket.

'Well, leave it where it is,' said Andrews. 'Here, use

these.' He proffered a handful of loose sheets of typing paper. 'One at a time. Take a seat. The suspect is having a slash, I'll have him back up here in a mo.'

Andrews departed. Roberts sat down at the table. Designed for the purpose of interrogation, the room was devoid of any decoration which might give the suspect the slightest emotional support. No pictures, no calendars, no posters, no tokens of normality. One single bare lightbulb. No windows. The walls were painted a neutral colour, the colour of the room where doctors take grieving relatives to tell them they did all they could, but.

Roberts wrote the date at the top of a sheet of paper and looked at his watch. It was 18.25. Almost seventy-two hours since Nestor had done a runner. His partner in off-duty security work had seemed to have some kind of grip on his emotions right up to the point where Mrs Bloom had said, quietly, 'So. Which of you pulled the trigger?'

Roberts said nothing. Nestor said, 'Ah, lookit . . .' For a moment it seemed as though he was going to go into his heart attack explanation. But Mrs Bloom said, again very quietly, 'Go. Now. Both of you, please.' Nestor turned and lurched out on rubbery legs. From the hall came a sound that might well have been a sob. Roberts said, 'It was an accident, he didn't intend to shoot the old bastard.' He surprised himself by making such an intervention out of simple pity for an associate.

'This isn't the first time someone has fucked up on a job,' said Mrs Bloom, staring hard at the floor. 'There's a routine clean-up process, to put some distance between us and the unfortunate occurrence. As long as no one runs off at the mouth, I don't see any need for panic.'

'Thank you,' said Roberts, and immediately felt a right gom.

'Give me the gun.'

'I was going to drop it in the river.'

'I have someone who will make a thorough job of it.'

Roberts suppressed a reply, took out the weapon and passed it over.

'Can we rely on Nestor?' asked Mrs Bloom.

'He's . . . he knows . . . I'm not suggesting . . . he's always,' said Roberts, starting and abandoning four replies. 'He's never let me down yet,' he finished, his voice dropping lamely.

'I see,' said Mrs Bloom. 'O yes.'

'What was it? . . . Maybe it's none of my business – but what was it the old bugger had that you wanted?'

'I suggest you run along after your colleague and impress upon him the importance of keeping his mouth shut and his nose out of places it doesn't belong.'

'Fair enough,' said Roberts. 'Fair enough.' He tried to think of something more assertive to say. 'Fair enough,' he said again. 'You'll be in touch, then?'

Mrs Bloom was reaching for her half-completed *Irish Times* crossword. 'You'll be informed if there's anything further required of you,' she murmured.

Nestor wasn't outside, nor was he at his flat. Roberts expected to see him next day at the station, but it didn't happen, he called in sick. A dozen phone calls and two visits to Nestor's flat had failed to locate the whingeing copper, and Roberts was about to make a third visit when Detective Superintendent Andrew Andrews collared him in the corridor of the station.

'I've a little gouger I've persuaded to make a statement,' he said. 'Come along in and take it down.' That was when Sergeant Roberts had said, 'Yes, sir, of course, sir. Just give me a minute, sir.' You didn't question Andrew Andrews.

'Here's the little gentleman,' said Andrews now, hooshing the suspect into the interrogation room. 'Sit down there and tell your story, in your own words, and the nice sergeant will write it all down. Then we can each go home to his own abode, humble or otherwise, and have a nice cup of tea – right, Jason?'

Jason Dunphy was about twenty-five, with very short hair and a thin moustache. He wore three-stripe fake Adidas ripaway leggings that he'd bought from a market stall, and a Nike top he'd picked up in a riverside apartment, just before departing through the bedroom window with a CD player, the complete works of Garth Brooks and a dozen-pack of condoms with only three gone. As he'd let himself onto a rail, Garth Brooks's entire *oeuvre* stuffed down the front of his jeans, the CD player had slipped from under his free arm and fallen to the ground, where it had smashed into several pieces.

Jason wasn't caught for that one, but he asked for the CDs to be taken into account when they were found in a raid on his gaff two days later and he was nicked for stealing a Sony radio from a Honda Civic parked in a lane off Pearse Street. The judge, a music lover, gave him a month for the Sony but took a week off for the theft of the Garth Brooks CDs.

'Ah, come on, you bloody eejit,' snapped Andrew Andrews.

Sergeant Roberts looked up, surprised. The superintendent was speaking to him, not to Jason.

'*One at a time*, I told you.' Andrews reached over and snatched the leaves of paper away. He looked at the date and time written at the top, folded the sheets of paper and tossed them aside. From a briefcase at his feet he took some more, placing them carefully on the table. 'One sheet at a time, nothing under it, lay it aside when it's full, go on to the next sheet.'

Roberts frowned, unsure if Andrews was taking the piss. Then it dawned on him. ESDA. Electrostatic Detection Apparatus, the box of tricks that reveals indentations on paper. It had been buggering up confessions since the early 1980s.

'Paper is an amazing material, you know, Sergeant. Every sheet of it tells a story. Nearly as sensitive as human skin. Did you know that?'

Roberts put a single sheet of paper in front of him, wrote the date and time, and then the words of the standard caution which warned the suspect that he wasn't obliged to say anything. Actually giving the caution out loud was officially mandatory but in practice optional (Andrews, for instance, found it tended to break the suspect's train of thought), but a statement which neglected to say that the suspect had been cautioned wasn't worth a toss in court.

'His name is Jason Dunphy, from the flats behind Traynor Street, I forget what they're called,' said Andrews.

St Anthony's Flats, Roberts said to himself, the patron flats of lost property. If there's something missing you can bet your life St Anthony's knows where it is.

'When were you born, Jason?' asked Roberts.

Jason looked at him for a moment, as though he was considering if maybe Roberts might be in the slightest way sympathetic. His face was pale, there was a slight tremble in his hands. There were no marks on him that Sergeant Roberts could see. After a moment Jason looked away and muttered, '16 June 1973'. Roberts wrote that down.

'Bloomsday,' said Andrews.

'What?' said Jason.

Roberts paused. For one frightening moment he thought he had heard Andrews say, 'Mrs Bloomsday.' But then he squared his shoulders and resumed writing.

'Tell us, Jason,' said Andrews, 'when did you decide to rob the place?'

Jason shook his head.

'On the spur of the moment, was it? You were just motoring around, looking for a likely target, and you came across this place?'

Jason shrugged, gave a half nod.

Roberts knew the drill. He carefully wrote:

> *On the day of the robbery, I was motoring around looking for somewhere to rob and I came across this place.*

'What did you think you'd find there, Jason?' asked Andrew Andrews.

'I dunno,' said Jason.

'Money, I suppose. That which is reputed to be the root of all evil?'

Jason shrugged again. 'Money, yeah, money.'

> *I intended to rob money, if I could find some.*

Mens rea. Good man, Jason.

'You broke in the door, did you?'

Jason nodded.

'Speak up.'

'I broke in the door.'

Actus rea. Attaboy.

'Empty, was it?'

'There was no one there.'

'What did you do?'

Jason just sat there.

'What did you do, you stupid fucker!' barked Andrews.

'I went in.'

'You went in?'

'I went in.'

'Bit of a dump, was it? Not much worth stealing, right?'

Jason shrugged.

'Say it, you little bastard.'

'There wasn't much in the place, it was a bit of a kip.'

'But still you thought there might be money, right? Maybe a bit of drink knocking around at least. Yes?'

'I . . .'

Andrews made to stand up.

'I thought there might be drink or something,' Jason said quickly.

'And there was a bottle of whiskey, wasn't there?'

'Yes. I drank some. When I was looking around.'

'Good boy, good boy. Where did you get the gun?'

'I dunno.'

'Did you bring it with you or was it there already? Was it on the table, maybe, or in a drawer?'

'I think so.'

Andrews pointed at him. 'Make up your fucking mind, little man. Make up your thick fucking useless mind or we'll have to have another one-to-one chat, won't we?'

'The gun was on the table.'

'And?'

'I picked it up.'

'Why?'

'It was just there.'

'Why did you pick it up?'

'In case someone came in, I suppose.'

'You'd have it to use, if someone interrupted you when you were robbing the place?'

'Yeah.'

Mens rea.

'Why did you shoot him?'

No reply.

'What were you doing when he arrived back?'

'I dunno.' Jason was growing more frightened.

'Looking for something to steal, maybe?'

'I *dunno*.'

'That's *it*, you little fucker!' Andrews leapt up, his chair making a harsh scraping sound on the dirty green lino.

Jason couldn't get the words out quick enough. 'Okay, I was looking for something to rob, I was. I think I was looking in a drawer when he came in.'

Andrews sat down slowly, staring at him. 'And that's when it happened? Right?'

Jason sat silent.

'Come on, lad, get it off your chest.'

Which, by way of being no coincidence whatever, was the first sentence Andrew Andrews had used when his interrogation of Jason Dunphy began the previous day. 'Come on, lad, get it off your chest.'

'Fuck off, I did nothing, you fat pig,' Jason had replied, quick as a flash. Jason had a bit of a reputation among his mates for sophisticated banter with the rozzers.

Andrew walked up to Jason and stood nose to nose. Jason leaned back. Andrew grabbed a fistful of Jason's Nike top and tugged Jason forward until he could feel the heat from the little bastard's red, sweating face.

'You little shit,' Andrew said quietly, and then in a roar that seemed to come from his belly, a roar that Jason, with a sense of shock, could feel literally rippling through the bones of his skull, the superintendent added, 'There is NOTHING inside your head that I cannot see! There is NOTHING that I ask that you will not tell me! NO ONE will hear you scream! And if anyone hears you NO ONE will listen! You – you pathetic little fucker – are MINE!'

Jason's face was still sweaty, but now it was pale.

The art of getting an inculpatory statement, or confession, involves three stages. Stages two and three, having the statement taken down and getting it signed, are a snap. The real work is in the first stage: breaking the will of the suspect.

These days, Andrews was somewhat cautious when it came to hitting suspects. He had rules, he had standards. Never hit on the face; the marks show up. The head is a good spot, the bruises are hidden, unless the gouger is baldy. Shins are good, kidneys too. Both open palms simultaneously clattering the ears as you stand behind the suspect, that's quite shattering, and whatever marks remain can quite credibly be dismissed as self-inflicted. You had to be careful, though. You never knew who might come in the door just as your fist was colliding with someone's kidney. Most of the members could be relied on to suddenly take an intense interest in something else, somewhere else, but there were some pissant gobshites floating around the force who had in their late teens watched too many episodes of *Hill Street Blues*. A few of them had got fluffy brains from reading rubbish about Nicky Kelly or that other shower of wasters who got done by the West Midlands lads. Mostly, a word in the ear would put such girlies back in their boxes, but there was always the chance you'd stumble across some little wanker who fancied himself as Frank fucking fair-play Furillo.

Anyway, as he gained experience, Andrew Andrews had discovered that he seldom needed to actually thump suspects in order to get a result. It is a fact of life that if a big, tough-looking man roars threateningly into your face you will experience an adrenalin rush and your body will involuntarily conspire against you. Your face will go pale, your blood pressure will rise, the acid in your stomach will erupt in all directions. After three or four minutes you will more or less regain your equilibrium.

Unless the big, tough-looking man has by then roared in your face a second time.

In which case your physical reactions will be compounded: you will probably be unable to stop yourself trembling.

If he roars threateningly in your face for a good five minutes you will probably not have a good five minutes.

If he roars threateningly at you repeatedly over a period of half an hour you will be mentally off balance, your brain will be scrambled.

'*Look at me when I'm talking to you, you pathetic little loser! I KNOW you did it, YOU know you did it! And every time you shake your head – there, Jason, you're doing it again, you insignificant heap of steaming crap, STOP SHAKING YOUR FUCKING HEAD – every time you shake your head you insult my INTELLIGENCE and I'm taking no more fucking insults from you, do you hear me? Nod! Right! NOD! That's it! When I ask you a question, you nod, okay? You nod your head, d'ya hear me? Shake your head at me again, by Jesus, I'll staple your bollocks to the back bumper of a squad car and drag you the length and breadth of Phoenix Park!'*

The big, tough-looking man is not only big and tough but he has you in his lair, where he is king and your own status in the scheme of things is somewhere just below a piece of shit. You can't leave, you can't have a cup of tea, you can't go to the toilet, without his permission.

'I'm trying to help you, here, Jason, and you're not making it easy on me. We're not talking about grabbing a handful of cash from the till in the local Spar, you know. We're talking about a robbery, a gun and a dead body. And, depending on how I treat things, that can come out as premeditated murder or it can come out as manslaughter. The difference is in whether you're slopping out your shite in Mountjoy for two years or going slowly mad in Portlaoise for fifteen. So help me out here, Jason.'

If, after hours of dominance, when your body is as ragged as your mind is frightened, just when you think he's taking a break, the big tough-looking man puts his face even closer to yours, when you didn't think that was possible, and he speaks to you in a roar that makes the initial roar seem a memory of a fond whisper, it's round about then that you start looking to please this monster so he'll let some kind of normality return.

'I didn't do it!'

'I fucking KNOW you did it, Jason, and you're not getting out of here until you tell me how it happened.'

You don't know if this will last hours or days. Even the most innocent citizen will start looking for a way out. And the people Andrew Andrews put through his own personal mangle were, on the whole, not the most innocent of citizens. Most were guilty of some crime or other, if not the one with which Andrews would eventually charge them. Guilt of any sort weakens resolve, and the persistent assertion that the big, tough cop knows you're guilty and there will be no relief until you agree to make a statement, ultimately presents you with just one way out. And, by and by, you agree to make a statement.

The second stage starts and you nod and shrug and say what's expected, reluctantly incriminating yourself but even more reluctant to give up the comparative comfort of stage two for a return to stage one. A policeman takes it all down in writing. Although you feel like backtracking hard, you're in so deep that getting you to sign the statement is no big deal.

Sometimes it didn't work; the suspect stared at a spot on the wall and Andrews and his like could rant and rave and give the odd belt in the kidneys and it all led nowhere. It might take forty-four hours and a bit of muscle before a frightened Provo's will would be bent, if ever; it might take half an hour to break a pickpocket. It took a little over twenty-seven hours, with time off for some kip (Andrews slept, Jason lay awake all night, listening to someone in the next cell weeping drunkenly about how he didn't mean to break his father's arm), before Jason Dunphy nodded that he was ready to do what was needed. Which was when Detective Superintendent Andrews called Sergeant Roberts to Interrogation Room number 2 to do the shitwork of scribbling down an approximation of Jason's words.

It's not the fear of a beating that matters so much as the reduction of the suspect to a thing of ragged nerves, humiliated, ashamed of his own reactions, his will peeled, cored and stewed by the dominance of the big, tough-looking copper.

The suspect doesn't believe that the confession will stick. If there is no way out except total submission, the suspect convinces himself that the smart thing to do is say whatever the copper wants him to say, to hell with it; and as soon as he gets away from the copper he'll tell everyone what happened and they'll know it was a ready-up and the confession will be thrown out. Except, no one believes that an innocent person would sign a confession. For to believe so would be to accept that a veteran police officer would do to a suspect that which civilised society knows it dare not permit. An appalling vista.

Mostly the suspect is guilty; for many, resistance is token, the occasional trip to prison is part of the job description. Some are innocent of the crime of which they are suspected, but they did something else the week before and it all evens out. It's when there's a big one, a major offence that lifts the suspect into a bigger league, with bigger penalties, that the likes of Jason resist making an admission.

But now Jason was in the home stretch, stage two, stitching himself into a confession. Agree to whatever the mad bastard copper says, get it over with, take your chances in court.

'You'll feel better when you get it off your chest.'

Jason sighed. 'Okay.'

'You had the gun in your hand when he came in.'

'Yeah.'

'Startled you, did he?'

'I got a fright.'

'You didn't mean to pull the trigger.'

'It kind of went off.'

'And all you got for your trouble, all you got for a man's life, was a fucking Superser.'

The pen jerked in Roberts's hand and made a little rip in the page.

'Are you . . . okay, Sergeant?' Andrews asked.

'Sorry, sir.'

'I wouldn't blame you for being shocked. The way we live now, what? The *Evening Herald* will enjoy this one: Killed For A Superser. You weren't dealing with the Reynolds case, were you, Sergeant?'

Robert's heart was thundering. 'Er . . . No, sir. Just what I read in the papers, what I heard around the station, you know. Died, shot, in a caravan, wasn't it?'

'Bloody awful, what Dublin has come to. The city of Swift and O'Casey and Joyce and Brendan Behan, and Yeats and little Jason Dunphy, and him scavenging on the likes of harmless aulfellas like Tommy Reynolds, shooting the poor man dead for the sake of a fucking Superser.'

'How did you . . . what . . . when did you . . . you know . . . how did you get on to him?'

'It's called detection, Sergeant. I got the names of a few of the wideboys who work that gig, little fuckers who drive out to the country, or to the periphery of the city, and knock off anything they come across, particularly from elderly victims, then run back to the rats' nest. Jason here has a history of preying on the helpless. Haven't you, Jason? I started paying visits to these tossers, and this one was number three on the list. Sure enough, as soon as I walked into Jason's very humble abode I saw the Superser. He claimed he bought it secondhand.'

Jason looked for a moment as though he was about to say something, but then changed his mind.

'So I Section-Thirtied him, found the gun in a suitcase under Jason's bed. He never saw it before, of course. By and by he admitted he knocked off the Superser, but he claimed he stole it from a building site out Artane way. It was only after Jason and myself got somewhat up-close and personal that he agreed there was no point making up silly stories, didn't you, tosser?'

Roberts looked at Jason. The suspect's eyes were focused on the floor.

'He gave me a bit of crack about being at home sick in bed on the day of the killing, but by and by we came to an understanding. Isn't that right, Jason?'

Jason bit his lip.

'Let's hear what you have,' said Andrew Andrews. Sergeant Roberts picked up the two sheets of paper on which he had scrawled the confession. He began to read, his mouth dry.

'*Statement taken by Sgt. Joseph Roberts. At 6.30 p.m. on 2/12/98 in my presence, the suspect was cautioned as follows by Det. Sup. Andrews. "You are not obliged to say anything unless you wish to do so but anything you do say will be taken down in writing and may be given in evidence." The suspect was identified as Jason Dunphy, St Anthony's Flats, Ansbacher Lane, Dublin 1, d-o-b 16/6/73.*

'On the day of the robbery I was motoring around looking for somewhere to rob and I came across this place. I intended to rob money, if I could find some. I broke in the door and went in. There was no one there, the place was empty. I looked around to see if there was anything I could rob. It was a bit of a kip. I had a good big drink out of a bottle of whiskey that was there. I saw a gun on the table and I picked it up. I wanted to have it in my hand in case I needed to use it if anyone came back and tried to grab me. I looked around the place but there wasn't much worth stealing. I was looking in a drawer when the door opened and a man came in. He startled me. I was holding the gun in my hand and I got a fright and I shot him. The gun just seemed to go off. All I took was the Superser.

'I have heard this statement read back to me and it is correct.'

'There you are, Jason. Put your signature to that, like a good man.'

Jason seemed to draw on a last ounce of will. 'I want to see my solicitor,' he said.

'Of course you do. So sign that there at the bottom and we'll take a little rest and I'll see if I can get hold of him.'

'Look, I think I should . . .'

'Sergeant, would you mind leaving the room for a few minutes?'

Roberts stood up. He moved reluctantly towards the door, looking back at the suspect.

Jason stared straight ahead. After maybe half a minute

a single tear ran down his cheek. He wiped it away with an anger directed more at himself than at his tormentor. 'Okay,' he said. 'Okay.'

'Sit down there, Sergeant, take the weight off your feet,' Andrews said.

Jason carefully wrote his squiggly signature at the bottom of the second sheet of paper.

'Good man.'

Now that Jason had signed away his soul, Andrews had a lever to prise out of him admissions to the further offences involved. Get the suspect to make one serious admission, then reel him in; don't ask him to swallow the whole shebang in one go. Just a matter of time and pressure and Andrew Andrews had a plentiful supply of both. Jason might baulk, mightn't admit anything further, but this was a two-for-one job and Jason was marked down for it.

The confession was beautiful, it had all the necessary elements. There was *actus rea* galore, admissions of law-breaking. And the necessary *mens rea* had been established, guilty intention. It's enough to get a suspect saying he broke into somewhere, but it's better to get the *mens rea* into the statement, the admission that he had the intention of stealing. Ditto when a gouger admits shooting someone; it's nice to have the *mens rea*, the admission that he intended using the gun if someone took him by surprise.

Andrew Andrews had learned the mechanics of getting a lawyer-proof confession the hard way, with smart alec barristers tearing holes in statements he had thought were watertight. And with new electronic trickery like the ESDA test, which could work all kinds of magic on the paper a statement was written on, and the impressions made on the paper underneath. Next thing you knew, some clever bollocks of a barrister was organising an ESDA test and finding out that page 4 of a statement was written before page 3, and that an incriminating paragraph was inserted on page 2 a couple of weeks after the statement was supposedly signed. Andrew Andrews fantasised about a new kind of paper, the kind that didn't tell tales. Sometimes there were rumours in the Dublin underworld that such a thing might actually be possible. One criminal boss had told him of a contact, a smalltime forger, who was working on a special kind of ointment which would age paper when applied to it, so the paper would show up nothing in any test, no matter how sophisticated. Andrews would make it his business to find out more. Such a substance would be as useful to an enterprising policeman as a criminal. Until then, there was a way to avoid all that defence lawyer's nonsense. One page at a time, nothing underneath to leave tell-tale marks, and let the Smart-Arse lawyers get out of that one.

'Okay, Jason, well done. You got that off your chest. We'll take a break and then have a go at the rest of the statement, the bit about how and why you shot the policeman.'

Sergeant Roberts's head jerked up.

Jason Dunphy said, 'Fuck sake.'

'Oh, I'm very sorry, Sergeant, of course you couldn't know,' said Andrews. 'I got word not more than an hour ago, just as Jason here was agreeing to spill the beans.'

Jason Dunphy said, 'Look, I . . .' and Andrews rapped him on the top of his head with his knuckles. 'Keep quiet, you impudent little fucker. You'll have lots of chances to talk before this is over.' He took Jason by one arm and led him out of the room and in the two minutes it took Andrews to return Sergeant Roberts just sat there, staring at the door, his heart hammering against his ribcage.

'Poor Garda Nestor, God rest him,' Andrew Andrews said as he flopped into the chair opposite Roberts. He offered the sergeant a cigarette. Roberts shook his head and immediately wished he hadn't done so, as the muscles at the back of his neck, stiff as pokers, shrieked with pain. 'Garda Nestor, I'm sorry to have to tell you, was found dead, shot through the head, in the same caravan we found poor Mr Reynolds, may the Lord have mercy on him. Initial reports suggest he'd been lying dead in that kip for at least two days. Christ knows what he was doing there, he had no connection with the Reynolds case, no more than yourself. Single bullet in the head. If I'm any judge of these things – and I am, Sergeant Roberts, believe me, I am – when Dr Harbison digs that bullet out of Garda Nestor we'll find it was fired from the same gun that sent Mr Reynolds to his reward. The gun that little tosser Jason had under his bed.'

Roberts could feel something moving in his stomach. He sat up straight and took deep breaths.

'It seems like Jason went back to the caravan for another look around – I expect that's what he'll say when I've had another chat with him – and poor Garda Nestor must have been trying some amateur sleuthing of his own and – bang.'

There was acid in Sergeant Roberts's chest.

'He was a friend of yours, I'm told,' said Andrew Andrews. 'Queer as a fourpenny bit, of course, but who are we to cast aspersions on a colleague so brutally taken from us? A tragedy, the only word for it.' He sighed and looked Roberts in the eye. 'I understand he never let you down.'

Roberts got up suddenly, a hand to his mouth, and staggered towards the door.

'A terrible loss to the force,' Andrew Andrews was saying, 'and a most unfortunate turn of events, O yes.'

Chapter Four: by Gina Moxley

She was silently thanking the inventor of completely seam-free tights when one of the sliced-ham boys thumped on the door. 'Phone, Dymphna.'

She had a lunchtime gig at a printer's near the Long Mile Road; a litho machine operator called Nosey Flynn was retiring. Dymphna had to dress up as that tennis player scratching her arse – Nosey's favourite printing job ever, apparently, though not as lucrative as the extra tickets he ran off for the annual Boyzone concert at the Point.

'Phone, Dymphna, love. Are you in there?'

She cursed the houseful of students and Mammy's boys fresh out of Templemore Police Training Centre.

'Coming,' she shouted back, then snagged her tights on the Superser. 'Bollix!'

The young police recruit stood in the doorway staring at her. He was so huge he caused a total eclipse on the landing. If he was meat he'd be destined for the export market. She edged past him, pressing the automatic light timer for the hall.

'Jesus Dymphna, but you're looking only mighty,' salivated the big boy from Bantry, leaning over the banister after her.

She waved her arms in the air and her dress rode halfway up her bum, just like her doppelganger in the tennis poster. He could imagine it but couldn't see it from where he was standing. She knew that. Nothing for nothing in this world, love. There was a Spar bag haplessly dangling from his wrist; inside, she'd bet anything, there'd be a couple of slices of wrapped, glistening ham and a pair of soft tomatoes. It was all these boys survived on between visits home. They were the kind that never learned to shop and probably wouldn't until they were well married. Then they would wander aimlessly in their husband jumpers after their organised wives through the foreign lanes of supermarkets, pushing the trolley with a puzzled expression like it's all news to them.

Dymphna Morkan waited till he shut his bedsit door before picking up the receiver. A ladder travelled up her thigh and a neat bead of blood settled on her calf.

'Joe,' she answered, knowing full well it would be him, even though she wasn't expecting the call. Real business was done on the mobile and Joe Roberts didn't have that number. Very few did.

'Dymphna,' he panted. 'There's trouble. Big trouble.'

'I know,' she said. 'Nestor. I heard.'

'Look, can you nip around to the Spar for me, they've a problem. I need time to sort something out.'

'It's something to do with the handle part, I think. That's what the youngfella on nights says anyway.' The woman who ran the Spar was trying to fix the broken door of the croissant oven. 'It affects the thermostat. A whole batch burnt to a cinder. What am I supposed to do, Dymphna?'

'Like I said, I don't know. I'm only doing Mr Roberts a favour. He couldn't come himself.'

Dymphna stopped herself being too snippy. The woman was a wreck. She was getting bored though; they'd been through it a couple of times already and to be frank her knowledge of croissant ovens was almost as limited as her interest in them. Poor old Roberts was really on the hop if he was getting her to run his errands. The shop was filling with the lunchtime crowd – women in bank uniforms, men in anoraks over their suits.

'Look at the queues. All looking for rolls. What am I supposed to do?'

The phone rang. The woman nodded to Dymphna to hang on a moment. Dymphna nicked a Kinder egg and went to read the headlines on the *Evening Herald*. Poor old Nestor. Nice picture of him, all the same.

Shot dead in a bloody caravan. What a way to go. A guy named Dunphy was up for doing it. Her eyes narrowed as they scanned the article. Fine officer . . . terrible loss. What was this? Some local hayseed witness had said he'd seen two old ladies with him in the field just minutes before the sound of gunfire.

As she waited for the manageress to get off the phone she noticed an aulfella going through the rubbish bin outside the door. He'd already pocketed a *Buy and Sell* magazine and was now going through the plastic bag Dymphna had just dumped there. He pulled out a grey wig and turned it over a couple of times as if trying to figure out what it was. He put it on, arseways, and started acting the gom with passers-by. People laughed but gave him a wide berth.

Dymphna watched, amused, remembering a time in Paris, or was it Amsterdam, sitting outside some fancy café, seeing an elderly man who made his living out of a big, mock, black rat. He would stand at the edge of the pavement, in view of the assembled coffee drinkers, with the toy rat hidden in his jacket. When he spotted somebody trendy or pretentious coming towards him, he'd give the crowd a collusive nod, wait for the innocent pedestrian to come level, then jump out in front of them, roaring and waggling the rat, scaring the living shite out of them. It worked a dream every time. Gas the way most people's decorum is so brittle that it can be shattered by something as stupid as a toy rubber rat. When his victim had stumbled off mortified he'd panhandle the café customers. Made a bomb, of course. Such a simple scam. A true entrepreneur. You had to be born one.

Back at the counter now, she eavesdropped on the manageress's phone conversation.

'Okay,' she was saying into the phone. 'Ring back in a quarter of an hour. I know, it's awful, Gary. Jesus. I'll be able to talk then.'

Gary was in Hayes Hotel, Thurles, birthplace of the GAA – a place in which he frequently felt particularly fat and unfit. But just at this moment he didn't know what he felt. He was actutely aware of his feet on the carpet; as if he could feel the flattened pile through his shoes. His heart was going like the clappers, his shirt collar grazing his neck, a maverick nerve hopping on his eyelid. Was he hungry? Maybe he should have a pint. He crossed the lobby like a somnambulist.

This time last week everything had been fine. Then his father had been shot dead and nobody knew the reason. And now a *cop* had been killed in his dad's caravan. What had the dead cop to do with his father? How could your life turn upside down so fast?

The lounge was fairly empty, bathed in nicotine light; a few old ladies wearing hats and sipping coffee, a scattering of office types with tomato soup moustaches. The weather forecast was on the radio. Gary settled on a stool at the counter. *Dry except for occasional showers today*. A stray shaft of sunlight caught cobwebs dangling over the bar. *Slack winds. A slow-moving cold front.*

Molly Ievers, the woman who ran the bar, kicked open the kitchen door, her arms lined with brimming plates.

'Where were *you*? We were expecting you Monday. Just as well Tipp fellas have a good aim otherwise that jacks'd be honking.'

'My father died,' Gary said simply. 'He was shot.'

He hadn't needed to say it out loud before. Not baldly like that. It sounded so grown up. But she wasn't even listening to him now. She was hurtling around the bar, giving people their lunches.

The *News at One* led with the story of the killing of Garda Nestor. There was a live report from Tommy's caravan, which looked sad and old in the television pictures. Gary tried to listen to what the reporter was saying but he couldn't make out all the words. Policemen were down on their knees, searching the grass. '*Tommy Reynolds*,' the reporter said. His father's name, there on the TV news. Suddenly the barwoman was back in front of him again with her order pad poised. 'Right. What do you want?' *Dublin mountains*. 'Soup is home-made cream of tomato, usual sandwiches.' *Garda Bartholomew Nestor. Fatally wounded.*

'And the hot plate is corned beef or shank of lamb.' *Gardaí are treating the death as suspicious.*

'The corned beef please, and a pint of Guinness.'

She was gone, through the doors to the kitchen like a bullet. *Dead man unmarried, but survived by his elderly parents. Investigations are continuing. No stone unturned.*

In the mirror behind the bar he watched the other customers. 'Excuse me,' he wanted to say. 'They're talking about my da on the news. I'm Gary Reynolds, Tommy's son. Yeah, *that* Reynolds, are you listening, missus, with your hat like a mushroom?' But nobody was even looking at the screen; too busy shovelling forkloads of mystery mush into their mouths, nodding and dabbing with paper napkins, content that Thurles was the extent of the world. Suddenly Molly was blocking his view of the mirror.

'Here you go. One corned beef.'

She was holding five plates. They all looked identical; he knew he was supposed to take one but he didn't know which. Oh Jesus. Why does every little thing have to be so hard? Half-heartedly, he went for one of the two plates on her right arm.

'That's the shank, you thicko. Beef on the left.'

How could she tell? He took it and his hand trembled, slopping gravy all over the counter.

'Easy boy, your pint is coming.'

He put the food down in front of himself and stared at his hazy reflection in the skin on the gravy. He really didn't know what he wanted to do: cry, puke or ring Madelene again.

Just then the barwoman called to him. 'Phone for you, thicko.'

He went down the bar and picked up the phone, blushing deeply, because everyone was looking at him now.

'Hello? Garret Reynolds? My name is Gertie MacDowell, you don't know me. I'm with MacDowell, Boylan and Mulligan solicitors. I got this number from your wife, Madelene.'

'Yes?'

'I'm the senior partner here and I represented your late father. He wasn't exactly a rich man, as you know, but he made it clear that he wanted to bequeath you something personal. Just a book, I think. It's in a sealed envelope. Would you be so good as to call into my office on Westland Row and collect it some time that's convenient for you?'

She hung up straight away. He could see in the corner of his eye that everyone was still staring at him. And for some reason, Gary kept on talking.

'Yes,' he said. 'Fine. I'll do that. Yes.'

He was determined to keep talking until they all looked at something else.

'Yes, I'll do that. Yes. Yes. Yes.'

Silently Dymphna left Jason Dunphy's flat, making sure to wipe her prints off the doorknob. Not that the cops would be bothered, she knew that. It was just a matter of habit, nothing more. The Superser had been in the corner; it hadn't taken long to find what she'd been looking for.

The taxi stopped at the lights just beyond the flats; the driver locked the doors and rolled up the windows. Here in spike-and-barrel land, he was taking no risks. Nothing much had changed since Dymphna had lived around here. From the back of the cab she could see where she grew up, her Auntie Julia Morkan's balcony just over there, her cousin Evelyn's place just down the road. She rarely came back here any more; before she died she'd promised her ma to stay clear of the place. Four years ago already; Dymphna had stayed clean for three. Jesus, the state of the place. The same plastic bags stuck up the trees, what bits of trees had managed to survive. The same swarms of youngfellas on bikes, whistling signals to each other, looking for something to settle themselves. A few on mobiles standing on the corner. Women with a firm grasp of their handbags huddled at the bus stop, simultaneously looking around and ignoring. The shops that won't sell tinfoil. A boy, maybe fifteen, slumped on the ground outside the chipper – Eight Chickenballs for a Pound! – gulping somebody else's methadone, the waves of heaven washing over his pale little face. Tell-tale heroin wraps fluttering around on the path. Some poor drink-weathered creature window-shopping outside the off-licence. The greatest range of cider in Ireland.

'Do you want me to go over the canal or along the South Circular?' the taxi driver asked.

'Canal,' Dymphna said, pulling her coat around her. Stop leering in the mirror and drive the bloody car.

'You're paying.'

'What does that mean?'

'The canal does be jammers at this hour.'

She checked her watch – it was only half-three, jammers my sainted arse – and didn't bother answering him. He flicked on the indicator. 'No skin off my nose, love.' As the lights changed and they began to move forward, a man stumbled out in front of the car. The driver braked and belted the horn. The man whirled on his heel as if only suddenly aware of the traffic, then gave a stoned, gap-toothed smile and a thumbs-up. That's the nice thing about heroin, Dymphna thought; it doesn't change your personality the way drink can. 'Scumbag,' Mr Jammers spat from the side of his mouth. The car took off around the corner and over the bridge. She herself had never injected, only smoked, otherwise she'd probably be a brilliant whistler by now.

Half an hour later, the taxi pulled up outside Dymphna's, or rather Roberts's house. When she first moved there she couldn't stop herself saying the word. Rathmines. Like a kid. Rathmines. *Rathmines*. Write a billion different sentences using the word Rathmines. There are trees in Rathmines. I have escaped to Rathmines. I love Rathmines and it loves me.

The meter was broken so the driver checked the fare from a chart.

'Nine-fifty.'

'Can I have a receipt, please?'

She passed him a tenner. He pocketed it.

'I just finished my receipt book yesterday.'

'I need a receipt for my boss. Write it on anything.'

At weekends, Bantam Lyons – one of Roberts's minions – drove her to her gigs. She rarely did the kissogram thing during the week. But the gig at the printer's had been almost enjoyable. Easier to get through when everyone is sober. Faster too when they haven't the Dutch courage to be glauming you. Annoyed, the driver rooted in the glove compartment.

'I've no paper.'

A couple of years ago a guy like this would've wrecked her head. She gave him some paper. He searched the door pocket, behind the sun visors and along the dash.

'I've no biro.'

She gave him one. He scribbled the receipt and stuffed it into her hand.

'Thank you,' she smiled and waited. He glared at her in the mirror.

'Are you not getting out here?'

'Change?'

He gave her the fifty pence in the smallest change he had.

'Thank you.'

Dymphna swung out of the cab and planted a huge kiss on the driver's window.

'Fuckin' slapper!'

She noted down his plate number. When things calmed down she'd get Roberts to have a word with them in the Carriage Office. He'd make sure he had a fucking biro then.

Twice a week she had a little cleaning job. Nothing huge. Keep the place shipshape, sort the books, do the front step. Mrs Bloom had a thing about the front step. She liked it immaculate. She liked everything immaculate. She was that kind of woman.

Later that evening, when Dymphna came in, Mrs Bloom and Mrs Blixen were in the front room, drinking wine and happily dunking Boudoir biscuits.

'Any joy today?' asked Mrs Bloom casually over the top of her glass.

'Bingo,' said Dymphna, tapping her bag. She was

relieved to have good news to report.

'Bingo is right,' chorused Mrs Blixen, with not even a trace of an accent today. A tiny clink with the glasses. Nothing excessive.

They were sisters. Half-sisters anyway. Neither of them had ever met her respective father. Pauline Bloom was the older of the two; fifty-eight, though she didn't look it, and she'd inherited her mother's handsome features and lustrous hair. Betty Blixen got what looks she had from some sailor whose name was never mentioned, if it was even known. Though there was a year between them, they acted as though they were twins.

As kids they were known as the Reillys; always together, there was no need to distinguish them by name. What set them apart from the other kids on the street was the fact that they were always reading and gaming on – playing the dozy princess or the wicked witch with equal relish, never letting their poverty prune their imaginations. Then, as teenagers, they'd sneak into the flicks, never once paying, never once caught, faces as innocent as buttercups in spring. Older again, they met and married a pair of brothers; the Breslins, Dennis for Pauline and Joe for Betty. Marriage didn't suit them, or maybe it was the men they chose. Without saying much – indeed, anything at all – by way of explanation they had simply upped and moved into this house together within six months of getting married. They hadn't budged since. The world came to them.

Dymphna took a folded, brown envelope from her bag. It had jaded sticky tape on either end. Mrs Bloom gave one of her half-snort laughs.

'Very good,' said Mrs Blixen, taking the envelope. She opened it carefully and had a quick look at the contents – a single sheet from a cheap jotter, covered in weird-looking scrawls.

'That was all? One page?'

'That was all, yes.'

'You're sure, girl?'

'Yes, Mrs Blixen, I'm absolutely positive.'

'*Shite!*' said the old woman. 'Shite and onions! Only one page and it's bloody well smudged!'

'Steady,' said Mrs Bloom. 'Isn't one page better than nothing at all?'

Mrs Blixen sat in silence for a moment. Then she nodded at her sister, who nodded back. 'Hand me down the receipt book, like a darling,' said Mrs Bloom.

Dymphna took the battered copy of *Ulysses* from the top shelf and passed it to Mrs Bloom while Mrs Blixen topped up the wineglasses. 'Will you have a drop?' Dymphna shook her head, 'Naw, I'm grand for now, thanks. I'll get on with the cleaning.'

She walked into the kitchen, put on her rubber gloves, and went to the only cupboard she ever opened. Nobody had as many cleaning products as Mrs Bloom and Mrs Blixen; they were great women for bleach, they had litres of the stuff, along with window cleaner, toilet ducks, furniture wax, brass polish, net curtain whitener, deck brushes, lily-of-the-valley-smelling mushrooms, wire wool, floor cloths, pot scrubs, all neatly lined up in case of an emergency of dirt.

'And where was it exactly?' Mrs Bloom shouted in to her.

'Exactly where you said it'd be, underneath the pilot light bit in the Superser.' Bleach, brush, basin.

Dymphna went back into the living room.

'To be honest, I was surprised the Superser was still there,' she said. 'I'd have thought the cops would have taken it as evidence.'

'Oh now,' Mrs Bloom chuckled. 'We arranged for them to have a little lapse of memory. In a manner of speaking.'

'But how did you know where it was?'

Mrs Bloom glanced at Dymphna and gave a little wink. 'Dublin's a small town. Our friend Sergeant Roberts sold it to an associate of ours. A business associate, you might say. And he sold it on to poor Jason.'

The two old women tittered.

'That's Roberts's weakness,' said Mrs Blixen. 'He's cheap. Can't help it.'

'O yes,' said Mrs Bloom. 'Cheap and sloppy. And it wouldn't have annoyed us half as much if they'd bothered cleaning up after them.'

Betty nodded in agreement, 'You'd want to have seen the state of the place, Dymphna. Terrible . . . messy it was.'

The three of them locked eyes and burst out laughing. Mrs Bloom drained the wine bottle into the third glass, 'Here love, don't mind that.' She took the basin and bleach from Dymphna. 'Those days are over for you, my girl. We have someone new starting tonight at the cleaning. We're going to give you a little promotion. Make more use of your talents, O yes.'

Organised as ever. That was Mrs Bloom. Not that Dymphna would have minded continuing, in fact she found the cleaning quite cathartic. But Mrs Bloom was right. Her apprenticeship had been long enough; the time had come to start seriously moving up the rungs.

When she'd started working for Mrs Bloom a few years back, the old lady had barely given her enough cash to cover her expenses; the rest was lodged in a Credit Union account for whenever she proved herself able to cope with it. Mrs Bloom held the account book; Dymphna had no idea how much was saved. She trusted Mrs Bloom. She had no choice. Soon enough she started the kissograms, and moved into the flat in Roberts's house in Rathmines. That was her own idea, a clever one too. Mrs Bloom had appreciated the neat touch, one of her little helpers living in a bedsit owned by one of her bent coppers. It was beautiful! Good to have someone smart on the ground like that, keeping an eye, watching proceedings. Roberts hadn't a clue of course, innocent as a sandboy, thinking he was cock of the walk.

Dymphna had moved on to the duty-free run. What a piece of cake; flying over and back to the Canaries, suitcases full of fags. She had a tan for that whole year – which was handy for the weekend job too. Towards the end of that time, she fell off the wagon, once, at her cousin Michelle Conroy's seventeenth birthday party. Mrs Bloom already knew before Dymphna arrived to clean the next day. She was straight and fair; every dog is allowed one bite. Though she made it abundantly clear that she wouldn't tolerate it happening again. Dymphna wasn't sure what that meant exactly, but was nervous enough not to want to find out. She went back to work, kept her bib clean, finally started as a courier on the Amsterdam run. Each time she came through customs she thought of the old man with the rubber rat. Steady, girl. Hold your nerve. Don't let them rattle you. Just keep smiling. She'd sail through as if she was on castors. Her own little game of cat and rat. It was good training.

The phone rang. Dymphna had never heard it ring before. She couldn't even picture where it was – although obviously they had one, since they rang her regularly. Mrs Bloom gave a tiny intake of breath. Mrs Blixen got up to answer it.

'You might as well bring down another bottle on your way,' Mrs Bloom called after her.

'My bloody knees. I'm getting old.'

Mrs Bloom and Dymphna sat sipping their wine. The stairs creaked as Mrs Blixen climbed them, as though in sympathy with her calcifying bones. The phone must be up in one of the bedrooms, Dymphna thought. They heard Mrs Blixen answer: 'Hello.'

Mrs Bloom took a folded envelope from her cardigan pocket, flattened it out and passed it to Dymphna, 'Something small, by way of thanks.'

What was this? The only other present she'd ever got from Mrs Bloom was a cashmere coat, recently shoplifted from Brown Thomas. It was far too old a style but she wore it anyway, of course. She felt the envelope. Money, maybe? No, something loose in there. She peeled it open. A single Yale key dropped on to her lap. Then she pulled out an estate agent's brochure, for a redbricked, two-up-two-down in Stoneybatter.

'What's this?' she asked.

'Like I said, it's only small.'

All of Pauline's gestures, grand or minor, were nonchalant.

Dymphna was gobsmacked. A house. Of her own. Fuck! But watch it. Careful. It could be a test. She read through the blurb quickly and calmly. *Mira electric shower. South-facing paved patio area.* Don't register any surprise. *Bedroom one.* No excitement. *Bedroom two.* She put the brochure back into the envelope.

'Thanks very much, Mrs B. You're very generous.'

'Fair is fair.'

Betty came back into the living room.

'Give us a minute on our own, would you, Dymphna?' She was looking very old and in need of a hairdresser.

Dymphna took her bag and went out. She heard Pauline ask 'Who was it?'

'Andr—' And the door clicked shut.

Dymphna stood in the kitchen looking out at the scrawny rosebushes. She was itching to have another look at the house, but she didn't want to get caught showing excessive enthusiasm. A *patio*, if you please. Jesus Christ!

Tomorrow morning, first thing, she would go into town to get a dressing gown. One with a big luxurious collar, nice and warm for having breakfast outside. She didn't normally eat breakfast but she thought she'd start. It was meant to be good for you, it set you up for the day.

Mrs Blixen came in carrying the basin and bleach. She had an anxious look on her face.

'Would you mind, love? The young one, Sharon, isn't able to make it after all. The new cleaning girl, I mean. That's her just after ringing.'

Brave girl, thought Dymphna as she took the basin. Not that she was fooled for even a moment. No way in the world was that Sharon on the phone. 'No bother, Mrs Blixen. Happy to help.'

She filled the basin. The water was boiling.

Given that the front step hadn't been cleaned for nearly a week, it wasn't too bad. But she scrubbed it anyway.

Chapter Five: by Marian Keyes

Micky McManus's day started badly and got worse.

First off, he woke up to find that he was still Caucasian. Despite the picture of Coolio sellotaped to his bedsit wall, there was no getting away from the stubborn fact that he was still the big-ass ol' white boy he'd always been.

Micky McManus wanted to be black. He knew that everything in his miserable, inadequate life would be somehow okay if he were big and shiny and graceful and ebony. Instead of short and stubby and freckled and ginger.

Kelly, the girl he'd met the previous night at Major Disaster's nightclub, was in the process of doing a runner. Not that she was much of a girl – a bit of a bargain-basement one really – but she was better than nothing.

Micky's sex life was unsatisfactory and unsettling. On the rare occasions he persuaded women to sleep with him – and money usually had to change hands – he suspected they did so just to see if he had ginger pubes, or to see if his lad was freckled. (It was.) To be fair, though, Kelly hadn't taken much interest in the colour of Micky's pubes. In fact, she couldn't have cared less. She'd only slept with him because she couldn't afford the taxi fare home to Bray.

'Are you going?' Micky asked anxiously from the

bed. As she was already fully dressed and halfway out the door, the question seemed a bit unnecessary.

'I've to go to work,' she said.

'Can I give you a call?'

Kelly shrugged her assent.

'But I don't have your number,' he pointed out.

'It's in the book.'

'But I don't know your surname.'

'That's in the book too.'

And then she was gone.

Desolate, Micky stared at the recently slammed door, then put on his Cypress Hill CD, very, very loud. After a couple of songs about smackin' his bitch up, he felt restored, even calm. While his floor, walls and stomach were vibrated by the bass line, he was at least briefly a Caucasian at peace.

Though there was no actual reason to get dressed as such, he put on his black shiny tracksuit; then the box-fresh trainers he'd managed to liberate ten minutes before being sacked from Crosbie and Alleynes, the sports shop he'd worked at until the day before yesterday. Actually, the liberation was *why* he was sacked.

He decided not to put on his gold chains just yet. It was too early. And lately they'd started to turn his neck green.

In the mirror over the sink, he experimented with putting gold foil from a bar of Dairy Milk over one of his teeth, then grinning at himself in various menacing poses. God, he wished he could afford the real thing. When Cypress Hill ended, he put on NWA – a few good shouty raps about killing rival gangstas with an Uzi. Great stuff! But hang on a second. Someone was knocking hard at his door. Probably one of those big-ass culchie bruddas complaining about the noise. 'Fuck off and ting, muddafucka,' he shouted.

When the knocking got louder and the door began to warp Micky lurched over rhythmically to open it. 'Yo! . . . Oh fuck . . . hello, Mr Roberts . . .'

It was the big bad bollocks looking for the rent.

Usually Joe Roberts sent a lackey to collect the rent, but as he was on the premises today – a quick visit to Dymphna – and as Micky McManus was in arrears by a week, he'd decided instead on a personal call. He felt the need to assert himself to someone, to remind himself that he was a powerful man. What better way than to bully a tenant?

'Mista Roberts, suh,' Micky smiled nervously, still with the gold foil stuck to his tooth.

'Turn off that racket!'

Micky did so with alacrity.

'What can I do for you, Mr Roberts?'

Roberts held out his hand. 'Money, Micky.'

Quaking, Micky tried to explain. He'd lost his job in the sports shop, it wasn't his fault, he'd be starting a new job on Monday morning. As soon as his P45 came through he'd have money to burn, honest to Jah.

'Micky, this won't do,' Roberts said, with horrible calm. 'I'm a businessman, you understand? An entrepreneur. If I put an ad in the paper this afternoon, there'll be fifty, sixty, a *hundred* people, queuing up to pay to live in this lovely bijou home.'

Bijou. He loved that word. He'd once asked Patsy, 'What's that French word beginning with B that means small and posh?'

'Bollix,' said Patsy.

'I don't think it can be that, pet. It doesn't fit.'

'Bijou,' she'd said, without looking at him.

'Bijou,' he'd agreed, pretending to write it in the crossword.

Micky's heart seemed to sluice through him on a wash of cold fear. If Roberts threw him out he'd have nowhere to go. There was no family bosom to be welcomed back into. And he couldn't go back on the streets again; the cold, dirt and tedium nearly killed him the last time.

'Mr Roberts, I promise . . .'

'Collateral, Micky. Provide me with collateral.'

Micky didn't actually know what collateral was, but he suspected he was in no position to provide it.

Roberts looked around the tiny room with mild revulsion. How could people *live* like this? The only thing of value was the bloody ghettoblaster. Well, nothing else for it, that would have to do.

'No, please, not that, Mr Roberts,' Micky said hoarsely. 'Why don't you take the kettle? Or the Superser? Or even the bed?'

'Because they're all *mine*, you tool.'

With a sense of deep distaste, Roberts crossed the threshold – Christ, the floor was actually sticky! – and unplugged the tape player.

'When you've paid me what you owe me, you'll get it back. Until then, it'll look lovely on my sideboard.'

Roberts felt he was being uncommonly compassionate. If he'd been firing on all cylinders, Micky would now be in the process of packing his few paltry possessions, and the phone would already be hopping with enquiries from potential tenants. But the events of recent days had knocked the stuffing out of him.

He departed, the tape player under his oxter, leaving

Micky utterly bereft. It was as though a part of him had been amputated, and without anaesthetic. Silence loomed. Oh, how he hated it. He could hear the chattering of his own tormented thoughts. Without the blanket of comforting noise he was brought face to face with his own ginger inadequacies. What was he supposed to do all day?

'Sheee-it!' he exclaimed. 'That . . . *muddafucka*!'

Not for the first time he wished he had a great big Uzi. He lay on the unmade bed, steeped in resentment. Incredibly violent fantasies began to flicker through his mind; they all seemed to end with Roberts begging Micky to put him out of his torment by using the Uzi.

In every man's life comes an inescapable moment where he has to choose between lying down to get trampled on, or standing up to fight for what's right. For Micky McManus that moment was now. Suddenly he knew what he was going to do. He was going to get his tape player back! He was going to go to Roberts's house and rescue his beloved. Or his name wasn't Gangsta MMC Manus.

As it happened, four miles away, Gary Reynolds was experiencing a similar kind of epiphany.

In the terrible week since his father had died, Gary had become uncomfortably aware that he couldn't get away with being a big, fat scaredy-cat any more. Even though he hadn't seen his father in recent years, he'd always been aware of him, always seen him as a protective membrane between Gary and adulthood. But Tommy's murder had shunted Gary forward into grown-up land. There were no more generations between him and death any more. He himself was next in the line of fire. The world was looking to him to be the adult. He had no choice but to oblige. He really hated that.

The package he'd collected from Gertie MacDowell's office had yielded no clues or consolations. No note, no letter from his dear old da, just a collection of thick faded jotters, all of them filled with strange, meaningless symbols and squiggles, a bit like the ones on the paper Margaret had found in the milk bottle, but in a large childlike scrawling hand. This time around, he'd checked the handwriting against a sample of his father's; but once again, the writing wasn't Tommy's.

There were 299 pages in all, each of them numbered. But all 299 pages seemed to be similarly incoherent and confusing – even deranged, if the truth be told. He would probably have thrown them out straight away if he hadn't noticed something odd: the very first page had written on it the same letters as the page from the milk bottle found at the caravan. *Y8S=+!*

For a moment or two he had found that exciting. But try as he might, he couldn't figure out what it meant. If it meant anything at all. And he knew in his heart that it probably didn't. The newspapers had been full of stories of the eccentric behaviour of Tommy Reynolds. Locals had seen him late at night, walking naked in the fields, smearing himself with grease by the light of the moon. 'He needed help,' one unnamed neighbour had said. 'A man like that should have been in a mental home. It wasn't right to leave him alone like that.' Gary wondered if his poor old dad had indeed gone loopy, all alone up there in the mountains. Sleeping in filth, living like an animal, collecting rubbishy papers that didn't mean anything. He had spent several hours looking through them – his one inheritance from his sad crazy da – and then, overcome by grief, he'd thrown the whole lot in the bin.

There was too much weird stuff going on with his father's murder investigation. It was all over the papers that the youngfella who'd hanged himself in police custody hadn't done it. TRAGIC JASON INNOCENT had been one of the tabloid headlines. There was nothing to corroborate Jason Dunphy's statement. No fingerprints had been found at the scene of the crime. And though he didn't have an alibi for when Tommy Reynolds had been killed, he had a rock-solid one for the day of Garda Nestor's murder – and yet, for some reason, he'd confessed to that too. There were hints in some of the papers that the cops had coerced the confession out of him.

Furthermore, a farmer had unexpectedly come forward, claiming to have seen two men visiting Tommy Reynolds on the day he'd been killed. Jason Dunphy didn't fit either of their descriptions – one had been in his late thirties, the other early forties. Both had been very well built. 'They looked like they might play rugby,' the farmer was alleged to have said. 'But one of them was wearing a Manchester United shirt.'

The cops had appealed for the two men to come forward, but so far no one had. Why would someone want to kill his father? Gary asked himself the question for the millionth time. Had he offended somebody? Assaulted them? What had he done? He was only some kind of innocent simpleton. Or did he have something that somebody wanted? There was nothing of any value in the shack, after all. Why would rugby players have been visiting him the day he died? His da hated rugby, he was always a soccer man. And why was a cop killed a few days later in his father's home? And why were the cops getting the wrong people to confess?

Though he would rather have stayed at home, in bed, eating crisps, for the rest of his life, Gary Reynolds had reluctantly decided that he had to grow up. It was time to do a little investigating of his own.

Freshly minted adult though he undoubtedly was, Gary Reynolds was not quite a natural hero. Or even a natural conversationalist. He didn't want to go and talk to whatever friends or neighbours his da might have had. But he had no choice. He could see that. It was the least he could do. After all, hadn't his poor dead da kept a photo of them taken the day they'd got the new car, one of the happiest days in Gary's lardy, anxiety-seeped childhood? Even if the sad and lonely Tommy had got the date on it wrong by several decades, it's the thought that counts.

So into his van and up into the mountains, the way the pretty woman cop had taken him and Margaret. He knew there had to be a pub near the caravan, because it had been a barman who'd noticed that Tommy had gone missing. He drove around the narrow lanes for nearly an hour. He was almost on the verge of giving up and going home, conscience cleared, or at least a bit clearer, when he finally stumbled upon a place called the Roadhouse.

Roadhouse, me arse, he thought, getting out of the van. It could have been sued under the Trade Descriptions Act. It didn't stand on a road and it was barely a house. The Trackshack might have been a better name for it. A flat-roofed, cheerless, window-free concrete bunker, with not even the faintest pretence of conviviality, it wouldn't have looked out of place in *Deliverance*. It seemed to radiate a powerful message: 'People don't come here to enjoy themselves.'

Gary was quaking as he walked inside. Three old men sitting grumpily over pints abruptly ceased their conversation. So far, so good, he thought nervously. Well, you had to expect that. In the detective films he had sometimes watched, the hero was always viewed with suspicion by the locals. But after the hero had bought a few well-targeted drinks, in no time at all some curmudgeonly old fucker would be singing away like Daniel O'Donnell.

Gary lumbered across the six feet of bare concrete floor, feeling more exposed than he ever had in his life. Behind the brown Formica counter, the barman watched his approach with steady contempt. Trying to exude casual *bonhomie,* Gary leaned on the bar. 'What do you recommend?' he asked anxiously, with a vague wave at the bottles on the shelf.

'That you get into your van, drive away and never come back,' the barman said, hostility lighting his beady eyes.

Gary felt as though his stomach was trying to leave without the rest of him. His scalp crawled and prickled with terror as a terrible realisation slowly dawned. What if these were the very men who had murdered his father? They looked weird enough to do it, they really did. You only had to take one look at that bar to know that it had a great big shotgun behind it. Oh, Jesus, why the fuck had he come? Why had he abandoned his fat-bastard coward life, an existence which suited him so much better? He should have just stuck to what he was good at.

One of the men stood slowly up. He lumbered over and thrust his face into Gary's. Slowly he said, in a hill-billy voice, 'You're not from round here, are ya, son?'

Gary's life began to pass before his eyes. (Well, it would have, if anything interesting had ever happened in it.)

'Yeah,' called another man, also in a deep-south drawl, 'we don't lak strangers round these heah parts.'

Never sweat-free at the best of times – the fat man's burden – Gary was positively bucketing it now.

'But . . . listen a second,' he begged. His voice sounded high and scared and incredibly urban. 'I'm not a stranger, I'm Tommy Reynolds's son.'

A nonplussed silence fell over the bar. 'Prove it,' one of them eventually suggested.

'Look at my van,' Gary suggested. 'It says "Reynolds Hygiene" on the side.'

'Go on, Tadgh,' the barman suggested. The oldest of the trio went to the door, checked and confirmed that that was indeed the case.

'You know,' another of the men said, eyeing Gary thoughtfully, 'you have the look of him right enough.'

Suddenly everyone was all smiles. A clamour of chat and laughter broke out. 'You're Tommy's son. Well, why didn't you say? Here, come on. Have a drink with us, won't you?'

Much hilarity was milked from Gary's terror.

'The look on your face when Henry said we don't like strangers round these here parts!' The barman, whose name turned out to be Peadar, convulsed with laughter.

'We do that to everyone,' Henry cackled. 'Oh, the crack we have when people get lost and come here looking for directions.'

'I thought you were going to piss yourself!' Peadar cheerfully told Gary.

'Ahaha,' Gary laughed lamely.

'Sorry about your poor father, all the same.' Tadgh had just remembered that uproarious mirth wasn't entirely appropriate.

'What was he like, recently, before, he, you know . . . ?' Gary asked.

They all exchanged glances.

'Not himself,' Peadar finally said.

'In good form, though,' Tadgh added quickly.

'Flying form,' another confirmed.

'The drink?' Gary asked.

'No,' Peadar said firmly. 'Whatever it was, it wasn't the drink.'

'What then?' Gary wondered at the awkward atmosphere.

'We don't know,' Peadar shrugged.

'Not . . . not . . . drugs?' Gary asked, haltingly. 'Where could he buy drugs around here?'

'Nowhere,' said Tadgh with finality. 'Believe me, I've tried.'

'Is the man who saw the two rugby players here?' Gary asked. He hated asking questions. He was afraid of asking too many and annoying everyone.

'That's me,' said Tadgh. 'And the rugby players are old news. It's been like Grand Central fecking Station in the last day. *Women* have been sneaking in and out, would you believe?'

Gary's head tightened. He didn't know if he could absorb any more information.

'Yes,' Tadgh said. 'Two aulwans.'

'Together?'

'No. First one, she looked a bit like a nun, well, she had one of those nun's hairdos, but she'd lovely legs. The legs of a young one. Then about an hour after she'd gone, another aulwan arrived. Jaysus, she was nearly as old as me . . .' – he paused for the laughter – 'wearing one of them French caps on her head, you know what I mean.'

Gary boggled at the thought of an old woman wearing a diaphragm on her head, visiting his dead father.

'A berry!' Tadgh said triumphantly. 'That's what I mean. She'd a black berry on her head.'

Gary began to wonder if he'd inadvertently taken some hallucinogenic drugs.

'She'd a blackberry on her head?' he asked weakly.

'What the French painters wear.'

Ah, a *beret*.

'I dunno at all,' said Tadgh gently. 'There was queer goings-on up in that field for a while . . . But sure we'll let the dead rest now, eh?'

'Yes,' said Gary.

'He's at peace now anyway, son. That's the main thing.'

'I hope so,' Gary said.

Tadgh nodded. 'Poor fella. The way he lived. You'd never have thought he was so well off. Potentially, like.'

'How do you mean?' said Gary.

'Well, y'know' – the old man lowered his voice. 'Did you get the book your dad left for you?'

'The book?'

'*The* book, yeah. That manuscript of his. Sure I often saw it meself. A pile of auld notebooks with funny squiggles and numbers in them?'

'Oh that, yes . . . I got that okay.'

'And did you have a good look?'

'Well . . . yes. Of course.'

'Well then . . . You're set up for life so.'

'What?'

The old man winked. 'You'll never have to work again in your natural, you jammy bastard. I envy you.'

'What?'

'Well, I mean to say – you do know what it was your dad left you? Right? I mean, you've figured that out, haven't you, son? I mean, only a prize fuckin' eejit wouldn't see the value of that. Your brains'd want to be up your arse not to see it.'

'Well . . . yes. Of course.'

'Exactly.' The old man winked again and touched his nose. 'As I say, them papers is worth millions and millions of pounds. Billions probably. You're on the pig's back, son. Sure it's better than winning the Lotto any day. Just what your dad always planned for you, eh?'

'I guess the drinks are on you, Gary,' Peadar said. 'It's not every day we get a millionaire in here.'

'Yes,' said Gary, thinking of how he had dumped his father's papers in the bin. 'Er . . . Yes . . . I'm on the pig's back now.'

Sergeant Joe Roberts's house was admirably situated right in the heart of three-piece-suite land. You'd think with all the money he extorted from the bedsits that he'd live in a mansion in Howth, Micky McManus told himself, instead of this modest road in Mount Merrion, all neat little conservatories, Austrian blinds and UPVC windows. There was a car in the drive, a crappy old Lancia. Micky loitered, waiting for its owner to leave. He found a football in a front garden, wished it was a basketball, kicked it up and back against someone's gable wall. After ten minutes, he saw a woman who must be Roberts's wife get into the Lancia and drive away.

As soon as she was gone Micky strolled up the gravel drive and slunk around the side of the house. Heart pounding, adrenalin coursing, he felt a terror that was almost pleasurable. Man, you could get addicted to this.

He'd broken into places before – well, you had to, it was impossible to live on the minimum wage – but he hadn't done any robbing since he'd moved into Rathmines. It wasn't a great idea to have a load of stolen goods under your bed when there's a trainee copper living either side of you.

Daytime was definitely the best time to go robbing on roads like this one. The men were at work, the children were in playschool and the women were out at their aerobics or their golf. He picked up a stone from the ornamental rockery, and quietly, almost gently, broke the glass in the back door, knocked away the stray shards, stuck his hand in and turned the key. Pausing for a second in case he could hear an alarm – he couldn't – he pushed the door open and crept inside.

He edged through the kitchen, smelling other people's smells, looking at the minutiae of someone else's life. Yellow kettle and matching yellow toaster, bills and letters stuck behind the radio, the wiped-down worktop, the J-cloth slung over the tap, the side plate and knife in the sink still with toast crumbs on them. Blood was pounding loud in his ears, his breath coming sharp and short. He always got a hard-on doing this.

Now he was here, the ghettoblaster wasn't the only thing he wanted. He decided to make this visit worth his while. He made straight for the freezer, the first port of call for the self-respecting house-breaker because it was where suburban housewives kept their jewellery. They thought they were so fucking clever. Jewellery in the freezer and telly in the oven. Efficiently, he rummaged through frozen chicken kievs, tubs of yellow-pack ice-cream, bags of meat, looking for gate bracelets and eternity rings.

'You let yourself in, I see,' someone said.

Micky's heart nearly went into spasm. A cold feeling licked down his spine. Slowly he raised his hands and turned around. A woman was standing in the kitchen doorway – the same woman who'd left in the car a few minutes ago.

He stared at her, sweat erupting from every pore in his body. 'Mrs Roberts?' he croaked.

'Call me Patsy.'

'I . . .'

'You couldn't have come at a better time,' she said. 'I was just thinking I needed a thug.'

Something was badly wrong here. She should have been begging him not to hurt her, to leave quietly. Instead, she looked at him appraisingly with her piercing blue eyes and said in an almost cordial voice, 'Close the freezer and sit down.'

'Ah no, missus, I'll be off.' He turned and made for the back door.

'Sit down!' she barked. And it was then that he saw the gun.

Micky McManus was no connoisseur of guns, other than his much-yearned-after Uzi. But he understood that what she was holding was no toy. It was black, heavy and evil-looking. It seemed to throb with a horrible authenticity.

'These yokes . . .' she looked at it and waggled it absently, 'can do a ferocious lot of damage. So sit down. And leave your flute alone. Men, you're all the same! Get nervous and you start fiddling with your equipment.'

'I was scratching me bollocks,' Micky said, with an attempt at dignity. 'They were itchy.'

'You were fiddling with your flute,' Patsy Roberts said, in a voice that brooked no argument. 'So. Anyway. What are you after?'

'Things.'

'You a junkie?'

'No.'

'Why not?'

'The gear made me puke.'

'What's your name?'

'Micky.'

Patsy sighed heavily.

'I thought you were gone to aerobics,' Micky found himself saying.

'No, just down to the shop.' She waved the newspaper at him. 'The witness thinks the two men were driving a Lancia. An old one.'

Micky hadn't a clue what she was on about – Witnesses? Men? Lancias?

Patsy sighed again and waved the gun at him. 'Stick on the kettle, there, would you, pet?'

She was scaring the living daylights out of him now. She was a handsome-looking woman, with a terrifying magnificence about her. Her blue eyes glittered with the absence of mental health.

'I'm a woman who's been pushed too far,' she said as Micky filled the kettle.

'Entrepreneur,' she said slowly and bitterly. 'Ent. Re. Pren. Eur. That eejit didn't even know how to spell it. It was *me* who had to tell him. Do you *understand*?'

'Yes . . . Course I do.' To be honest, he didn't, but he thought if he admitted that, she'd blow him away.

'That's right. He owes *everything* to me. I've had all the ideas, and he thinks they're all his!'

Micky shot her a nervous look. She was a bit too young to be going through the change. Seemed like an open-and-shut case of good old-fashioned lunacy. Just his fucking luck. A madwoman from Mount Merrion.

'What I've had to put up with,' she went on. 'Police brutality? I'll tell you about police brutality. You'd want to smell his socks. You'd want to see how much he gives me for housekeeping.'

'I . . .'

'Fourteen years we've been married. Fourteen years. If I'd murdered someone I'd be out by now! The tea-bags are in that press.' She waggled the gun again. Micky's bowels felt as though they were melting.

'And it's not that I mind that he's riding that Dymphna one,' Patsy insisted.

'What do you mind, missus?' Micky asked, his voice sounding muffled to himself. He was beginning to feel like he'd strayed into someone else's nightmare. This kind of thing didn't happen in suburbia.

'I mind, Micky,' she hissed, 'that he's fucked up. I mind, Micky, that I've been waiting for what is rightfully mine, for a long, long time. And now it's all in danger of unravelling!'

Micky forced himself to nod sympathetically. What the fuck was she on about?

'Get two mugs there, good man,' she said. 'Do you like it strong or weak?'

'Weak.'

'Do you know what Joe Roberts is, Micky?' She was pouring the tea.

'No.'

'He's expendable, that's what he is. And you're just the man to expend him.'

'I couldn't expend my way out of a paper bag,' Micky protested in terror.

'You'd better learn. Fast.'

'You're mad, missus.'

'Very probably. I come from a long line of mad people. You'd want to meet my mother.'

'Please can I go?' Micky begged.

Patsy laughed. 'If only life was that simple. No, the arrangement is, you do a little job for me, and I won't shop you for house-breaking.'

'I can't kill someone.'

'Maybe I won't need you to kill him.'

Micky relaxed slightly.

'Just hurt him an awful lot,' Patsy continued. 'Have you ever gouged anyone's eye out? No? Well, there's a first time for everything. Anyway, it's not as bad as it sounds, there's a special little tool that's quite useful for doing it. A melon-baller.' She rummaged in a drawer and handed him an implement. 'Here.'

Micky's forehead prickled with sweat. He felt as though he might faint any second.

'I really should be off, missus,' he said hopefully. 'Thanks for the tea and good luck with the . . .' – he faltered – 'y'know, the eye-gouging.'

'Nice try, Micky, but you're coming with me. Or

else you're going to be gouged yourself.'

Holding the gun in one hand and a comb in the other, she began tidying her thick black hair in the little mirror in the kitchen. 'Isn't it a crying shame?' she complained, examining her face. 'You spend your entire life hating your mother, and the next thing you know, you turn around and *you've fucking become her.*'

Micky shrugged helplessly.

'Okay,' she said, checking her handbag. 'Keys, lipstick, gun. Off we go.'

Outside the day was breezing up. Micky got into the passenger seat of the 87 Lancia. Patsy grinned at him. Buoyant. Upbeat. Bonkers.

'Just like *Thelma and Louise*,' she laughed.

She started the car, the gun in her lap. 'So tell me, Micky, have you ginger pubes?'

Miserably, he nodded.

'God love you. And is your flute freckled?'

He nodded again.

'I thought so,' she said with a devilish grin.

Patsy Roberts was lambent with fury. Glittering and gorgeous with psychotic rage. Surfing its waters, *cruising* on it. It was time for her to *get involved*.

Obviously the old woman couldn't hack it any more. She was starting to make mistakes. And it looked like Joseph Pius Mary Roberts was beginning to make stupid slip-ups too. Maybe she should never have told the old woman to take him on.

They drove towards town. Micky's mind was on escape. At a set of traffic lights, he suddenly realised he might be able to jump out.

'Don't even think about it,' Patsy warned. 'I'd have your legs blown off before you were out of the car.

Have you ever seen someone being kneecapped? It's ugly, Micky.'

Micky swallowed and hoped he wouldn't puke.

'You'd be arrested,' he pointed out.

'Hardly,' she said cheerfully. 'I'm married to a copper. Does the word "cover-up" mean anything to you?'

Micky decided he'd died and gone to hell. Roberts was a *pig*? Could that be *true*? He'd gone and broken into a cop's house. Could this day get any worse?

They drove on without speaking. 'Why do you hate your mother?' Micky eventually broke the silence to ask. He'd read somewhere that it was best to befriend your captors, talk to them, remind them that you're a human being.

'What are you talking about?'

'When you were looking in the mirror you said that you hated her. And then, you know, you said you'd turned into her.'

She shot him a glare of hatred and rage. 'Because she fucked off and gave me away when I was a baby. And do you know something? That really, really annoyed me. It really, *really* got on my nerves.'

She gave a shudder of suppressed anger. Although it wasn't suppressed enough for Micky's liking.

'But I found her. O yes. And she's making things up to me. Guilt is a marvellous weapon, Micky. Although not as marvellous as this, of course.' She stroked the gun fondly.

They drove through town, over O'Connell Bridge, heading north. Along Dorset Street. Following signs for the airport. They turned off the main road, on to a smaller road, then on to a smaller road again. Finally, they stopped outside a small, redbrick terraced house.

Its windows sparkled, its curtains were snow-white; the front step gleamed as though recently scrubbed.

'Out,' Patsy ordered.

Betty Blixen, tall and elegant, her hair in a bun, answered the door. Her face hardened to an expression of loathing.

'Mrs fucking Danvers,' Patsy greeted her contemptuously, pushing Micky into the tiny hall. 'I want to see Old Mother Time and don't give me any guff about her not being here. She never leaves this place.'

'She's out the back,' Mrs Blixen said.

'Plane-spotting, I suppose,' Patsy replied. 'Keep an eye on the jaffa, he might try to escape.'

She had to go through the kitchen to get to the back garden. As she passed the blue Formica table, she was surprised to see their 'recipe book' sitting on it. She knew it normally lived on the top shelf in the living room.

She paused. A powerful instinct made her pick up the battered copy of *Ulysses*, hold it by its spine and give it a good shake. A page of cheap jotter fell out, and Patsy had a quick read. Meaningless words. Sums. And what looked like a witch's recipe. Eye of toad and leg of newt kind of stuff. Patsy folded it quickly and stuck it in her bra. She had a feeling this might come in very handy.

She opened the back door, and stood for a moment watching the grey-haired woman in the mauve duffel coat sitting on the papal throne. Her eyes were skywards, her biro poised over a copybook. She looked across, her blue eyes blazing over Patsy, who moved slowly forward out of the sheltering shade of the kitchen and into the cold sunlight of the garden.

'Mammy,' she said, making her way to Pauline Bloom. 'Would you mind telling me just what the fuck is going on?'

And just at that moment, on the other side of town. Gary Reynolds was more than a bit upset. The bin into which he'd thrown the mystery papers worth millions of pounds had been emptied, not half an hour before he got back to the house. They were gone. He was fat. He'd fucked up again.

He wondered how the hell he was going to break it to Madelene.

Chapter Six: by Anthony Cronin

Detective Superintendent Andrew Andrews paused for a moment outside the door. It was not a long pause; his hand was already on the knob; but it was one of those moments that reveal a man to himself, the normally hidden fear, the usually concealed sense of inadequacy, the latent feeling of powerlessness in a world full of strong and utterly ruthless bastards.

Then he twisted the knob and stepped inside. As usual, the Assistant Commissioner did not even deign to look up. He had a file on the desk in front of him and was studying it intently – or pretending to, the bollocks – the well-groomed top of his head confronting his visitor.

'Sit down, Superintendent,' he said affably, waving his hand vaguely in the direction of the chair in front of his desk. Andrews advanced reluctantly. He wanted to pick up the chair and smash this man's skull with it. Instead he sat down and hitched up his pants to spare the crease. As always, he did not know what to do with his huge and useless hands. The perennial rage of the subordinate possessed him, in concert with the perennial unease.

The Assistant Commissioner went on reading, the bastard. There was nothing for Andrews to do except sit there and look at the painting on the wall behind the desk. He knew it already, having been in this position before. It was, to his eye, an incompetent, smudgy yoke, but he knew too that it was meant to be a portrait and he knew that the fellow with the big nose and glasses on the end of it was the poet Patrick Kavanagh. From where he sat he could make out the signature – Michael Kane. He remembered Paddy Kavanagh, a big, ignorant latchiko who never had an arse to his britches. A colleague had once caught him in the act of stealing a milk bottle from a doorstep in Pembroke Road. When he told the story he had made great sport of the culprit's defence – 'I put it there myself when I went to get the paper' – but Andrews had felt there should have been a prosecution. Now he knew better. You had to go along with a lot of fuckology nowadays. He read the *Irish Times*, he knew about Bloomsday. Once, he'd tried reading Joyce, but found his work totally impenetrable. He'd tried some of the other Irish writers, he'd even been to the Abbey Theatre – the wife was always mad to go there. But he knew that no matter how much he picked up he could never compare with this smoothie in front of him, a mother's boy who had absorbed all this arty stuff with his mammy's milk.

He tried to read the title of the file without seeming to, straining forward in the chair. Ah. He had thought so the minute Horan had said to him with a smirk – 'Cuthbert wants to see you, you'd better get over there quick.' *Reynolds Murder* said the pasted-on label inside the cover.

The time passed slowly, as the Assistant Commissioner had intended it should. Andrews found himself slipping off the chair. His hands, dangling in front of him, seemed to be getting bigger. But for five minutes at least there was no relief from his discomfort. Then the AC closed the file, pushed it to one side and fixed him with what seemed a mild enough gaze. Andrews's hopes began to rise. Perhaps it would not be too bad after all.

'Your men seem very keen, Superintendent,' said the AC pleasantly. He waited for a response.

'Well, yes sir, they are,' said Andrews eventually.

'Very keen indeed,' said the AC, his tone still mild.

'I hope they are,' said Andrews. 'I believe on the whole they are.'

'Oh, very,' said the deputy. 'Sergeant Roberts, for example, volunteers to take a statement from a suspect in a case he is not even assigned to.'

Again he waited for a response.

Andrews felt he had to say something, but he was beginning to suspect a trap.

'Sergeant Roberts is a very keen and helpful officer,' he said.

There was another pause. And then he added: 'A very good man.' Immediately he said it he knew how foolish it was. Roberts was a slag and a crook and the AC probably knew that.

'And then there's Officer Nestor, God rest him,' said the AC. 'He was so keen he went poking around at the scene of a crime which had nothing whatever to do with him. And got a bullet in the head for his pains, the Lord have mercy on him.'

Andrews tried to recover something of the lost ground. 'As a matter of fact I don't quite understand that yet myself, sir,' he ventured. 'I've been trying to find out what he was up to.'

'Or thought he was up to, eh, Andrews?'

'Exactly sir.'

'You've been inquiring of his colleagues, I suppose?'

'Oh yes. As part of my general inquiries.'

'And what do they think? Roberts, for example, what does he say?'

'They, er, think it is very strange. Like myself, they are mystified. It would seem that he hadn't given any indication of his interest in the Reynolds murder.'

The AC was enjoying himself. If there was one thing he enjoyed more than any other, it was putting a bully on the spot. It was the aspect of police work which gave him almost unadulterated satisfaction. Most professional criminals, and certainly all gang-leaders, were bullies, the terrorists of the playground. Contact with them brought back involuntary memories of the taste of tears, of blood and snot commingled, of his shameful weeping. And of course some of the policemen whom it was his job to oversee were bullies too. That, as much as anything, was why he had tried to get to the top. Of course he hadn't quite succeeded yet. He was only the Assistant. Like most people in this sad world, he still had a bully above him. Well, what odds. In time he would square that too. And meantime he would take it out on this prime example of the breed.

'This Dunphy fellow hanging himself. That's a bad business,' he said pleasantly, almost conversationally, as if he was discussing a neutral topic with an acquaintance.

'Very bad,' agreed Andrews after the inevitable pause.

'Particularly when he had no more to do with the matter than the man in the moon. Makes it a bit worse, don't you think, Superintendent? Bad enough when the guilty ones hang themselves in our custody, but when we bring people in off the street and hound them to their deaths it always looks a bit worse.'

Andrews remained silent. He had nothing to say.

'You never found the gun or associated him with the gun. You got no forensic evidence of any description. But you got a confession. A signed statement. Now that was clever, really clever, Superintendent. And now you've given the media the biggest fucking field day they have had since the fall of the Roman empire.'

'Sir, I know how it looks or can be made to look. But I assure you on my word of honour that it isn't that way.'

His boss reached into a drawer and took out a bottle of Irish whiskey, which he placed carefully on the beautifully polished desk.

'Would you like a drink, Superintendent?'

'No, thank you, sir. Not when I'm on duty.'

'You know where I got that bottle, I suppose?'

'Well' – the question confused him and he gave a nervous laugh – 'no sir, I don't know that.'

'That bottle was found in the dead man's caravan.'

The trap was being sprung now, Andrews could tell.

The Assistant Commissioner took a document from the file and began to read aloud from it.

'Statement given by Jason Dunphy . . . "I looked around to see if there was anything I could rob. It was a bit of a kip. I had a good big drink out of a bottle of whiskey that was there."' He peered at Andrews over the rim of his spectacles. 'Odd, that. Don't you think, Superintendent?'

'Sir?'

'There are no suspicious fingerprints on that bottle, Andrews. Only the dead man's. How would you begin to explain that strange fact?'

'I suppose young Dunphy must have been wearing gloves, sir.'

'Oh?'

'Now that I think of it, I believe he told me he was.'

'I see. Tell me, Andrews – did he also tell you that he was violently allergic to alcohol? As a result of a serious medical condition?'

Andrew Andrews found himself speechless.

'Because he was, you know.' The AC nodded thoughtfully. 'One sip of alcohol – let alone "a good big drink" – would have landed Jason Dunphy in intensive care. And yet he includes the claim of freely drinking whiskey in his signed confession. Strange, isn't it? Don't you think that is strange?'

He looked his subordinate in the eye, waiting for the flinch, which duly came.

'This will not be forgotten, Superintendent,' he said. 'The boss is hopping mad about this. The minister is hopping mad. You may think I am hopping mad about it. You would be wrong. The only emotion I feel about it is an absolute determination to see that you get full credit for your part in the affair so far. I have to make a report about this business to the boss. Tomorrow morning he and I have to go together to see the minister. She will not be easily mollified. But in my report the name of Superintendent Andrew Andrews will figure prominently, so prominently that it will never be forgotten in the annals of the Garda Siochána, even among all the other strange and remarkable things that are recorded there.'

He stood up. Andrews, believing himself to be released, sprang up on the instant.

'Sit down, Andrews,' said the AC. 'We're not quite finished yet, you know.'

He walked round the spacious office he had furnished

with such care, by dint of alternately badgering and browbeating the Board of Works to produce the charming little bookcase, the oak table on which stood John Behan's bronze boar, the more bijou one with its strangely luminous Frances O'Connor vase, the Patrick Swift painting, the Nano Reid, the Patrick Collins. During this perambulation, Andrews was constrained to sit in a forward-facing position, watching him out of the corner of his eye, but when the AC spoke again it was from directly behind the other man's back.

'What did you intend to do when you retired, Superintendent?' he asked, his tone now mild and pleasant again.

'I've never really thought about it, sir. I've been too taken up with my work on a day-to-day basis. It seems a long way away.'

'Well let me give you a piece of advice, Superintendent. Think about it now. Think about it seriously. It will not be time wasted, I assure you.'

Now he was back behind the desk again, his tone quite serious.

'You may go now, to meditate on your retirement. But before that happy event comes to pass, you will let me have your thoughts, in writing, on this case so far. To be quite frank, I don't expect them to be of much value, but one never knows.'

Andrews rose with such relief that he knocked over the chair. While he was putting it to rights again, the AC said mildly, 'Oh and by the way, find Sergeant Roberts and send him in to me.'

Anxious to get to the door though he was, Andrews felt he had to say, 'He's not on this case, sir, and he may be hard to find. He may be out on another case.'

'I do not currently happen to need any advice or reminders, Andrews,' the AC responded blandly. 'You brought him into this case to the extent that he took the statement. I want to know more about the circumstances in which it was taken for the purposes of my report. You will find him within the next twenty minutes and you will have him here within the half-hour. Goodbye, Superintendent.'

After Andrews had gone, the Assistant Commissioner sat moodily at his desk, tapping the closed file with his fingers. He was not looking forward to the meeting with his superior, nor to the subsequent meeting with the minister. He would get no comfort from the first and little from the second except for the privilege of observing the discomfiture of his superior officer. Kick arse though we may, he reflected, there is always someone above us to kick ours. The minister could kick the chief's; but she could get hers kicked by the Taoiseach and he in his turn had to reckon on a good kicking by the electorate. Nobody escaped this process. Even the Pope of Rome could have his arse kicked by Our Saviour Who is in Heaven. It was sad, but it was also comical; and the fact that there was no immunity all the way to the top should be a source of great consolation and encouragement to everybody lower down. Brightening again, he picked up his telephone and buzzed the outer office.

'Get me the personnel file of Sergeant Joseph Roberts, will you, Sinead,' he said, 'and make them be quick about it. Oh and don't let them put any calls through for the moment. None whatsoever. I want to think.'

He pulled a pad towards him and unscrewed his pen,

but, like most people in such situations, he didn't think. Instead his mind flitted about. The officer who got shot. What did he think he was up to? And what was his connection, if any, with the Tommy Reynolds murder? Roberts had taken the statement from the unfortunate little fellow who committed suicide. The AC knew how it had been obtained. He knew Andrews's methods and he knew Roberts's type too. Rack-renting and sleaze, that was Roberts. The world was divided into those who tried to avoid the sordid and those who revelled in it, like dogs rolling on dead seagulls. He hated sordidness. He hated low-grade, low-life money-grabbing, whether criminal or not. Always he had sought to avoid the sordid, even in his deceptions and – he smiled to himself – his love affairs.

All his life he had rejoiced in order, discipline, precision of thought and action. It may be that the sordid cometh, he thought, but woe to them by whom it cometh. In their number he included many contemporary novelists. He read a fair bit of contemporary fiction because he wrote the book notices in the *Garda Review* under a pseudonym, and he had strong views about it. There were great writers, Joyce among them, who dealt at length with the seedy as an aspect, an inescapable aspect, of human affairs, but this was to throw something else into perspective. They did not rejoice in it for its own sake. And they were men with wide experience of life. They did not have this weak fascination with the sordid. Most of those who dealt in it now though, he thought, were actually sheltered middle-class males and females, playing a game, trying to be toughies, to show their laddishness. And they really knew very little about it, very little about the criminal and his mind, or the mind of his symbiotic twin, the policeman. This Roberts, he thought, was probably the sordid personified, with no sense whatever of anything finer in life than to cheat and impose, except possibly to brag about cheating and imposing. The Assistant Commissioner wanted his policemen and his criminals to have style and even a sense of tragedy, of necessary doom. What a hope, he thought.

When Sinead came in, he saw at once from her expression that there was something wrong. The clear gaze that he so loved was clouded. The features, usually so serene, and seeming, to his besotted heart, to reflect an inner composure of soul, were puckered slightly.

She handed him the file. 'I'm sorry to interrupt,' she said. 'But I felt I had to. Something awful has happened.'

'Sit down, Sinead,' he said tenderly, indicating the chair where Andrews had so lately sat and suffered.

She obeyed automatically, frowning and still pre-occupied with whatever it was.

'Now tell me about it.'

'I went down to Personnel myself to hurry them up and collect the file and I was just on my way back with it when I met Sergeant Timmons. He told me . . .' She broke off, as if in shock.

'Yes, dear? Told you what?'

'About Sergeant Roberts.'

'What about him?'

'He's been shot. Shot dead. I'm sorry, it was a shock – the coincidence. I was just on my way back from Personnel with his file.'

'Do they know any details?' His tone was businesslike and his face displayed no emotion.

'It seems he was at his girlfriend's flat in Rathmines,

somebody called Dymphna Morkan. It seems he owned the house.'

'Was she there? Are there any witnesses? Is she a suspect?'

'No. Though I didn't get all the details. Somebody at the top of the stairs saw a dark-haired woman hurrying down after they had heard the shot. But it wasn't the woman who lives there, this Dymphna Morkan. And there was also a man, the witness said, a red-haired man, I'm not quite clear about this, but he seems to have been driving a car, maybe a getaway car. A Lancia. But he drove off before the woman got down the front steps. It appears that she stood there and shouted something after the car, then she hurried around the corner. The witness didn't follow her.'

'They never do nowadays. She presumably still had the gun. Who's there at the moment, who's at the scene?'

'Sergeant O'Brien. Superintendent Andrews is said to be on his way.'

'Well, he can make his way back again and save himself any further trouble as far as I am concerned.'

Sinead had now recovered herself and something of the businesslike relationship which they liked to alternate with exchanges of tenderness had returned to her manner. 'Is there anything I should be doing?'

'I want somebody in homicide who is not tied up in anything else at the moment, somebody young, with a lot of cop-on. Get me the murder roster from outside, would you please?'

'Of course. But can I make a suggestion?'

'If it's a good one, and yours usually are.'

'I have a friend. As a matter of fact you met her. You may not remember. It happened when we decided to go out for a drink one night' – she felt like saying 'for once', but thought better of it – 'and she came into the pub.' She was going to say, 'You were covered with confusion', but again she thought better of it. This was no time for banter. But she couldn't help adding: 'You were quite impressed.'

'I remember,' he said drily. He recalled a tall, dark-haired girl with dark eyes and a nice smile, wearing a white suit.

'Grainne O'Kelly. Inspector Grainne O'Kelly she is now.'

'I know. She was promoted a couple of weeks ago.'

Sinead stood up, her neat blue shirt tightening over her breasts, smoothed her skirt and looked at him from under her brows in the way that he had first found irresistible.

'She's really clever,' she said. 'She's a graduate in forensics and she's aching to be in something big.'

'Hmm. It would be the first time a woman had charge of a murder. But that might not be any harm. The way we're going at the moment, it's beginning to look as if only drastic new departures can save us. And besides, it would soften the media's cough for them. The trouble is, though, that this could turn out to be something very big, with a lot of media interest and pressure. Is she up to that?'

'I'm sure she is. She's a very tough girl.'

'Good. I like tough girls.' As a matter of fact he didn't, but it seemed an okay thing to say in the circumstances. 'I have a funny feeling about this case,' he said. 'Roberts had only a peripheral connection with the Tommy Reynolds murder. But another officer died because of that and now we have two officers dead. I have a strange feeling that all three killings are connected. But if that's the case, there will be a lot of dirt flying. Other officers may be implicated and others will have to talk. There will be a lot of arm-twisting to be done. Is she up to that?'

'When you meet her I think you might agree that she could get answers. And perhaps by using new approaches. I think she would be quite prepared to do a little arm-twisting, but there might be other ways.'

'All right. I think you may have won. Send her to me.'

He stood up. He longed to take Sinead in his arms, but they had agreed there would be no caresses in the office. It was too dangerous.

'I'll have to get my reward for this,' he said. 'Thursday still all right?'

She smiled her assent and mouthed a kiss.

'Perhaps you'd find Inspector O'Kelly for me.'

Inspector Grainne O'Kelly was in Bewley's café when her mobile phone rang. She was waiting for Paddy Dignam, her ornithologist boyfriend, who was as usual half an hour late, and she had just been reflecting on a curious phenomenon of our time. Bewley's customers, she noted, were getting bulkier. Soon there would be no room for them in their favourite place of resort. All around her people were wearing heavily padded jackets and voluminous woollen garments. Most of them, male or female, wore knapsacks on their backs, so that they required a considerable space to turn around in. If they did it suddenly you were in danger of being knocked down; and this was to say nothing of the backpackers, with whom the danger was even greater, since they had all the materials for encampment on their backs, or, as all around her at the moment, on the floor, leaving hardly any room to move about between the tables.

She noticed this phenomenon particularly because she had spent the last hour or two in the Horseshoe Bar of the Shelbourne Hotel, where she had also spent part of the night before. The people there wore wafer-thin, svelte clothes which fitted closely and added very little bulk to their already thin bodies. They could pass each other and move around each other with ease.

Last night she had been entertaining, and this morning seeing off, an English detective who had been delivering a warrant for the arrest and deportation of an Irish building contractor wanted for tax fraud in England. He would be back, for the proceedings were likely to be contested and he would have to prove the warrant in court, but she was already making vague plans to avoid having to entertain him again. She had gone to bed with him somewhat against her better judgement, largely because latterly she had been feeling a little guilty about not being more experimental in her sex life. The experiment had not been a success; and though she spent a cordial morning with her overnight partner, she was already blotting it from her mind.

At this point in her meditations a middle-aged grey-haired woman approached the table. She too was occupying a lot of space, with her two shopping bags, her voluminous leather handbag and the bulky coat and scarves which she now proceeded to loosen. She smiled at Grainne and Grainne smiled back, returning what seemed to be a message of good will.

'Do you mind if I sit here, love?' the woman asked. 'Is there anybody else here?'

'No, not at all,' Grainne replied. 'I'm waiting for somebody, but there's room for him too,' she added, indicating the chair beside her.

'So he's late, is he? They usually are, in my experience. But there you are. We like them just the same.'

Grainne smiled again. She did not want to encourage too much intrusion, but she liked this woman, with her long grey hair, which had tumbled loose when she took off her beret, her lower middle-class Dublin accent, her faintly harassed air. She liked such women, who had usually had a hard enough time of it; and this one seemed motherly and kind as well as intelligent.

'I see you're reading a book, dear,' the woman now said, indicating the paperback on the table beside Grainne's plate.

The book was Karen Blixen's *Anecdotes of Destiny*, which Grainne was currently carrying in her bag and had taken out and laid on the table beside her, but had not actually been reading.

'Do you read a lot?'

Grainne gave the answer which everyone gives. She wanted to think her own thoughts. 'I'm afraid I don't have time to do as much reading as I would like, but then who has?'

'I think books are wonderful,' the woman said, evidently bent on conversation. 'If they had never been invented and somebody thought of them now, they would be the greatest things ever. I can't think of anything that has given so much happiness to humanity. Or could do, except maybe a pill to make us live longer. Books are so simple. No batteries, no wires, no earphones. Absolutely silent, don't interfere with anybody else, you can take them anywhere with you, into bed, into the bath. And they can't be broken. You can lie on them, sit on them, prop the door or the window sash open with them and you still can't damage them.'

Grainne laughed.

'I'm very fond of books,' the woman continued. 'My friend and I read a lot of books.'

Friend, Grainne thought, idly. Male or female? Could be either.

'I often pretend to be characters in them,' the woman said. 'For a few days. My friend and I like that. I pretend to be Mrs Bennet, or Jane Eyre, or Emma. I've even pretended to be Karen Blixen,' she said shyly.

Grainne laughed again, a little uneasily this time. Maybe this woman was a bit cracked. She didn't want that. She wanted her to be a brave, intelligent, middle-aged woman who had come through the mill.

Then, in the depths of the woman's bag, a mobile phone rang. At first Grainne thought it was hers; but it wasn't. The woman took it out. 'Excuse me, love,' she said.

God, I hope mine doesn't ring, thought Grainne. It's bad enough to have one person at a table in Bewley's talking on a mobile phone. But two complete strangers doing it – that would be ridiculous.

She pretended not to listen, even opening Karen Blixen, but she did.

'Oh no,' the woman was saying. 'What a terrible pity. And him in the prime of life too. Of course not, dear. I always am careful. He was little more than an acquaintance really, wasn't he? I mean we hardly knew him at all.'

Grainne was now listening a little more intently. She was, after all, a detective. She had been on very few big cases, and then only as a dogsbody, treated as such by her male colleagues, but she was practising. And she always tried to piece together the context of overheard conversations.

'In the papers,' the woman was saying. 'I see. Of course you probably don't know very much, but can you tell me how it happened? Oh dear. *Cherchez la femme.* He was being unfaithful, I presume. Well, that's men for you.'

Grainne was finding this interesting, if only in an academic sort of way; but then her own phone rang. She took it out, smiling foolishly at the woman. It was an excited Sinead.

Strangely she found herself using some of the same phrases the woman had used: 'Oh dear. What a pity. How did it happen? In the papers, yes. Am I? Wow. Well, of course I'm not to know till I see him. I always am careful, you know that. Okay. I'll just finish my coffee and come straight away. Can you tell me anything about the circumstances?' Finally she said, 'I'm waiting for Paddy here in Bewley's, but never mind. Of course I'll come at once.'

After she had rung off, the thought struck her that the woman, who had now also finished her call and was calmly munching a rock bun with her coffee, could have been talking about Sergeant Roberts and his death too. She was a great believer in the long arm of coincidence as an adjunct to the long arm of the law. So strong was the thought that although she was already standing up and saying a smiling goodbye, she very nearly sat down again. She could at least ask the woman's name. Then she dismissed the idea as just too fanciful. It was impossible to imagine a woman like that having anything to do with such a murder, or having any significant acquaintance with the victim. She was too eccentric, too human, too womanly.

'I hope we meet again,' she smiled.

'I'm sure we will, dear,' said the woman; but Grainne was already turning away. She would add a few touches to her face in the office. She remembered meeting the AC that night with Sinead. It was not quite true she had not liked him. She had not approved of him, or at least she had not approved of him having an affair with her Sinead. Sinead should not be having an affair with a married man who was also her boss. She should be going to places where she might meet a nice, intelligent, upwardly mobile fellow, get married to him and have children. Ah well, she thought. People never did what was right for them. She turned towards Harcourt Street. She knew exactly how long it took to walk from Bewley's to the Garda headquarters, but today she hurried a little more than usual.

The Assistant Commissioner and his superior officer got rather stiffly into the back seat of the car together, both wearing their blue uniforms with plenty of braid on display. The AC had already had a bollocking and he felt the worst was over. Now they were going to see the minister. His superior would have to take most of the flak.

'Now remember,' the Commissioner said as they were driven out into the Harcourt Street traffic, 'keep it simple. Keep it within her grasp. If it was one of the old gang, now, Burke or somebody who understood human failings and complications, then you could tell the whole story. But this gang are not like that, the

Fine Gaelers in particular. They have a limited grasp of the human aspect of things. They're limited both mentally and morally. They don't understand the grey areas, what you might call the ambiguities. They don't really understand human nature. They want everything cut and dried. There's no use saying to any of this gang that it looks very complicated and it's all a bit of a mystery because of the general oddness and confusion of human affairs. They're not prepared to admit that aspect of things, what you might call the grotesque aspect, the unprecedented, the bizarre, you know what I mean, the unpredictable, no two situations ever being the same from the dawn of time. They want everything cut and dried, the reason for this, the reason for that, who's to blame and who's not to blame.'

He straightened his cap on his head and stared gloomily at the traffic in Stephen's Green, where a large force of uniformed officers was occupied in clamping and unclamping cars. He was a stout red-faced police chief of the old school and, truth to tell, the AC rather liked him, in spite of their differences.

'That's not to say,' the chief continued, 'that you don't have a villain of the piece. So far, as far as she's concerned, and in the absence of any other, your villain is Andrews. You can lay it on thick about him. Your report makes it obvious to me that you don't have a clue otherwise, as far as the actual crimes are concerned. But this lot have a great appetite for blame. They're avid for villains.'

At the corner of Grafton Street an *Irish Times* poster was on display. CALL FOR GARDA INQUIRY, it said.

The chief regarded it sourly. 'That'll be the next thing,' he said. 'We'll all be up before a tribunal. God alone knows what will come out.' He gave his assistant a playful dig in the ribs with his elbow. 'I hope your lifestyle passes inspection,' he said, 'and that your private life is on the up and up. And I hope the same is true of that gobdaw, Andrews. His private life better be squeaky clean. When this shower get to digging we could all be in Queer Street. I hope to God he has nothing to hide.'

Chapter Seven: by Owen O'Neill

For one split second amid the chaos, Andrew Andrews realised that everything was spiralling out of his control. Why did he take these incredible chances? If things were to go wrong now – if he were to be double-crossed – it would mean the end of his career. Everything for which he had worked so hard would vanish in a puff of smoke.

He knew that the handcuffs had been fastened far too tightly – much, much tighter than usual – and the situation had become quite disturbingly violent. But he also knew that this was why he was here. The danger was part of the overall pleasure, and just at this moment he didn't care. Out of the corner of his moist, hot eye he watched her raise her hand and whip the belt through the air. His whole body convulsed as the leather slashed across his buttocks.

She pulled him around by the hair and dived between his legs, taking him in her mouth, her head nodding frantically. *Yes! Yes! O God yes.* He arched his back as he orgasmed, letting out a deep and guttural roar. Trying to rise from the bed, he felt the handcuffs bite into his wrists. He cried out in pain and ecstasy, and sank back down, his breath coming in gulps.

'You're such a noisy bastard,' she said. 'You never used to be this noisy.'

* * *

Jason Dunphy's father was consumed with grief.

It had come upon him suddenly, hitting him in the face like a wave. As it washed over him, he felt as if he was drowning; and he didn't want to drown, not here, not in Bewley's café. He hated Bewley's, hated its claustrophobic mahogany interior, its slow black-clad waitresses. And yet he always seemed to end up here whenever the black dog of depression was pissing down his back. Bewley's was not unlike the inside of a church, he thought. If the Catholic church had a canteen for nuns and priests it would look almost exactly like Bewley's café.

His heartbeat was pounding hard in his ears; pins and needles prickled along his arms and across his chest; a trickle of cold sweat was forming on his forehead. The clatter and chat from the crowded café was becoming a strangely distant murmur. He gripped the sides of the little table, then clenched his teeth and his stomach muscles to stop himself from screaming. But it was to no avail. The word forced its way up his throat.

'ANDREWS!' He roared the hated name from the pit of his knotted stomach. '*ANDREWS!*'

His shriek brought Bewley's to a total standstill – every last person in the place was staring at him now. 'ANDREWS! . . . *I WANT ANDREWS!*' He was howling and barking like a wounded dog.

A grey-haired woman at a nearby table dabbed rock-bun crumbs from the side of her mouth. She studied the unfortunate screaming man and made a mental note never to come into Bewley's again when it was so crowded.

Through his tears he became vaguely aware that two

anxious waitresses were standing by his side. 'Is it liver salts you're after, sir?' said the one with red hair and apple cheeks. 'I don't think we stock that,' said the dark-haired one with the crooked teeth. 'I'm not sure. I'll go and ask.'

He rose from the table and ran stumbling for the door.

He only stopped running when he got to Stephen's Green, where he collapsed, shaking, on a bench beside the pond. His lungs seemed to be on fire; excruciating pain skewered through his upper body. Three ducks came closer and laughed at him. Sarcastic laughs. Dirty as well. *Wark! Wark! Wark! Wark! Fuck off, Mister!*

He remembered when he used to bring his son here, back when he was only two or three. He could still see that silly little boat he had bought him in Dunnes' toy department – in his memory he saw it, floating on the pond. 'Don't go too near the edge, Jason son, you'll fall in.'

His grief was quieter now, darker; it began to roll over him slowly, a heavy dead wave. Tears welled up again and he sobbed like a child.

This was the worst he had ever felt in his life. It was even worse than having to identify Eileen's body when it was eventually dragged from the rail tracks and brought to the morgue. When was that? So long ago now. WOMAN DIES AT PEARSE STREET STATION. He remembered the stark brutality of the headline in the *Evening Herald*, the efficiently diplomatic words of the city coroner. 'A painful case, a painful case.'

What had hurt so much was that he had always expected it to happen; she had threatened it often enough. 'I can't stop drinking, Eamon!' she'd wail. 'I can't live with it and I can't live without it. I'll fucking kill myself one of these days.' Jason was sixteen when she finally did. Eamon had never even been able to talk to him about it. Without his mother, the kid had gone wild, and Eamon, numbed and helpless, had ignored all the signs.

Maybe suicide was hereditary. He wondered if it was. Everything is genetic, that's what they said nowadays. Gay genes, violent genes, alcoholic genes. But no. No – that was too easy. It was Andrew Andrews who had killed Jason, Eamon Dunphy was convinced of that. Jason may have put the belt around his own neck, strapped it to the cell door and jumped off the chair, but it was that cruel bastard Andrews who had driven him to it.

Eamon sat on the bench and allowed memories to come. Every time there was a burglary or a mugging in the neighbourhood Andrews would haul Jason in and terrorise him. Jason would confess, just to get out of the place. The bastard had been hounding Jason for years, barging into the house whenever he felt like it, and always the same stupid sarcasm about Eamon's name 'Ah, Mr Eamon Dunphy, you're not the football man, are you? No, of course not, you wouldn't be living in this shithole if you were.'

But Eamon knew more about Andrew Andrews than the merciless bastard realised. Dublin was small, you got to hear things. He knew, for instance, that Andrew Andrews was having an affair with another policeman's wife. He knew where they went, he had followed them on several occasions, never knowing exactly why, only knowing that one day the knowledge would come in handy. The same grotty little place every time, the Araby

Hotel on Northumberland Road. They always arrived in separate cars. Eamon had watched, he knew their routine. The woman didn't look like much – a bit Costa del Sol, he thought, no class. But then Andrews himself had no class. For all his pomp and braided arrogance the man was a mucksavage who would only ever understand one language – the language of violence, of hate, of revenge.

A calmness began to descend on Eamon. His sobbing subsided, his heart seemed quieter. He dried his eyes with the sleeve of his coat and looked out across the shining pond. A plan started to form in his mind. He visualised himself doing it. It felt good. He ran it over again. He sat on the bench until it was dark, until he couldn't see the ducks any more, replaying the idea like a favourite film clip.

'Yes,' whispered Eamon. He sighed contentedly.

Wark! Wark! Wark! came the distant laugh.

Micky McManus caught sight of his reflection in the window of a trendy boutique in Grafton Street.

He had to admit that he liked what he saw. For once in his miserable life he had spent his dole money wisely. A droplet of rain smacked his cheek. He hoped that the black face-paint was waterproof. The girl at Action Props – a theatrical supplies shop behind the Olympia – had assured him that it absolutely was. The dreadlock wig was making his head itch, but the girl had told him he'd have to expect that for a while. He'd get accustomed to it before too long. It was a bit like wearing in a new hat, she said.

The canary-yellow flares were slightly tight around his plump little arse, but the satin zebra-skin-pattern jacket was a perfect fit, and the blue silk shirt could have been tailor-made for him. The secondhand bongo drums had been a lucky find in a charity shop, a real bargain at twelve quid, even with a cigarette burn hole in the middle of one of them.

He couldn't believe how easy it was to play the bongos. He'd always known he had fantastic rhythm, always felt there was a black man inside him just begging to get out. But here he was, actually doing it, busking on his bongos in the middle of Dublin. He felt good. He felt *baaad*. He also felt safe. That mad murdering bitch Patsy Roberts would never find him here. In fact no one would ever find Micky McManus again. Because Micky McManus didn't exist any more.

'Yo! Make dat noise muthafucka.'

Andrews looked at Patsy Roberts. A wave of revulsion and self-loathing swept over him. He wanted to die, simply not to exist. He knew he would feel like this, he always did afterwards; like a drunk racked by a hangover, it was the price he had to pay.

Why the hell was he here? It couldn't just be the sex. He often felt there was something deeply wrong with him psychologically. Maybe he needed counselling, or therapy. Perhaps he needed to go back to the Church – he often thought he did. Was it too late, he wondered, to take Holy Orders? How could he trust a woman who had just murdered her husband in broad daylight? Clearly she was insane. Jesus, how he hated her. He knew that this was why he needed to be handcuffed when he was with her – so that he couldn't kill her, couldn't strangle her with his bare hands.

She slid off the bed. 'Do you want coffee?' Andrew

Andrews took a deep breath before he spoke, hoping his voice wouldn't betray his true feelings.

'Can you take the handcuffs off please, they're just a tad tight.'

He was surprised, even pleased, at how calm he sounded; there was no hint of the murderous rage that was boiling in his heart. She undid the cuffs and kissed him gently on the forehead. Christ, he had to give her credit – Patsy Roberts knew just how to handle him. The kiss on the forehead was exactly the right thing to do. It was normal, bland; it extinguished his anger. He rubbed at the red welts already forming on his wrists, got out of bed and began to get dressed.

She gave him a wild look as she plugged in the kettle. 'Why are you in such a rush? You said you were going to help me sort this mess out.'

'Okay!' He turned on her, snapping. 'Relax! I hear better with my clothes on – now just make the coffee.'

Andrew Andrews liked what he had just said. It felt good. He was back in control. He zipped up his flies and allowed himself to watch as she bent to get the carton of milk from the minibar. The glimpse of her ample ass, that tuft of pubic hair, made him harden. 'Let's go over it again. Are you absolutely sure McManus's prints were on the murder weapon?'

She rolled her eyes and sighed. 'Yes, I put it in his hand myself.'

'How?'

'We were driving along and I unzipped him and took out his little freckled dick. I told him if he didn't do what I said I would have it cut off – and then he gripped the handle of the gun until his knuckles went white.'

'And you're sure you were wearing gloves?'

'*Yes*, for God's sake, how many times . . .'

Andrews grabbed her roughly by the arms and pulled her towards him. The milk carton flew out of her hand and splashed against the television screen.

'Now you fucking listen to me, you crazy bitch! If you had followed my instructions you wouldn't be in this fix. I *told* you I would take care of Roberts for you! What the hell were you thinking about? Not only did you kill him in broad daylight but you brought along a complete fucking stranger as your getaway driver, some fucking eejit who's just burgled your house . . .'

Sobbing like a child, she began to tremble in his arms.

'Please . . . Don't be angry with me, Andy.' Her eyes were streaming now. 'When he . . . when he broke into the house I just thought . . . I thought I could make him kill Joe . . . scare him into it. But I couldn't . . . so I . . .'

'It's all right,' he sighed.

'I wanted that bastard dead after what my mother told me about his . . . tendencies. The disgusting, sex-crazed pervert! O.'

Pervert was good, thought Andrew Andrews, considering what they had just been doing.

'I couldn't . . . I just couldn't stop myself . . . I told McManus to keep the car running . . . but the little ginger fuck drove off . . . What am I going to do?'

Andrews sat down on the bed and buttoned his shirt.

'I think we have enough to pin it on McManus. His prints are on the gun, they're also all over your house. He had a motive too: Roberts swiped his precious tape player. Right?'

'That's what he said, yes.'

'I'll find witnesses who'll confirm they heard him say that he was going to kill that husband of yours.'

Andrews checked his gun, snug in the holster. 'By the way, what did you do with the wig?'

'The wig . . . it's gone. I threw it in a litter bin. I watched the dustman take it away in one of those little carts . . .'

'Good.'

'This is all my mother's fault. You know that, don't you?'

'We can bloody take care of her too. If we need to.'

'I was hoping you'd say that. I picked this up at her house.'

She handed him a DHL courier receipt for £755.

'What's that for?'

'She sends stuff all over the world. My dear little mammy. Mrs Bloom.'

'What kind of stuff?'

'Well,' she laughed hollowly, 'I'm not talking about holy pictures, am I? The bitch was selling heroin in Leitrim before it was heard of in Dublin.'

Andrews stared at the receipt, then put it in his pocket.

'I'll take care of everything,' he said. 'You go home and start playing the grieving widow.'

He was beginning to lose his patience now. A powerful urge gripped him to be out of the cheap hotel. This madwoman was bad for him. She was bad for everyone around her. If he wasn't very careful she could make him do something stupid. She was going into one of her spiels.

'The bastard,' she snapped. 'It was *me* who told her

to take him on, you know. Without him even knowing she was my mother. But then he got too big for his boots, the bastard. You know he was in love with her? My own *mother*! What kind of a man is that? I didn't mind him shagging that slut Dymphna Morkan behind my back, but he also wanted to bed my mother. The sick fuck! He wanted me to wear the grey wig in bed! . . . I'm glad he's dead. I did the right thing, didn't I, Andy?'

'Patsy, finish getting *dressed*. We have to . . .'

But she wasn't listening.

'She was going to make him the main man, that's what he told me. He was going to do all the major runs. She denied it when I confronted her but she was lying, I knew it. She was starting to involve too many people. She'd stopped telling me what was going on. That Reynolds thing was driving me nuts. I mean what the fuck was *that* about? Reynolds was almost a tramp, a gypsy for Christ's sake, living in a caravan. But he had something. And I think it was this.'

She pulled a jotter page out of her bra.

'I know her hiding places. It wasn't there the last time I was in the house. It only appeared there after Reynolds was killed.'

Andrews stared at it. 'What? What am I looking at?'

'I'm not sure. I do know that Reynolds used to be some kind of chemist. It might be a recipe. For drugs or something.'

Andrews was now fully dressed. 'Patsy, this is not time to be worrying about fucking recipes! Now listen to me and listen good. Here's what we're going to do. I'm taking you in.'

'What?' She pulled away from him.

He grabbed her arms. '*Listen!* This is what happened. McManus kidnapped you and forced you to take him to your husband. You both went into the house. He shot Joe and ran back to the car – you chased him but he drove off. You didn't go straight to the police because you were in shock. And don't worry, I'll have McManus picked up – in fact I'll do that right away.'

He reached into his blazer, pulled out his mobile and tapped out a number.

'By the time I've finished with him he'll sign anything. He'll confess to the theft of fucking Shergar!'

Patsy bit her lip. 'Why are you doing this for me?'

Andrews picked her blouse from the floor and threw it to her.

'O'Brien? Andrews here. I want a Micky McManus picked up in connection with the Roberts murder. He's a tenant in Roberts's house in Rathmines. Get on it right away, it's top priority.'

He threw his phone on the bed and stared at Patsy.

Just then came two sharp raps on the bedroom door. 'Room service.'

Patsy and Andrews exchanged nervous glances. Andrews whispered, 'We didn't order anything. Did we?'

Rap rap rap!

'Room service for 106. Compliments of the management.'

Patsy shrugged. 'Hold on a moment,' she called.

Andrews went to the window and checked the street. Everything seemed calm, but you could never be sure. 'Get rid of them,' he hissed.

But Patsy had shrugged on a dressing gown and was already opening the door.

In one smooth movement he was into the room. A man in a black balaclava. He whipped out a gun, kicked the door shut, grabbed her hair, lifted her almost off her feet and wheeled her around to face Andrews. This man was strong and meant business.

'What the . . .'

But Eamon didn't let Andrews finish. 'Shut up! Hands behind your head. Do it! NOW!'

Andrews did what he was told.

'Andrew Andrews. You dirty murderer.'

He thought he knew the voice but he couldn't place it. The eyes seemed vaguely familiar too. But what did he mean, calling him a murderer?

The man eased his grip on Patsy's hair but kept his gun trained on Andrews.

'All right. Now be a good girl and go get his gun . . . Go on.'

Patsy had never known fear like this. He sounded so horribly calm – almost relaxed.

'Hurry up. Go on. Get his pistol.' He said it like he was sending her to the shop for sweets.

She reached in and took Andrews's gun from its holster.

'Good girl. Now walk backwards slowly until I tell you to stop. That's right. And don't make any sudden moves. If you do, I'll kill you.'

With a sense of crawling, abject horror, Andrew Andrews now realised who the man was. His bowels began to loosen and liquefy.

'Did you – go to school with me?' he said.

'What?'

'Aren't you Padraig Donohue? You used to call me Randy-Andy-Soft-As-A-Shandy.' He tried to laugh. 'We had a little falling out about it. But I never meant to tie you up in that grotto, honest. I was only – y'know – acting the maggot.'

At this moment Eamon Dunphy wished his own gun was real and not some stupid replica that he had bought Jason for his fifteenth birthday. Slowly, theatrically, he removed his balaclava.

'Jesus,' tittered Andrews anxiously. 'You've changed over the years, Padraig. How's all the crowd down home anyways?'

'My name is Eamon Dunphy,' said Eamon Dunphy. 'You murdered my son, you merciless cunt.'

Andrew Andrews swallowed hard. He could feel his heart pumping, keeping him alive.

'Look, Mr Dunphy – I swear to God I didn't have anything to do with your son's suicide.'

'Do you know any prayers?' asked Eamon Dunphy. 'Because if you do, I'd start saying them fast.'

'Now look . . .'

Dunphy lunged forward and slapped his face hard. 'A bully is always a coward,' he spat. Then, grinning, he turned his attention to Patsy. She was standing very still with Andrews's gun in her hand.

'Turn on the TV,' he ordered. 'Do it slowly.'

Trembling, she crossed to the bed and picked up the remote. She pressed a switch and the screen flickered into life. The other Eamon Dunphy was on a panel discussion, talking about football. There was no excuse for that kind of naivety, he was saying, not at this level of the game.

'Turn it up. Loud. As loud as it goes.'

She did that.

'Okay. Shoot the bastard. With his own gun.'

Patsy almost passed out. 'Come on now . . . for fuck's sake.'

He shoved his gun into the underside of her ear. 'Shoot the fucker or I'll kill you both! I'll count to three and you better have done it!'

Andrews was backing away towards the window. 'No please . . . Please . . . Look, I can explain!'

Eamon started counting. 'One . . . two . . . thr . . .' Patsy fired, hitting Andrews just below his right eye. The bullet went through the back of his head, through the cheap plywood bathroom door, bursting open the toilet cistern.

Eamon Dunphy on the TV boomed, 'WELL THERE'S NO POINT IN HAVING LOTS OF CHANCES IF YOU CAN'T GET YOUR SHOTS ON TARGET. WHAT THIS SIDE NEEDS IS SOMEONE WHO CAN FINISH.'

Superintendent Andrew Andrews had crumpled in a heap, eyes and mouth wide open, spatterings of his blood on the cheap mustard wallpaper. Eamon Dunphy switched off the TV. He listened for any movement outside. But everything was quiet. Nobody had heard.

Shaking uncontrollably, Patsy dropped the gun. 'Please don't kill me . . . Here, take this.' She pulled a jotter page from her bra. 'It's a secret formula . . . for manufacturing drugs . . . it could make you a lot of money. I know it doesn't look like much but—'

'Shut up!'

He snatched the page from her and put it in his pocket. He didn't know what the fuck she was on about, he just wanted to keep her quiet.

'Stay here for at least an hour after I've gone. Do you understand?'

She nodded.

'Good.'

He left, closing the door quietly behind him.

Patsy dropped to her knees and sobbed. 'Mammy, oh Mammy. Help me, Mammy.'

Detective Superintendent Andrew Andrews stared back at her, a black bead of blood bubbling slowly from his nostril.

Chapter Eight: by Hugo Hamilton

'You should always judge a book by its cover,' her father used to say. 'And you should always judge a man by his clothes.'

Somehow this simple maxim never failed – not just in her personal affairs, but also in her work. Inspector Grainne O'Kelly had a way of building up a profile on men – lovers, colleagues, victims and suspects – through their wardrobes. Suits, ties, shoes, pullovers with holes, trousers with shiny seats, socks with diamond-shaped patterns: all these details were worth entering in the record. A person's dress code became a vital part of an investigative methodology that brought to her profession the obsessions of the novelist. After all, police work had everything to do with the imagination.

She was never disappointed. Each search through a man's wardrobe offered a remarkably clear view into his life, his state of mind at a moment of crisis, his level of organisation or utter disarray. Sometimes her work revealed men who seemed to be in a constant state of flight, men who lived like refugees, men who got undressed with great resignation, with sadness, as though they were leaving everything behind them, shedding a life and embarking on a voyage into the unknown. Or meticulous men who folded away their lives neatly before heading into exile. Others who discarded their clothes with great disdain. Men who craved the anonymity of nakedness.

In the past few weeks, she had examined a lot of clothes – dead men's clothes mostly. There were three police officers, to begin with – Nestor, Roberts, Andrew Andrews – as well as the unfortunate Jason Dunphy. Not to mention Tommy Reynolds, the man in the battered caravan whose inexplicable murder she kept coming back to. Each of the victims had left behind a signature, a kind of memoir or autobiographical legacy, a story contained in one or two black plastic bags. Who needed Proust or Gorky or even Frank McCourt when you could go through one of those revealing bags, pick out a pair of shoes or sneakers, reconstruct the urgency of a man's last walk from the angle of a worn-down heel?

Relatives were often the only people who understood these items. They tended to attach sentimental value to things that merely looked like secondhand clothes to everyone else. Stuff you'd see in Oxfam shops. Anonymous tweed jackets that held the hunched shape of a former owner long after he was cremated and scattered. Shirts that stored his bacteria in a kind of life-after-life; the ghostly immortality of his DNA. The sort of thing you could deduce from a man's underpants was staggering. Criminal was often a better word. Some day she would write a new chapter in the textbooks on this one.

The sartorial searches of the past few weeks had rewarded Inspector Grainne O'Kelly not only with great insight, but also, importantly, with tangible evidence. There was, for example, a spectacular discovery in the rather sad navy blazer that Superintendent Andrews had died in. A crumpled invoice from DHL couriers, made out in the name of one Pauline Bloom, of almost legendary criminal fame. It had cost a whopping £755 to send a parcel all the way to Sri Lanka. At that price, it was definitely urgent.

The document she had recovered from the blazer with gold buttons was a poor-quality duplicate, so the weight of the parcel and the address of the recipient were illegible. Perhaps the customs declaration would reveal the contents; if it didn't, she might have to dig around some more. In the meantime what mattered was that the invoice connected Andrew Andrews to this Bloom woman. A major breakthrough, you might well say.

At first she thought the invoice might have been part of Superintendent Andrews's own investigations; something he had come across in the course of the murder inquiry. But then why would he have kept such an important item in his civilian clothes, the very clothes in which he had died? Why was he carrying it around with him? Why had he not placed it in his files? Or made even passing reference to it in his case notes? Peculiarities had begun to emerge from this case – they tended to place Andrews himself centre stage. Why would anyone be so stupid as to murder a Garda Superintendent? Was every police officer on this case a target? That just didn't feel right. It made no sense.

Unless Andrew Andrews was involved in some way.

On the one occasion that she had met Andrews, she had noticed obvious features that should have aroused some suspicion. He was wearing a double-breasted suit for a start. And the tie was very colourful; loud, almost tropical. Alarm bells should have rung when she saw his slip-on moccasins. It was as though he'd been demanding respectability beyond his stature, trying to marry some bogus statesmanlike frontage with rock and roll cool. As though he wanted to look like a Fine Gael politician. And what could you say about a blazer with gold buttons?

'Dodgy' was really the only word for it. But that was easy to say with the benefit of hindsight. After a man was connected to some crime or another, you almost always said to yourself: 'No wonder; *look* for God's sake, he was wearing white socks.'

There were other interesting clues emerging from these black plastic bags. The young man who had killed himself seemed to cry out for justice from beyond the grave. Those curious stains, those tell-tale marks: police brutality was written all over his trousers in urine and blood. And then there were the clothes of Sergeant Joe Roberts; he had left behind a list of lovers' telephone numbers in the pocket of a shirt stained with grey hair-dye. Inspector O'Kelly hoped his poor wife Patsy could be spared that information; she had more than enough to worry about now, having been hospitalised with a total nervous breakdown.

Yes, people's clothes could be endlessly fascinating. Officer Bartholomew Nestor had died in a ragged CHOOSE LIFE T-shirt that was several sizes too small for him and clearly not his own – yet his prized and personalised Manchester United shirt was missing from his room, and his poor grieving mother had been unable to explain its absence. Perhaps most interesting were the clothes of Tommy Reynolds – or, at least, their thought-provoking contents. A poor, sick, malnourished man, who, the autopsy confirmed, had eaten nothing for several days – but with a crisp £10 note hidden in his sock. Why hadn't he gone out and bought food with it? She took out the tenner and looked at it closely. The face of James Joyce seemed to grin back at her. His tartan bow-tie looked a bit too tight. Indeed, from her knowledge of Irish literature, she didn't think Joyce had been the kind of man who would wear a tartan bow-tie at all. It just seemed wrong. All these dead men and their clothes.

Most of her colleagues would have had a good laugh if they had any idea of what she was up to, if they had any inkling of her wardrobe-based pathology. They were all backward, of course; and as uptight as hell. A Fine Gael ethos permeated the Garda establishment, its favourite music the whip-crack of rectitude. All these recent tribunals and media revelations of political payola had given Fianna Fáil, their historical opponents, a permanent image of self-serving gents in party hats pulling Christmas crackers. But at least there was an air of generosity and fecklessness about them. Yes, Fianna Fáilers were just as likely to wear double-breasted suits. But when all was said and done, they prepared Ireland for prosperity. They showed us how to *enjoy*!

Clothes were like political beliefs, you could say. Like a manifesto of sorts.

Inspector Grainne O'Kelly was a plainclothes inspector with no political leanings. She had risen up the ladder without any connections – a little too rapidly perhaps. She was constantly amazed that they had allowed a woman to reach this level on the kick-arse hierarchy. Her vigilant detective work, not to mention her innovative criminal theory, could no longer be completely ignored.

Yes, perhaps the study of men's clothes could be seen as a fetish. You could take it to extremes, of course. Certainly it was open to misdiagnosis. You could get carried away with it sometimes.

To Inspector Grainne O'Kelly, sartorial conformity was beginning to arouse more suspicions than eccentricity. The man without the earring or the nose-stud was a marked man. Often she had to keep her suspicions in check. Ultimately, what linked a criminal to his crime was not his clothes or his looks – nor even his idiosyncratic twitches – but his actions. Even if a man was called Adolf or Augusto and ate raw liver and kept animal pornography in the fridge and listened to REM and loved all of Steven Spielberg's movies and drank his own urine and shoved holy statues of Saint Christopher up his arse, he was still innocent.

Unless you could connect something specific to him.

The DHL docket was the only piece of hard evidence that Inspector O'Kelly had come up with so far. It would have to be pursued all the way to the terminus. The contents of the Sri Lankan parcel could end up being crucial.

One of the rookies, Garda Paschal Greer, came in.

'I've just been down to DHL about that invoice, Inspector. They say the contents were declared as books and magazines.'

Books? Magazines? Who could believe that a woman in Ireland would send books and magazines out to Sri Lanka by courier and then hand the docket to a senior police officer? What kind of books? The lives of the saints, maybe? Religious magazines? Or something more political? According to Greer, DHL were defending their ignorance in the matter. What right had they to ask what people wanted to send abroad? If a woman wanted to sent multiple copies of *Republican News* to far-away friends, then who were DHL to stop her?

'It doesn't add up,' Grainne said.

'Do you think – maybe – it wasn't books and magazines at all?' Garda Greer asked cautiously. He was a bit of a bright light, Grainne thought.

Maybe the Bloom connection was the one to follow. It was time to go and see her, that much was obvious. She would go herself, rather than use an emissary. But first she would need to study the file.

'Garda Greer, can you get on to records for me, please? I'd like to see everything they have on Pauline Bloom.'

'I took the liberty of getting this – her file – on my way up,' said Greer anxiously. 'I hope that's all right. Here it is.'

He handed it over, red in the face. Sometimes this boy could look kind of cute, Grainne thought. She opened the folder and began to flick through the contents. Despite the lack of successful convictions, Mrs Bloom had a long and interesting history. She had been under Special Branch surveillance a number of times and had come to the attention of the Criminal Assets Bureau. The Inland Revenue had tried to take her on, but had failed.

'She started with robbing shoplifters,' Garda Greer informed her. 'They say she used to sell kids back their own lunches at school.'

'Thank you for that,' Inspector O'Kelly said and smiled.

'There were rumours about serious furniture larceny.'

'I'm sorry?'

'A papal throne went missing from the Phoenix Park. Nothing was ever proved, but she was definitely . . . in the frame.'

'I see.'

'I know it's hearsay and all that,' Greer continued, 'but they say she owns half the Cayman Islands.'

'Interesting.'

'She's a formidable woman,' he finally added, like a warning.

Inspector O'Kelly was already putting on her coat.

'Do you want me to go in with you?' Garda Greer asked, when they arrived outside the small terraced corporation house with the almost frighteningly clean front step.

Inspector O'Kelly shook her head. She felt in her coat pocket for her spiral-bound notebook, checked that she had brought her pen.

'It's all right. I'll try the subtle approach first.'

'I'm . . . concerned,' he said, making another attempt. 'These are dangerous people here. And after all, you're . . .' His voice trailed off.

'What?' She laughed in mockery. 'A woman?'

'Well . . . Y'know.'

'I'm also a senior officer, Garda.'

It irritated Grainne how many of her male colleagues insisted on subtly implying her vulnerability all the time. And now Garda Greer was doing it too – going on as though she was unable to get out of the car without the protection of a male escort, when all she was doing was going into a house to have a polite talk with another woman.

Garda Greer sat beside her with sad, hangdog eyes.

Was this a discreet come-on? she suddenly wondered. Was it desire masquerading as concern? Another colleague trying to get into her knickers? Wishing she would be a little more submissive and frightened, and allow him to act as some kind of hero? Well, after all, if it came to that, there was nothing wrong with the idea of a brief romance with Garda Greer. If he took off his uniform, he could be quite handsome. She wondered if he knew that she had always found him attractive.

'I'll tell you what,' she finally agreed, as she opened the door of the unmarked car. 'If I'm not back in an hour, send in reinforcements. Send in NATO. Will that keep you happy?'

'NATO,' Garda Greer chuckled. 'That's a good one.'

She crossed the street and knocked on the door. A radio was blaring through an open window upstairs. 'You're forgiven, not forgotten.' *Come on*, she thought, *open the door*.

No answer came for a long time. Then the curtains shifted in the window and the sound of shuffling could be heard from inside. She knocked again, a little more vigorously. Finally the door opened and a woman glared at her. That fake long-suffering mother-of-fourteen look. Inspector O'Kelly could see through it immediately.

'Are you Mrs Bloom?'

'Blixen.'

'I was looking for a Mrs Bloom. Is there a Mrs Bloom living here?'

'Hold on.'

The woman turned on her heel and disappeared, leaving the hall door wide open. Grainne stepped into the narrow hallway and closed the door behind her. She walked past the living room and peeped in. There were piles of books from the floor to the ceiling, filling every inch of space. Perhaps the parcel to Sri Lanka did contain books, after all. Either that, or those shelves were part of the cover-up.

In the small kitchen at the back of the house a woman was sitting with a jotter on her knees. There was a red biro lodged behind her ear. She had a wide haystack of grey hair. For some reason her face seemed very familiar.

'Mrs Bloom?'

The woman looked up, startled, and nodded. Her facial expression could only be described as shifty. The Blixen woman shuffled in.

'I told you to wait outside,' she barked at Grainne.

'It's all right,' the other murmured.

Inspector O'Kelly stared at Mrs Bloom. Like most police officers, she had an accurate databank of faces and names. But sometimes the signals went astray and you mixed them up. You connected people to their habitual environment. You fixed them in a definite background – Spar checkout counter, doorman at the Omniplex cinema, bus driver on the 13 route. Out of context, you could mistake somebody. If you saw Bill Clinton in the back of a butcher's shop with a red face and a white hat, stuffing black pudding, you'd say to yourself: 'I know that face. But I don't know how.'

'Bewley's,' she said at last, with no help from Mrs Bloom. 'That's it. We met in Bewley's.'

Mrs Bloom smiled back.

'Very good. You're not as stupid as I thought.'

Grainne could hear Mrs Blixen guffawing in the

background. But she refused to turn around to see what she was up to. Instead she stared straight at Mrs Bloom, ignoring the insult. People only implied their own criminality with such unnecessarily offensive behaviour.

'I'm an inspector with the police. I'd like to ask you a few questions if you don't mind.'

'Fire away.'

She took out the DHL docket and placed it on the table. Mrs Bloom laughed. The laugh grew louder. Before long she was killing herself laughing. Grainne could see all her fillings as she rocked back on her chair. She allowed this little paroxysm of mirth to work its way through, and then sighed.

'Something funny about this docket? Like to tell me what was in the package?'

Mrs Bloom gave another burst of helpless laughter, echoed by further clucks of gaiety from Mrs Blixen in the background. But then, Mrs Bloom's laugh began to sound a little forced. It fizzled out and became a fake laugh. It went all the way along the spectrum of Irish laughter from the innocent, hearty, jolly ho-ho to the hollow, knowing chortle. The mechanical laugh. The wind-up-toy laugh.

'Can you explain how this document got into the hands of a murdered police officer?'

Grainne had decided it was time to go in heavy.

'How the fuck do I know?' Mrs Bloom replied. 'And if you don't mind, it's none of your business what I send to Sri Lanka.'

'Running a little export operation here, are you?'

Grainne was met with a wall of derision. Okay, that was it. It was time to take this woman into custody. This whole meeting had been frustrating, but also illuminating. It had given her a chance to examine Mrs Bloom and form an impression – her clothes, her make-up techniques, her domestic situation. Even a casual study in wardrobe pathology was telling her that Mrs Bloom was a very dodgy adversary. A silk blouse and three-stripe tracksuit bottoms. Purple nail polish. The signs were clear.

It was when Grainne finally picked up the DHL docket again that things began to get very interesting.

'I'd like you to accompany me to the station,' she said and tried to stand, only to be pushed back down into her seat by the strong, farm-in-Africa hand of Mrs Blixen behind her.

Mrs Bloom nodded with her eyes. Grainne felt the cold print of a double-barrelled shotgun on her neck.

Mrs Bloom got up from the table and began to root in a drawer. Finally she produced what looked like an electrical cable. It was grey and had a brown earth-wire protruding at one end.

'I'm afraid we're going to have send you to Sri Lanka. It's not a bad place actually, Sri Lanka. Except it's a bit humid. They say your money goes mouldy in your pocket.'

Grainne was determined to put up a struggle. She tried to recall the first principles of self-defence. Go for the shins, gouge the eyes, stamp on the toes. But before she could even move she found herself gagged and bound. The cool, ring-main wire was tightened around her neck. If only she had brought Garda Greer with her. He was such a nice man, he really was. If she ever got out of this situation, she would definitely sleep with him.

The wire tightened harder. Inspector O'Kelly felt her tongue getting larger, almost bursting in her mouth like an unmanageable piece of steak. Her eyes were starting to moisten and bulge. It was just as she looked out of the kitchen window that she saw Garda Greer climbing, or, rather, scrabbling, over the back wall and dropping down on to the patio.

A shot rang out, right beside her ear. The window blew out. Glass beads spraying all over the garden. Then another shot.

Inspector Grainne O'Kelly passed out.

Chapter Nine: by Joseph O'Connor

It was not in Paschal Greer's nature to bandy opinions, nor had it come into any branch of his training.

Even for a new recruit, he was a little shy; some in the station described him as effeminate. One or two of his crueller colleagues referred to him as 'Germaine' behind his back, but the nickname was a comment on his hairstyle rather than his assertiveness. So when the Minister for Justice put down her teacup and asked for Paschal Greer's ideas on fighting crime, the best he was able to do was grin, shrug and take a small bite from his gingernut biscuit.

The Assistant Commisioner gave a nervous laugh. 'Our Greer can be a little quiet,' he said. 'We're trying to bring him out of himself.'

'You're a great man, Greer,' the minister said. 'A fine man altogether. A credit to the force.'

Paschal Greer's face felt like it was burning.

'Thank the minister, laddie,' whispered the Assistant Commissioner.

'Um . . . Thank you very much, Mrs Kinch.'

'You're welcome indeed,' the minister replied. 'If we had more like yourself in the ranks, the war on crime would be over.'

'And don't forget to thank the minister for your promotion too . . . er . . . Sergeant.'

'Thank you, Mrs Kinch. I'm really . . . very honoured.'

'Ah, stop,' scoffed the minister. 'You deserved it. You're a hero!'

Freshly minted Sergeant Greer, the Minister for Justice, Assistant Commissioner Staines and a triumvirate of anxious-looking civil servants were sitting in a large office which boasted a window looking down on to Merrion Street. The meeting had been hurriedly arranged to celebrate Sergeant Greer's promotion, given in recognition of his exemplary bravery in the heroic arrest of Mrs Bloom and Mrs Blixen, the return to enforced tranquillity of Mrs Patsy Roberts, not to mention the timely liberation of Inspector Grainne O'Kelly, who was making a good recovery from the bullet wound to her thigh. The minister was smoking a small cigar and sipping brandy. Rain spattered softly against the window.

'It's on occasions like this,' said Minister Kinch, 'that I feel we in Ireland should have an awards system. Would you like to win an award, Sergeant?'

'I've won awards,' said Sergeant Greer.

'Oh?' said the minister.

'For macramé,' said Sergeant Greer.

In truth, he didn't feel he deserved an award for what he had done that fateful day. He had been listening to his new Tammy Wynette tape in the police car, dreamily fantasising about what Inspector Grainne O'Kelly's face would look like close up if you were kissing it very softly. All of a sudden, he had observed Mrs Patsy Roberts, relict of the late Sergeant Joe, skulking along the road with a handgun. He was taken aback to see this particular lady, as last thing he'd heard she was in the Central Mental Hospital, recovering from a breakdown brought on by the grotesque murder of her husband and the similar cancellation of his superior, Detective Superintendent Andrews, a long-time friend of her family.

A man called Eamon Dunphy but not *the* man called Eamon Dunphy was the main suspect for the shocking double homicide, and was thought to be on the run, or even to have fled the country. He sounded very nasty indeed; the coroner had detected handcuff marks on the dead officer's wrists, and rumour had it that Mr Dunphy, crazed by grief, or maybe just crazed, had subjected Detective Superintendent Andrews to some kind of bizarre sado-masochistic fuckfest before shooting him down like a dog. Holy God. It was like something you would read about in England.

Horrid innuendoes about Mrs Roberts and D.S. Andrews had spread through the station; it was whispered that they'd been having a sordid affair for years. Garda Greer told himself it couldn't be true. He had too much goodness in his heart to believe it, too much respect for the departed Sergeant Roberts, for the legendary if occasionally controversial Superintendent Andrews and for the tragically bereaved Mrs Roberts herself. Such behaviour was unthinkable. Why, it was like saying that a Taoiseach, a priest or even a bishop might be corrupt! Typical gossipy nonsense, that was all. What an Irish poet had once called 'the daily spite of this unmannerly town'. He might be a policeman, but there was no need to be suspicious of people. There was good and bad in everyone, after all. The Irish were a nation of knockers, no doubt about it. But Paschal Greer would be nobody's knocker. No way.

Unhinged by the murders and the slanderously wagging tongues of Dublin, poor Mrs Roberts had been legally, indeed forcibly, lodged in a place where the doors had no handles. Or so everyone thought. But no – here was Mrs Roberts now, large as life and twice as nasty, and, to judge from the gun, open for business. Up she'd tottered to the Bloom–Blixen residence, and next thing Greer knew she'd begun bawling at full tilt, 'Come down here, Mammy! *Come down, you fearful Jesuit bitch!*' and she dribbling all over the lovely clean front step.

Paralysed by fear, Garda Greer had watched from the car, his toes curling in sheer, existential panic. There were moments in the career of every young garda when quick decisions had to be made. Night and day they had drilled this into them in Templemore, and there was little enough doubt that this was one of those fabled moments. Mrs Roberts raised the gun and loosed off a shot at an upper window. 'Die, Mammy, yeh larruping mowldy bitch!' she yelped, whipping a carving knife out of her handbag.

Garda Greer found himself doing a rapid cost-benefit analysis of his potential intervention in the unfolding scene. Cost: a brisk de-bollocking from a violent madwoman. Benefit: the fleeting gratitude of the Irish people.

Sod this for a haircut, he thought. I'm off.

But then there was Inspector Grainne O'Kelly to consider. He loved her with every fibre of his being, every atom of his reticent soul – if only he had the courage to tell her. He had worshipped her for many months. His love was primal, occasionally quite frightening. But there was nothing cheap or unpleasant about it. He worshipped the very ground over which she hovered. But how could he even dream of saying this to her? She would scoff at his love, no doubt, and who could blame her? In the Darwinian league table, his Grainne was a thoroughbred. Whereas he himself – at best – was a donkey.

Late at night, in his dank, lonely bedsit, he had composed technically incompetent but tremendously heartfelt poems extolling her beauty, her grace, her almost unspeakable sexual attractiveness. Sonnets, lyrics, epics and haikus, he had given them all a lash. ('Oh, Inspector Grainne O'Kelly/ how I want to kiss your belly' was one of the haiku.) He had even attempted to write a few songs for her. Some of them weren't half-bad either. One of these nights he would go to a pub he knew and see if they'd let him try them out on the punters.

It was true love. There was no doubt about it. He would wake early in the mornings, sweating, shaking, from dreams of feverish, nerve-shredded longing, the damp sheets wrapped around his twitching limbs like manacles. Inspector Grainne O'Kelly was the bee's knees. She was, he often thought, the other half of his soul. Without her, his continuing existence in the corporeal realm would be meaningless. How in the name of God could he abandon her now, in a situation of possibly mortal peril?

Ah, fuck her, he thought. She had a good life.

He turned the key in the ignition, started up the car and jammed it rapidly into first. And it was at that precise moment that Mrs Patsy Roberts had seemed to notice him.

In the days to come, Paschal Greer would often recollect the subsequent chain of events in something like slow motion. Slowly she had turned, like a cartoon bulldog suddenly aware of a tippy-toeing pussycat, a snarl of concentrated hatred etched into her ruined, crazy face as she raised and shakily aimed the gun. 'You useless fuck,' she seethed, as though she knew him personally. 'You snot-grovelling, sweaty-arsed, insignificant little runt.'

'*Yew'll have bayed times, and yew'll have good times*,' sang Tammy Wynette.

BLAAM! The windscreen shattered. BLAAM! BLAAM!

As though hearing the sound from the bottom of the sea, he would remember the piercing squeal of the tyres and the awesomely cinematic grind of the gearbox as he'd somehow managed to get into reverse, gunning the car backwards around the corner, and, just his luck, into a blind alley.

He grabbed his radio. The channels were jammed. Reached for his truncheon. Prayed he wouldn't have to use it.

His graceless hands were soaked with sweat. His tongue was stuck to the roof of his mouth. Mrs Roberts had come tearing around the corner after him, screaming, 'Come here and take what's coming, you shitkicking culchie! I HATE YOU ALL!'

Gibbering with dread, Garda Greer had leapt from the car, tottered backwards and executed a Fosbury flop over the back wall of the Bloom–Blixen garden, landing on what seemed to be a papal-style throne and shattering it into many pieces.

Through the kitchen window he could see Mrs Bloom and his beloved Grainne, either slow-dancing or all-in wrestling, he could not be sure which. His heart was pumping like the Kilfenora Ceilidh Band on ecstasy.

BLAAM! A shot rang out from behind him and shattered the window. Mrs Roberts was attempting to climb the wall now, screaming 'Mammy! Mammy! Mammy must die!' It was like something out of a horror film.

Somehow he'd lost his truncheon. He'd seized the nearest object to him, the mahogany foot-rest of the papal throne, and bashed repeatedly at her scrabbling fingers with it. '*Aieeee!*' she had screamed. Gravity and Mrs Roberts had entered into conflict, and, as devotees of the late Sir Isaac will confirm, out of such a negotiation may emerge only one victor. Downwards she had fallen into the alley, muttering terrible oaths and imprecations. Greer had grabbed his radio again. This time it was working. Trembling, he'd called for back-up and an ambulance. Next thing he knew, shots had rung out from the house, the back door had whipped open, and out had rushed two old ladies, cantering through the side gate like a pair of greyhounds at Shelbourne Park.

Inside the remarkably clean kitchen was Grainne, trussed up like a yuletide turkey, gagged and bound, her beautiful dusty-blue eyes popping like gobstoppers. Falling to his knees, almost weeping with desire and affection, he had torn her free, the inspector of his dreams, his long fingers trembling, coins spilling from his pockets. He was close enough to smell her musky perfume now, to see the tiny blonde hairs on her long lithe arms, her soft, moist, proud yet yielding mouth only inches, nay, millimetres from his own. This, surely, was the moment for which he had prayed.

'Inspector . . . I mean, Grainne . . . I'm so . . . so deeply . . .'

And then she'd fainted.

And now the minister was congratulating him, shaking his hand, pumping it vigorously up and down, clasping his forearm tightly, even kissing him on the cheek. As a matter of fact, Sergeant Greer felt she might even fancy him. Ordinarily, he wouldn't have minded this. Yes, she wasn't exactly a beauty, but Greer – he had to admit it – was more than a little desperate.

Despite his virginity, he found himself shamefully imagining sex with the minister, in all the different positions, or, at least, in both of them. It wasn't the worst of all possible prospects. He imagined that she would make love like he himself played the piano, not skilfully as such, but with great enthusiasm – and occasionally to entertain groups of appreciative drunkards at parties. But she had a mad look, he thought, a certain lunatic glimmer behind the eyeballs. There had been a lot of innuendo in the Sunday newspapers lately about her state of mind and unpredictable moods.

The minister crossed to her desk, muttering softly under her breath. Dark, secretive looks were exchanged between the civil servants; it was as though they expected trouble to break out.

'Come here, would you, Sergeant?' Mrs Kinch suddenly called. 'I want to show you something interesting.'

Paschal Greer gaped nervously at the Assistant Commissioner, who motioned with his enormous boulder of a head for him to do as the minister asked. 'Go on, you fool,' he urged, 'she likes you.' So across the floor minced the sweating sergeant, his brand new brogues squeaking maliciously.

The minister led him to a corner, where she turned her back on the other men. Grinning, she handed him a copy of her party's manifesto with a mobile telephone number scribbled on the cover.

'Give me a bell some time,' she whispered.

Sergeant Greer held the manifesto lightly, as though its edges were on fire.

'Oh . . . Well it's very nice to be asked, Mrs Kinch . . . but you see . . .'

She moved closer and brushed a stray hair from one of his epaulettes.

'You're a fine figure of a man,' she said. With a smile.

Mrs Bloom sat bolt upright in the front bench of the courtroom, with the air of a woman who owned the place and wasn't about to sell it. Surrounded by solicitors, barristers and concerned-looking Fianna Fáil members of parliament, she sat very still, staring up at the sleepy-featured judge, an expression of sculptural inscrutability on her face.

The courtroom was almost completely full. Journalists, prison officers, members of the public all sat around, enraptured by the unfolding proceedings. Among the police officers was Inspector Grainne O'Kelly, her leg still heavily bandaged from the day of the arrest. Fat Gary Reynolds was also on the premises, standing alone down at the back, his massive girth crammed with difficulty into the doorway, and his small brain sadly wondering if these two frail old dames were truly the architects of his father's demise.

What a dog's breakfast he had made of things lately. Throwing out the mysterious and apparently valuable document bequeathed him by his dear old daddy. After staring for ten whole minutes into the empty bin outside his house – as if by the very act of staring he could summon the document out of nothingness – he had gone inside and spent several hours looking in places where he absolutely knew it couldn't be.

Then he had driven to the city dump, and searched around in the mounds of black sacks and broken tellies, of deceased domestic pets and mangled supermarket trolleys, while the squawking seagulls had dive-bombed him, and the scuttling rats had nibbled his trainers, and the wriggling maggots had slithered up his trouser legs, but he couldn't find his own rubbish bags no matter how hard he tried.

Guano-splattered, slurry-smeared and generally banjaxed, he had squelched from the dump a discontented man. Holy God, what had those valuable pages been? If only he knew. All he had left of his father's scribblings was the one strange page that little sis Margaret had found in the milk bottle outside the caravan. The pages numbered 1 to 299 he had chucked for ever.

Y8S=+!

That was the phrase the two documents had in common. But what on earth could it possibly mean? He had taped the remaining jotter page to the kitchen wall, had looked at it often and pondered it deeply. *Y8S=+!* With a circle of red ink around it. Lately he had begun to see the cryptic figures in his dreams, flashing before his eyes like the Lotto numbers on the television.

Alone in a corner, hardly noticeable, was a frail little nun, Sister Dymphna of Stoneybatter. She too had things on her mind. She had gone to ground since the arrest of her bosses, things were worrying, she'd even thought of fleeing the country. Back to the

Canaries, but for good this time. What the hell was going to happen next? Would Mrs Bloom and Mrs Blixen crack under police pressure? More to the point, would they turn her in? Every time she'd closed her eyes lately, she'd found herself picturing that large rubber rat.

Up in the dock, Mrs Blixen was being cross-examined. A portly, alarmingly tanned senior counsel was on his feet. He peered around the court, his nose upturned in arrogant contempt, his glittering eyes refusing to meet the witness's angry gaze. Staring up at the ceiling, he put his next question.

'When the late Mr Thomas Reynolds was killed, he had produced some kind of scientific formula. What is the purpose of that formula, Mrs Blixen?'

'I don't know what you are talking about.'

'I think you do, Mrs Blixen.'

'I was never any good at science in school. I preferred literature.'

'Mrs Blixen, the police removed a number of notebooks and other papers from Mr Reynolds's caravan for analysis. After they were returned to Garda headquarters from the mathematics department of University College Dublin, they were stolen. That happened just the other night. Were you behind their theft?'

'How dare you, sir! I've never stolen anything in my life.'

The little nun was smirking now, safe in the knowledge that she had the missing documents safely stashed beneath the floorboards of a certain bijou residence in Stoneybatter. It had been little enough bother to sneak into Garda headquarters and find them. Particularly because she had been dressed as a Garda herself. Three hundred pages of the same old rubbish, the pages numbered 300 to 600. But she knew they meant something. They *had to* mean something. And no way was she handing them over to Mrs Bloom and Mrs Blixen. The two old ladies might be going down, but she would not be going down with them. No way in the world. A little insurance was a great thing to have in these troubled times.

'I put it to you again, Mrs Blixen, that you and your sister were deeply involved – indeed that you are so involved now – in a major criminal conspiracy. And that the formula discovered by the deceased Mr Reynolds has something to do with your illegal activities. And that you know very well what that formula means. And that you plan to continue your criminal career by use or marketing or development of same.'

'Neither of us has ever even got a parking ticket,' she said.

'Neither, madam, did Al Capone.'

'Objection,' called one of the defence barristers.

'Yes,' sighed the judge. 'Lookit, Mr O'Madden-Burke, this is not some kind of . . . stand-up comedy venue.'

Bowing briefly to the judge, the counsel continued. 'A docket from DHL made out in Mrs Bloom's name was found in a garment – I believe a "blazer" is the word – belonging to the late Andrew Andrews. Can you explain that to us, Mrs Blixen?'

'No.'

'I see.' He smirked. 'What a surprise.'

'Objection,' said the defence lawyer again. 'My Lord, it is hardly up to my client to explain what Superintendent Andrews had in his pockets.'

'Yes,' said the judge. 'I often find strange things in my own pockets.'

The prosecution counsel nodded and peered at his notebook. 'And what, Mrs Blixen, were you sending to Sri Lanka in conditions of such . . . morbid security? Holy pictures, was it?'

'Novels,' she said.

The barrister flinched. 'Novels?'

'Limited editions. Joyce. Flann O'Brien. Beckett. That kind of thing. It's only a hobby for us really – for myself and Mrs Bloom. We just . . . we do it for love, I suppose. Love of literature. We have a good customer in Sri Lanka.'

The barrister gave a sardonic, Clongowes Wood chuckle. 'Come, come, Mrs Blixen. You don't expect the jury to believe that expensive couriers and high-class security are required to run a part-time book-selling business?'

'A signed, first-edition copy of *Ulysses* can be worth a lot of money. Thirty thousand pounds or more. A senior counsel would need to work nearly a whole week to afford one.'

There was laughter now, in the back of the court. Even the jury members were laughing.

The barrister waited for the amusement to die down. And then he started to laugh himself, a soft, mocking, sarcastic chortle. 'And you, Mrs Blixen – you and your sister had a copy of that to sell, did you? An autographed copy of the first edition of *Ulysses*?'

'We had better than that once.'

'Oh, I see. You had the Holy Grail, I suppose.'

'We had even better. In former times.'

'Elucidate, why don't you? We're all ears.'

Mrs Blixen shot him a glare of defiance. 'We had the manuscript of James Joyce's last novel. Written in his own hand. Totally unique. Almost priceless.'

'Do you allude to *Finnegans Wake,* madam?'

'I do not.'

'Mrs Blixen, my education is not, of course, on a par with your own. But I believe *Finnegans Wake* was indeed the title of the late Mr Joyce's final masterwork? No?'

'No!' she said, her small eyes gleaming like diamonds. 'There was one more complete novel. He meant to publish it, but tragically died before he could. In Zurich. We acquired the manuscript, my sister and I.'

'Oh, I see. And where is it now?'

'It was stolen from us. By the dead man, Thomas Reynolds.'

A loud gasp filled the courtroom. Even the judge woke up.

'I thought you didn't know Mr Reynolds,' snapped the counsel.

'I know what I hear, that's all. I know we received letters from him, demanding ransom money.'

Another gasp was heard now, a great whoosh of democratic outrage.

'You can produce those letters, I assume, Mrs Blixen?'

'No.'

'Oh. I see. How very convenient. And what was it called, this missing Joycean masterpiece?'

'It was and *is* called *Yeats Is Dead!*'

The barrister snuffled with cynical mirth. 'Lord above now, that is a new one on me. *Yeats Is Dead!* Holy mother. I wonder whether the professors have heard of that one.'

'Its title is a puzzle. A kind of pun, if you like.'

'Do tell us more, Mrs Blixen. You are quite the expert.'

'The title is spelled Y8S=+! Do you see? Yeats equals a cross, and then an exclamation mark. Therefore, together, *Yeats Is Dead!*'

Somewhere inside his blubbery body, Gary Reynolds felt his heart suddenly stop beating and then start again. A sound not unlike rushing water filled his ears. Sister Dymphna Morkan, similarly shocked, nearly jumped right out of her habit, which, given her extensive professional experience, would have been well within her capabilities.

'And what is it about, this so-called last novel of the great Joyce?'

'It is beyond language,' said Mrs Blixen. 'It has no story, no character development, no purpose at all.'

'I see,' said the barrister. He nearly made a joke about Jeffrey Archer, but thought better of it.

'It is pure conceptual literature,' continued Mrs Blixen witheringly. 'Mathematical ideas, scientific symbols, biological formulae. Six hundred beautiful pages. All written out in the master's own hand. *Yeats Is Dead!* The novel released from the narrow cage of meaning. Abstract art in literary form. A new literature for the new world.'

'What palpably unbelievable nonsense,' scoffed the senior counsel.

'It is the most prized and sought-after relic of Irish literature,' continued Mrs Blixen, her voice insistent, riding over him. 'And it was robbed off us by that bowsie, Thomas Reynolds.'

'The West Brit *fucker*,' cried one of the Fianna Fáil deputies.

'I've heard enough,' said the judge.

'My Lord, I must protest,' said the senior counsel.

'The police are after making a right bags of this,' the judge continued.

'My Lord, if I could just sum up my case, I'd be . . .'

But the judge waved his hands dismissively and shook his head. '*I* shall sum up for *you*, Mr O'Madden-Burke. This man Reynolds is shot dead in a caravan. Two days later a police officer who has nothing to do with the case, Garda Batty Nestor, is killed in the same unlucky location, we don't know by whom, but, to judge from the witnesses, it seems by two ugly transvestites. Then the man arrested for the *original* killing, Jason Dunphy, kills himself in police custody, having signed a confession to two murders he certainly didn't commit. Then Sergeant Joseph Roberts is slain, allegedly by some strange woman and a mysterious male accomplice. Then Jason Dunphy's father – Eamon Dunphy if you don't mind – allegedly murders the investigating officer, Andrew Andrews, and disappears. And in all this grotesque inefficiency and confusion the *real* Eamon Dunphy, the footballing man, journalist and noted broadcaster, is almost wrongfully arrested! And *then* Sergeant Roberts's unfortunate wife escapes from the Central Mental Hospital and is detained while fleeing from the house of these two ladies, having shot the place up and tried to kill *them*.'

'My Lord . . .'

'It's getting to the stage,' the judge continued, 'where I open the *Irish Times* obituaries column in the morning and if I'm not in it myself, I get up and eat my breakfast!'

'But My Lord . . .'

'But my head! It is clear what has happened here. It would be clear to a chimpanzee. These two innocent elderly ladies were attacked in their own home by an overly eager young policeman who suffered some kind of brainstorm. And at least he *had* a brain to storm, which is more than may be said for some of his colleagues.'

'But Your Lordship, I really must protest . . .'

'The jury is dismissed,' said the judge. 'This case is over.' And he turned to Mrs Blixen.

'You and your sister are free to go, dear lady.'

'Thank you, My Lord,' said Mrs Blixen in a trembling, tearful voice. She struggled to her feet and shuffled painfully down the steps, her bony fingers gripping the handle of her recently acquired walking stick.

There was uproar now in court number seven. The journalists were on their feet, the Fianna Fáil members of parliament were punching their fists in the air and attempting to start a manly chorus of 'A Nation Once Again'. So mighty was the tumult that nobody noticed Mrs Bloom shooting the judge a surreptitious wink and a thumbs-up. He nodded back, while under the bench his plump fingers were already counting the banknotes in the fat brown envelope emblazoned with the Sri Lankan postmark. Down the aisle limped aged Mrs Blixen, into the arms of the weeping Mrs Bloom.

'There there, pet,' said Mrs Bloom. 'We'll have peace now, please God, O yes.'

And off they went, out through the door, pausing only to mutter to a shocked Sergeant Greer, 'You're a dead man now, you little mulchie bollocks.'

Flabbergasted, gobsmacked, he turned towards the courtroom. Grainne came limping towards him, Venus on crutches. He held his arms out towards her in a gesture of longing.

'Grainne,' he said. 'I'm really, really sorry.'

She slapped his face hard and limped straight out the door.

Equally unnoticed in the courtroom was Gary Reynolds, who had sunk to his knees, his idiotic face turning white with shock.

The page stuck to his kitchen wall was from James Joyce's last novel, written in the great artificer's own handwriting! 299 pages he had thrown out; they were mouldering away in the Dublin city dump! But what exactly had the old biddy said? There were *six hundred* pages in all. He had only ever seen 299. Where were the rest?

'Oh my God,' he murmured. 'What am I after doing?'

And nobody noticed either that the little nun in the corner was practically hyperventilating with glee. Under her floorboards, in lovely Stoneybatter, were pages 300 to 600 of pure literary gold.

'Oh my God,' grinned the little nun, sitting down now with her head in her hands. 'Things seem to be looking up.'

As he sat at the cocktail bar in Corporal Punishment's nightclub, a little down the street from Major Disaster's, Sergeant Greer presented a frankly pathetic figure. It had been Country and Western Fetish Night at Major Disaster's, but even in full police uniform he had not been allowed in. Perhaps this was because he'd had to confess that the only leather item he was wearing was a scapular.

He wasn't drunk, but he was getting that way. To add to his dark sense of lust and unease, all the cocktails on offer in Corporal Punishment's had sniggeringly sexual *double entendres* for names. It was as though even the drinks were conspiring to mock him. Already he had consumed two Slow Screws, three Coitus Interruptuses and a double-strength Spank Your Monkey. He was beginning to feel highly unusual.

Up on the stage, a strange Rastafarian in an emerald green codpiece was doing a rap routine of his own devising, accompanying himself in a rudimentary way on the bongos.

'*Oh Danny boy he down cos he don't gotta job,*
But he gotta submachinegun dee siza his knob . . .'

'What d'yeh reckon?' asked the ancient barman.

'Very nice,' said Sergeant Greer uncertainly.

'Not sure meself,' said the barman. 'I prefer the auld ballads.'

'Mmmm,' said Sergeant Greer.

'Another Multiple Orgasm?' said the barman.

'Please,' said Sergeant Greer. 'With a packet of nuts.'

Where, oh where, was Tammy Wynette now? What on earth was the country coming to? Who put the bomp in the bomp-deebomp deebomp, who put the wang in the wanga-langa-dingdong? Yes, Sergeant Greer's mind was haunted by questions.

As he blew the cherry foam off his Multiple Orgasm, he pondered the events of the last few weeks. Things were not going at all well. Grainne had been avoiding him, despite all his pleas, but the Minister for Justice had been ringing him up at all hours, inviting him around to her house – or, once, on to her yacht. So far he had managed to invent excuses, but he knew they were beginning to sound increasingly implausible.

Women were a puzzle, there was no doubt about it. How the blazes could you ever understand them? Think of a man, then subtract reason and accountability – that was what his father used to say. But Sergeant Greer didn't really think that was right. Such reactionary and sexist views had no place in the modern world. Even in these days of equality and progress, he felt women were deserving of special respect. Sometimes, after all, it was hard to be a woman. Giving all your love to just one man.

The Rastafarian had finished his set to a trickle of applause and was standing a few feet away from him now, trying to attract the barman's attention. It seemed to Sergeant Greer that there was something strange about him. Suddenly it struck him. He was the only black man Sergeant Greer had ever seen who had ginger eyebrows. It was quite extraordinary. It was a bit freakish, really. Shamefully he found himself wondering if the man's pubes were ginger too.

'Yo, Mista Luvva Luvva,' called the Rasta to the barman. 'Gimme a Blowjob in a Taxi. And make it quick.'

'Excuse me,' said Sergeant Greer. 'May I ask you something?'

'Me's only got me a small amount, mon . . . for personal use.'

'Oh, no.' Paschal laughed. 'It was nothing like that.'

'Me no usually rap wit de Babylon pigs,' said the Rasta cautiously.

What strange and exotic language was he speaking? Was it Welsh?

Perhaps it was the alcohol that made Sergeant Greer bold. 'I'm in love with this woman called Grainne O'Kelly,' he found himself saying. 'And I don't know what to do about it. I was wondering if you might have any advice for me. A man like you . . . so full of confidence. So secure, you know . . . in your sexuality.'

'What's the problem?' asked the Rasta.

'It's just . . . well . . . she doesn't seem to notice me.'

'Yer chat-up lines must be arseways,' said the Rasta, lapsing oddly into Dublinese. 'Just go up and say "Me don't believe we've met, Shooga, I'm Mista Right." '

'I'm not sure she'd consider an approach like that appropriate.'

'Oh it's appropriate,' sniggered the Rasta, clutching his codpiece.

At this point, Sergeant Greer found himself wondering if the russet-browed reggae-boy truly understood the meaning of the word 'appropriate'. But he knew it wasn't right to make value judgements based on idiosyncratic language use. He had recently volunteered for a departmental training course about understanding the needs of ethnic minorities. Deep in his heart he felt sympathy and solidarity for these new migrants to his adopted city. It touched him profoundly, as a citizen and a policeman, that he was in a position to help these people, to show them the hospitality and understanding they deserved. All they wanted was a chance, after all, the same chance the Irish had been given all over the world. And how much more beautiful Dublin would be, he reflected, when there were people from all over the world living here.

The Rasta held his hand up in what seemed to be a gesture of greeting.

'The name's MC Micky Mac,' he said.

'Er . . . Yes. Groovy,' said Sergeant Greer, remembering some of his training course.

'Nah. Whip me some skin, homeboy.'

Sergeant Greer slapped his upheld palm, which hurt a bit, and the Rasta slid on to the barstool beside him.

'Now mon,' he said. 'You wanna bitta advice about the chicks, just osk.'

'Well then,' said the sergeant. 'How far do you think you should go on a first date?'

The Rasta's eyes narrowed. He emitted a lascivious cackle. 'Depends on the broad, mon. Carlow, however, seem to be generally acceptable. Thurles at an absolute push. Anywhere south of Kanturk should be avoided. Rastaaaa!'

'Are you . . . talking about sex now, Micky?'

'Mon, what else? The horizontal boogie-woogie.'

'You see, Micky, the thing is . . . I've never even kissed a girl in my life.'

'Get outta here.'

'No, really. I'm . . . y'know . . . a virgin.'

'Well, knock me down and spin my decks. I say, I say, I say. What 'ave we 'ere, mon?'

What had we here? That was the question. Sergeant Greer took a deep breath and opened his heart and mouth simultaneously. His one excursion into the boggy field of courtship had occurred in the Connemara Gaeltacht, *circa* 1985, where his parents had sent him ostensibly to learn Irish but actually just to get him out of the house so that they could rent out his room to a number of pubescent Spaniards.

He'd had a teenage crush on a girl called Siobhan, the eldest daughter of the family of native speakers with whom he was lodging. Siobhan was fifteen, two years older than Paschal, a beautiful sloe-eyed loose-limbed colleen whose startling attractiveness was only slightly diminished by the dental brace she'd had to wear.

Sometimes he would try to get to know her, but she'd only laugh, refusing to make conversation except in Irish. But one night after a *ceilidh*, they'd gone for a walk together on Spiddal beach. By the silvery light of the Connemara moon, she had linked her arm in his and started to kiss the corner of his mouth. 'Kiss me, Paschal,' she'd said, in the first national language. And he had tried to. But at the crucial moment, the tip of his tongue had got caught in her dental brace. Try as he might, he couldn't get it free again. He and Siobhan had staggered around Spiddal beach, bonded by something more than love. The pain had been astounding. But it was the trip to the casualty department that had really traumatised him, the pair of them stuck together, shrieking in agony. His eyes still watered today whenever he heard Irish spoken. People sometimes took it for national pride.

All this he confessed to his new friend, MC Micky, the pain and humiliation scaldingly fresh in his memory.

'Two pints of Doggy Style and a double Bill Clinton,' called the Rasta to the barman. And he put his arm around Sergeant Greer's shoulders.

'See, the trick with kissin,' he kindly advised, 'is to remember, whatever else you do, don't kiss the poor broad like you's trying to remove a fishbone from her throat, mon. That's all.'

'But I get so nervous when I'm around her. She's so . . .'

'Nah, look, look. You worry too much.'

'You know something,' said the sergeant. 'What would really impress her would be to sort out this case.'

'What case is that, mon?'

'I need to find Eamon Dunphy. Fast.'

'Well . . . he's sometimes gettin' down funky in Lillie's Bordello, brudda.'

'Where?'

'It's a nightclub on Grafton Street. Saw him there once myself.'

'No, no – not *that* Eamon Dunphy.'

'Not the guy on the radio?'

'Another one.'

'Hmmm.'

'I need to find Eamon Dunphy. And I need to find that manuscript by Joyce.'

'Joyce who, mon?'

'*James* Joyce, of course! And I need to find out what Mrs Bloom and Mrs Blixen are *really* up to.'

'Righteous,' said the Rasta. 'Hey, order me a double Brewer's Droop willya,' and he tottered off in the direction of the Gents.

'Yes,' said Sergeant Greer with a new and steely determination. 'I'll solve this case single-handedly! And that'll show everyone! Yes. Oh yes.'

It was just at that moment, or, certainly, close enough to it not to make much difference, that Sergeant Greer noticed that a remarkably striking girl was looking at him from the edge of the dance floor. Her eyes glittered prettily in the wash of neon, the flashing light emphasising the smooth curves of her body. She had an anxious and oddly weary look. When he glanced back at her, he saw that she was still staring in his direction. Holy God! Now she was coming over! He grabbed his glass and stared into its treacly depths.

'Excuse me,' she said.

'Yes? . . . Do I . . . ? . . . That is . . . Can I . . . help you, miss?'

'Hi. My name's Dymphna,' she said, pleasantly. 'I was wondering if you could give me a ride home?'

'I . . . well . . . that's to say . . . Where do you live?'

'In Stoneybatter,' she said. 'I wouldn't ask only I've had my purse robbed. And, you know . . . I saw you were a policeman, so . . .'

'Oh,' he said.

'I wouldn't want to put you to any trouble or anything. But I'd be tremendously grateful if you could help me out.'

'Oh, it's no trouble. Not at all. It's on my way, in fact. Practically.' (And it was, practically; it was only a six-mile detour.)

She smiled, a beautiful, warm beam that illuminated her face. 'Maybe . . . I don't know . . . maybe you'd come in for a coffee or something when we get there?'

And just at that point, the club doors opened and in marched Mrs Jacinta Kinch, the Minister for Justice, followed by a trotting, uniformed chauffeur who had once, many years ago, been a Fianna Fáil Taoiseach.

'Hey, Germaine!' called the minister, in delight and surprise. 'Get over here, sexy. I feel like DANCING!'

'Yo, bitch,' said the Rastafarian, bumping into the minister on his way back from the facilities. 'You fancy a Fuck in a Phonebox? I'm payin.'

Two dull thuds sounded through the room.

The Minister for Justice hitting Rasta Micky McManus.

And Rasta Micky McManus hitting the lino.

Chapter Ten: by Tom Humphries

'Come over here, Sergeant' smiled the Minister for Justice, reclining seductively on the sky-blue nylon sheets.

Wow!

Even in the grip of his terrible drunkenness, Paschal Greer found himself getting excited. Where would you *get* sheets like that? Guineys, maybe. Guineys of North Earl Street. They were lovely sheets, they truly were. Look at them. So smooth and nice. Probably drip-dry. Maybe he would get some in the January sales. Sheets like that were really . . .

Ouch! Aaarrghhh!

The minister had him by the short and curlies. Literally. She was hurting him more than any mere metaphor could. His eyes filled with salty water, what felt like a scrotumtightening sea of it. Involuntarily he surveyed the body politic. It was not what he had imagined. It was beyond imagining. Oh, Lord. *Forgive me, Grainne.*

'Well,' he observed anxiously, 'you're . . . er . . . some woman for one woman, Minister.'

'Listen, Greer,' she said. 'Let's drop the Cary Grant shit. I want to play Bill and Monica. Only get this. *You're* gonna be Monica!'

She sucked half the life from her slim Havana and waved it menacingly. *Swoosh!* Hot ash fell on the blue nylon sheet and burned crinkly little holes through it.

'C'mon, Sergeant. Don't be a shy little pullet now.'

Against his better judgement, his eyes wandered again over the peaks and vales of the ministerial form. Treacherous bastard eyes. Sinful eyes. In the dark recesses of his inebriated mind he seemed to hear his mother saying, '*Don't look, Paschal, don't look, son,*' as they passed an accident between an oil tanker and a herd of sheep in Drumshanbo, County Leitrim, in April 1976. But he *had* looked on that occasion, just as his father had chucked a fag end out the window. Jesus. Talk about mutton *flambé*.

He looked again now. He couldn't help it, try as he might. Oh, Sergeant Paschal Greer, but you're a slow hoor to learn a lesson.

He gazed at the minister's awesome body as one of the forensic boys might – indeed, if truth be told, as several of them had. Jesus. *Don't look, Paschal.* He felt dizzy. He felt sick. Impure thoughts gushed through his brain. *Don't look, sonny, please don't look.* Sweetmotherofholysufferinjeezus. If only me friends could see me now.

They were in a strange room in a strange house. Snotgreen wallpaper and seablue sheets. Downstairs in the living room was Dymphna Morkan and a chap from the papers she had picked up on the way home, along with Rasta MC Micky Mac and the minister's laconic, stressed-looking chauffeur.

Oh God, my stomach. Shouldn't have had that last tequila.

Mammy. Mammy. Where are you, Mammy?

Cree-akk.

He thought he heard the bedroom door open behind

him. The room seemed to swim before his eyes. Blood was pounding hard in his temples. Another strange sound rent the air. *Zippp!* The minister was chuckling naughtily, peering over Greer's shoulder.

It was just as Rasta Micky clambered into the bed to join them that Sergeant Paschal Greer fell into a drunken faint.

A Map of Sergeant Greer's Night

They had all been thrown out of Corporal Punishment's by a man who looked like Hannibal Lecter. He had threatened to call some of his friends in the press if they weren't gone in two minutes flat. DRUNKEN COPPER ON RAMPAGE WITH MINISTER was only one of the headlines he envisaged.

'Chill out, dudester,' said Rasta Micky Mac.

'Out,' the man repeated. 'Or I'm ringing the Sunday papers.'

'I am the Sunday papers,' said a six-foot tall and skeletally skinny redhead who had somehow insinuated himself into their company.

Grabbing Hannibal Lecter's crotch on her way out the door, the minister had said, 'Don't ever speak to me like that again. Or I'll have *your* liver with Heinz beans and a bottle of cider.'

'Ungggghh.'

'Say, "Yes, Minister."'

And he had. Several times. In various amusing accents.

They'd all left and laughed together and adjourned briefly down the street to General Mayhem's Late Nite Hooch-House, where the geezer with the red hair had introduced himself as Eddie Lambert, social columnist.

'Hey bro,' said Rasta Micky to Lambert. 'Bet ya get really sicka havin the red pubes jive laid on ya.'

'Fockin roight,' said the social columnist, in a Southside Dublin monotone. 'Rasta Far Eye.'

'Been there brudda,' said Rasta Micky.

'Off we go,' cried the minister, downing her double vodka. 'Next port of call! Chop-chop!'

Despite her earlier assault on his person, peace had broken out between Rasta Micky and the minister. Even before his bruises had emerged as bumps he and she were fast friends. Allies, you could say. Soulmates maybe. Part of a fab five of intoxicated friendliness. Eddie Lambert, Paschal Greer, the Minister for Justice, Rasta Micky and little lost and lonely Dymphna, all dandering along and bearing no grudges.

'You know what?' the drunken minister said many times as they wandered between clubs, mid the labyrinths of nighttown. 'You're my main man, Micky. You really are.'

'Ah now, Minister, don't be talkin.'

'You da *maan*, Micky. Is that a black pudding in your caks or are you just pleased to see me? Heh heh heh.'

Following at a distance was the minister's chauffeur, a saturnine-looking fellow whose eerie little snake-eyes Sergeant Paschal Greer remembered vaguely. He'd been drummed out of prime-ministerial office for running a black market mail-order organ transplant scam. The Mayo Clinic had blown the whistle when some of the livers and lungs he'd been sending them had started to seem a bit familiar. One of the professors had looked into the matter – only to discover that their Irish supplier was secretly buying the organs they'd taken out and selling them back for putting in. His indignant line of defence had gone down in history. 'I swear to God, the alcohol must have been put there by somebody else as a preservative.'

The minister was acting a little gamey, goosing one and all as they poured into Private Members' Gin Joint. Greer had never seen her like this before.

More drink. And more. And yet more again. Sergeant Greer licking salt off the minister's neck as part of a game called Tequila Slammers. Eddie Lambert taking snaps. *Pop! Pop! Pop!* The minister feeding Rasta Micky a fat white worm from the bottom of the bottle.

'Roight, say feta cheese, goys,' called Eddie Lambert.

Gulp! The worm slid down Micky's throat. *Pop!* The Instamatic imprisoned the moment. *Whoa!* Paschal Greer was on his feet and dancing. He had friends. He was happy. He was OUT ON THE TOWN. He checked the ointment of his life for a fly. Not a one in sight. He was over Grainne O'Kelly. He was about to lose his virginity.

He did the birdie-song-dance with the beautiful Dymphna. Every time they came close she'd say: 'I want you to come back to my place. Please.'

And he'd flap his wings and duckwalk away.

Man, this was living. This was the *business*. This was a life he had never expected to be revealed to him. A life of glamour, a social whirl. He thought about the letter he would write home soon.

Dear Mammy. Guess what. I'VE MADE IT.

The tequila was busily boiling up his brain. He knew

now, with absolute certainty, that he, Paschal, would be the most successful Greer ever. It was his destiny. Decadence and high living. Hob-nobbing with influential friends. No more would he be the village wuss. No more would everyone laugh at him and call him names. He threw back his head and laughed out loud, happy as two mutant dogs with four mickeys between them.

It was, perhaps, little enough wonder that Dymphna Morkan had never held members of the Garda Siochána in high esteem.

She could take the red necks and the flat feet. She could even go with the bad dress sense. But why wouldn't they recruit somebody with an IQ greater than that of a mangle? That was really what disturbed her the most.

Look at him, she thought. A neck you could roast chestnuts on.

'I'm off home,' she said. 'I really have to go now.'

Big mistake, as it had turned out. The minister had decided they would all go back with her.

And for the two-mile drive back to Stoneybatter in the ministerial limo, Dymphna had been forced to grit her teeth and listen to the wind-him-up-and-see-him-talk guff of Eddie Lambert, social columnist.

'I wroit all my own stuff,' he droned and dribbled. 'Dot integrity is important to me. Oi've got to be naked in front of the readers.'

Poor sap thought he'd be getting naked when they got back to her place. She could tell by the creepy way he kept trying to find reasons to touch her. Hand on her shoulder, hand lingering on her back, pat pat pat, seeing if she was wearing a bra. Yawn.

Her head was rewinding old episodes of *One Man and His Dog*. How cleverly the mutts used to separate one sheep from the gang and pen it. She eyed Sergeant Paschal Greer. It might require a scalpel rather than a sheepdog to separate him.

They had staggered out of the Merc on Manor Street and stood around on the kerb as she'd fumbled in her bag for the keys.

'Noice pad,' said Eddie Lambert. 'Moight crash if you get lucky.'

And cackling he had led them all into the hallway.

Straight up the stairs went the Minister for Justice, dragging Greer behind her, his hand clawing at the banister.

That had left Dymphna, MC Micky, the disgraced chauffeur and Eddie Lambert together in the living room, sipping tea and gawping at each other, while loud moans and roars had drifted down through the floorboards. And after a while Micky had left too. She heard his footfall on the way up the stairs.

Grunts and groans, shrieks of wild pleasure, rhythmic pumping and bedsprings creaking. Lambert and the chauffeur had fallen asleep.

Fuck it anyway. Her scheme had failed. Pick up some drooling hayseed copper, seduce him; make him help with the plan to discover who had the other half of the manuscript. Yes, they were thick, but they had contacts all the same, a certain way of finding things out. Now it was time for plan B. And fast.

From under the loose floorboard she took out the three hundred pages.

'Yes, yes, o yes!' came the howl from upstairs.

Who the hell had the other half?

* * *

As the morning sun rose high over Dublin, a gimpy little darkglassed man with a taptapping cane was slowly walking up Dawson Street towards St Stephen's Green.

All things considered, he was in good spirits. Time had passed. He was still free. Yes, he was in the frame for the offing of Andrew Andrews, but there was so much untreated sewage flowing out about that case that he couldn't believe anyone cared any more who had rubbed the bastard out. If they had ever cared. Which was by no means definite.

Commenting on the death on the *News at One* recently, the Minister for Justice her eminent self had said that the passing of Andrews had given the Police some much-needed inner cleanliness. Ho ho. The papers were saying it looked like a professional job. Chancers.

Fidgety. Yes. He was happy but fidgety. There were things to get done and no time to waste. The trim beard he had grown on the point of his chin was still itchy but already he was becoming accustomed to the moustache. The little wire-rimmed John Lennon glasses gave him the blissful comfort of a mask. He pulled the brim of his boater down and made a right turn into South Anne Street. He liked the feeling of having a new identity. It made him feel young again, at some kind of beginning. Jason's death had been an end. But this was a beginning. O yes.

This morning Eamon Dunphy was taking another small step along the road to avenging his son. Small step? More of a giant leap forward. Getting what was his, what should always have been his. Green folding stuff and lots of it too. Most of it wasn't green any more of course. But he was old-fashioned about money.

He could feel the satisfactory heft of his wallet in his breast pocket, pressing lightly against his calmly functioning heart. In there with all the old bus tickets and receipts he had the page which would turn his life around. Fifty long years and everything he touched had turned to shit. But not any more. No way José. Now he was going to be Midas Dunphy.

He wandered up the wonderland of Grafton Street towards Even Adam's Cocktail Heaven where he had arranged to meet a prominent Dutch chemist. A respected man. A true professional. A man who understood the awesome potential of chemistry.

Around him the street traders were putting out their wares. Since the publicity in the papers about the Bloom–Blixen court case 'Yeats Is Dead!' T-shirts were all the rage, Y8S=+! emblazoned on the front, NOT SLEEPING! printed on the back. He had to hand it to the hawkers, they were quick off the mark. Other souvenir T-shirts had a picture of Lester Piggott on the front, the words PASS BY on the back and the Y8S=+! logo on the sleeve. Credit where credit's due, thought Eamon Dunphy. I'm not the only one thinking. I'm not the only entrepreneur.

It had taken only one phone call to lure the Dutch doctor into a meeting. *No I'm not THAT Eamon Dunphy. Here's what I have. A formula to make drugs so powerful that heroin will seem like fucking toffee.* He had seen the chemist on the 'Late Late Show' once, campaigning for Ireland's bedraggled swimming community. They needed facilities. A 50-metre, eight-lane, Olympic-size pharmacy. Eamon Dunphy had liked the cut of his jib.

He sat down in the corner of Even Adams and waited for Dr Derek de Wet to arrive.

When Sergeant Paschal Greer woke up, his head hurt, his limbs ached, and his mouth felt like a wino's gusset. Beside him on the floor was Rasta Micky McManus.

'This can't go on,' Rasta Micky was whispering.

'Ungh,' said Greer.

'Can't go on like this,' said Rasta Micky.

'What? Like what?' said Sergeant Greer.

This was the morning. Nobody respected him in the morning. Nobody respected him any of the time but in the mornings they respected him even less.

'We'll have to split up,' said Rasta Micky.

'Huh?' said Greer.

'Split up. Like fucking soon. Like right now, Homie.'

Sergeant Greer grabbed Rasta Micky by the dreadlocks and pulled his nose close to his own.

'Look, pal,' hissed Paschal Greer. 'I'm not a sophisticated man. And I'm still not sure what went on here last night. But I know one thing. Whatever happened between you, me and Sleeping Beauty over there' – he nodded across at the Minister for Justice, her dozing face yoghurt-white in the morning sun – 'there is no *we* to split up. There is no parting and there is no sweet sorrow. God forgive me, but whatever happened, well it happened. And there is no scene. There is no we. There is no item that is we. There is me, Sergeant Paschal Greer, getting up and leaving.

There is you, Michael fucking Jackson, staying here and keeping your big freaky mouth shut. Got that? Yes?'

He let go, but the grotesque black face somehow welded on to a bog-standard Irish body stayed uncomfortably close to his.

'Don't flatter yourself, Plod,' scoffed Rasta Micky. 'I said *spliff* up. I'm not sure what happened last night either. But I've some shit here that'll make you so high you'll need a giraffe on stilts to wipe your arse. So start looking around for some skins, man. Then we'll get our heads around the rest of this shit.'

'Some what?' said Paschal Greer.

But Rasta Micky wasn't looking at him now.

'My head hurts, Micky. I feel bloody awful.'

'Hang on a sec,' said Rasta Micky.

The minister was lying on the blue nylon eiderdown, her handbag under her head as a pillow. Rasta Micky was touching her gently. Hand on her forehead. Now feeling her wrist.

'Oh no! Oh Jesus! *Shite and onions.*'

'What's the matter?'

Rasta Micky's eyes were wide with terror.

'Jaysus,' he gasped. 'She's fucking dead.'

Gary Reynolds was in a bad way.

He was hot, he was hefty, he was moist and palpitating. He was after spending the whole morning in a room no bigger than a prison cell with an eminent Joycean scholar for company. Gary was sweating like a sow in a sauna. Four hours had millimetred by, with Professor Doonan Durrus holding the sheet of jotter paper up to the sunlight, then poring over it with a magnifying glass, transcribing the hieroglyphics, fingering through dusty textbooks, making copious notes, exploring the internet.

'Hmm,' he kept saying. '*Most* unusual.'

Get on with it for fuck's sake, thought Gary Reynolds. Please Professor. Hurry up.

Back he went in his memory, to kill the time. For no good reason he thought of his wedding day, that chalkstripe suit he'd poured himself into. Madelene had left him now, and who could blame her? The news that he had chucked away his inheritance had simply proved too much to take.

'Jesus,' she'd said bitterly. 'Jesus Christ. And I thought it was a joke when I saw "LOSER FOR LIFE" tattooed on your arse, Gary Reynolds.'

He tried to picture his arse. It was difficult to do. He envisioned the terrible mocking words emblazoned across his flabby cheeks. Cadet Camp had been supposed to make a man of him. Instead he'd got soused along with his comrades and somehow ended up in a tattoo-and-piercing parlour in the bad part of downtown Ballincollig.

He vaguely remembered the tattooist telling him he'd once put dolphins onto a swimmer's crotch. But had he imagined that? Was he making it up? Certainly he remembered nothing else; ten pints of anaesthetic had done their terrible work. Several years later in a guest-house on the North Circular Road he had bent down low to pick up a condom and, laughing, Madelene had told him the news. He had been, quite literally, the butt of the joke.

A memory of his father's funeral loomed up; a remark he'd overheard outside the church. 'Hey Fatboy, try not to eat the flowers off the hearse.' There was no need for the priest to speak to him like that.

All his life he'd been chasing down long shots and all his life he'd been pipped at the post. His father's precious manuscript was just another empty promise. Look at how it was making him behave. No sooner had he got the maggoty smell of the rubbish dump out of his polyesters than he'd been seized by the thought that maybe – just maybe – his rubbish had gone to a recycling skip. His inheritance on the way to the Hades of pulpsville. Joyce submitted to a commodious vicus of recirculation.

For the last three nights, he'd been sucking his gut in and literally *posting* himself through the round windows of recycling skips all over Dublin. But no joy. And no Joyce.

Finally he had taken the one surviving page from the kitchen wall and hightailed it into Trinity College, where he'd sought out the internationally renowned Professor Durrus, explained his plight, begged an audience.

'Extra-AWED-inary!' boomed the Joyceman at last.

'What?' said Gary Reynolds, grateful to have the silence finally broken. His stomach had been rumbling for half an hour and he'd been hoping that the learned scholar couldn't hear it.

'You tell me this was written by Joyce?'

'I have good reason to think so, yes, Professor.'

'Amazing, truly. I can't be sure myself. One has only ever seen the master's handwritten *words*, you know. The numerical aspect of this – all these formulae and graphs – one can't be certain. But if it is genuine it is really quite astounding.'

'Why is that?'

'Well,' said Professor Durrus, drawing himself to full height, 'Joyce, as we well know, was not a clean man in college. He confessed to a total abhorrence of soap and used to joke that even lice would find his skin repellent.'

'And?'

'But this – this document – it appears to be . . .'

'Yes?'

'Well . . . a formula for some kind of . . . skin cream. Yes.'

'*What?*'

'Indeed. So I am told by email by a colleague in biochemistry. If what you tell me about its provenance is true, then it seems that Joyce – the great maestro – spent his final years working on . . . cosmetics.'

'Huh?'

'Old artificer.' The professor shook his head as though in disbelief. 'Extra-AWED-inary. The sheer extent of the master's talents.'

'But . . . what does it mean? It isn't part of a novel?'

The professor gave a startled chuckle. 'Oh no, my good man. Of course it isn't. What you have brought me is of no literary value whatsoever. It does however change our . . . perception of Joyce and his general orientation. Still, you know, it may change your life.'

'How?'

'Well – for example – I am no businessperson of course – but you may be able to license and merchandise an entire range of Joycean toiletries. If you can get your hands on any more of this stuff.'

I chucked three hundred fucking pages of it into a plastic bin with a picture of Pocahontas on the side, thought Gary bitterly.

'But now good luck and good day, sir. I must bid you adieu.'

Professor Doonan Durrus handed back the piece of paper and rose to his feet.

'You know, it's been quite a revelatory week for us Joyceans,' he said, as he led Gary towards the door.

'Oh. Has it?' said Gary glumly.

'Yes it has. Do you know, I had a sweet little nun in here Wailsday or was it Thumpsday and you'll never guess what she had for my perusal.'

'What was that?'

'Well now' – the professor gave a merry wink – 'I'll let you in on the little secret. Not a word, mind, to anyone else. But she waltzed through that very door with three hundred pages of the great and famous lost novel – the one the dogs in the street are talking about lately. A wondrous work donated anonymously to her order. People *are* kind, you know. Oh what bliss to feast one's eyes on something like that. Absolutely authentic too.'

Gary stopped, rooted to the spot.

'You wouldn't have her name, Professor?'

'Morkan . . . Sister Dymphna Morkan. I remember it very well . . . because of the coincidence.'

'Which coincidence?'

'Well, Morkan is a very Joycean name. It appears in one of the stories in *Dubliners*.'

'And which story would that be?'

'Well . . . "The Dead", of course.'

'I don't suppose she would have left an address?'

'Oh, Lord. What was it now?' The professor scratched his head. 'I think she said something about Stoney-batter.'

Gary Reynolds turned quickly towards the door. Professor Durrus watched him go. And quietly laughed.

Chapter Eleven: by Pauline McLynn

It's funny how quickly you can go off a place, thought Dymphna Morkan. And she had definitely gone off Stoneybatter.

It was brilliant to have a house given to you free (or, to be more accurate, for services rendered). But to have it filled with drunken gobshites, one of whom had now departed for gobshite heaven, was nothing short of fucking calamitous. And when said corpse happened to be that of the Minister for fucking *Justice*, then really, you were on the wrong side of the law. Whatever they drummed into them in Templemore, it certainly wasn't imagination, because the first thing the gobdaw sergeant had done was phone the cops from the bedroom extension. Now there could be no damage limitation. It was time to skedaddle.

She could hear the sound of crying coming from the bedroom as she changed into her navy shellsuit and packed a small bag. Most of the bag was taken up with her portion of *Y8S=+!* It was a heavy bugger too. Still, there wasn't much else to pack. She hadn't ever moved her personal stuff into the house – maybe a premonition of the dark things to come. She was used to travelling light, accustomed to quick getaways; the habit hadn't left her just because she'd been set up in a cosy hideyhole.

She had absolutely no idea of how to handle the

situation with Mrs Bloom and Mrs Blixen. They were impossible to hide from, they had spies everywhere. But she'd try to go to ground while she formulated a plan. The main thing now was to get away from here as quickly as possible.

To be honest, Dymphna had never truly felt as though she'd settle in Stoneybatter. She liked the house but the area it stood in was too full of arty types, actors and the like. Loveybatter, she'd heard it called on one occasion. Bitterbatter, more like, she thought sourly. Given her own aptitude for disguises and lying she could act any of the so-called luvvies off any stage.

Social diarist Eddie Lambert and the minister's chauffeur were still conked out in two of the armchairs. She hoped the racket upstairs wouldn't wake them before her getaway. She didn't want to have to kill them.

She took one last look around the home she'd always wanted. Then, not sure of where she was going, she let herself out into the bright sunshine. Before long she was moving through the warren of streets. She quickened her pace, then broke into a trot. Dymphna Morkan was on the run again.

Inspector Grainne O'Kelly was beginning to get the hang of her walking stick.

Her leg was still bandaged, very stiff and sore; but she could get around nearly as quickly as that woman doctor in *ER*. What she couldn't do, despite her best efforts, was walk, carry a coffee mug and answer her mobile simultaneously. And so, when Sergeant Paschal Greer phoned, she dropped the stick, reached for the mobile, and fell sideways over on to the photocopier in the Incident Room, spilling the scalding liquid not only over her good leg but also down the light-blue suit she had collected from the dry-cleaners the day before. As a consequence, she was less happy to hear his voice than she would have been at other times and in other circumstances.

She lay on the photocopier as comfortably as she could, the machine making multiple copies of her splendid side elevation, while Greer reported the shocking news of the Minister for Justice's death.

'Good God! We'll be there as soon as we can, Sergeant, and well done. It's good that you were first on the scene. You know the drill. Preserve the evidence. Don't let anyone into the house.'

In Stoneybatter, stony-hearted Paschal Greer hung up – sick that he had lied to the woman he loved.

In Harcourt Street, Grainne O'Kelly struggled to her feet, happy that Greer had followed his snitch's lead and raced to the crime scene. What a copper he was. Surely that boy was headed for another promotion. Yes, there were a few good ones out there still. Not for the first time, she hoped he was single – it was high time she checked that out.

She radioed all units in the Dublin 7 area, retrieved her walking stick and squelched to the car pool.

Micky McManus had some quick decisions to make. He gazed over at the bloated corpse of what had once been the Minister for Justice. Jesus Christ. What was going on? First Joe Roberts and now Jacinta Kinch. No way was *this* one getting pinned on him either. How had it all gone so wrong? Again.

He would have to make a run for it. Again.

He checked himself in the dressing-table mirror. What

gazed back at him wasn't great. Bits of pillow-stuffing were embedded in his Rasta wig. His streaked and smudged make-up gave him the look of a piebald pony – some sort of strange breed with big ginger eyebrows. He rubbed at the face-paint to even out the effect, but it didn't work, it only made things worse. Well it would have to do. There wasn't time. The main thing was to split before the forces of Babylon arrived. He would find some sort of sanctuary or safe house. He'd change his look and go from there. Pity – the threads were righteous, mon.

He tiptoed past the sergeant, wondering why he was crying so hard. Greer hadn't even got a ride off Mrs Kinch; he couldn't have been *that* fond of her.

At least Micky had seen to it that she'd died a happy minister. Jesus, I must be one mighty shag, he thought, as he made his way out on to the street.

Gary Reynolds was feeling energised, positive. Okay, the morning had been long and tedious, but he'd survived it, and he'd got a great lead. This little nun was the woman he wanted. He would track her down, explain his situation, beg her to hand over those three hundred pages.

A youngwan in a navy shellsuit darted into the road, causing him to swerve and stand on the brakes. He leaned hard on the horn and shouted: 'Maybe you should watch where you're going in future.' She swung her holdall at the passenger door and gave it a good wallop. 'I'll have the law on you if you're not careful,' called Gary in reprisal. Yes, he liked the new plain-speaking him.

He had two distinct problems now. One was that he

had an erection. He'd had one for some time. It was physically dangerous to have an erection for too long, or so he'd once read in *Loaded* magazine. Well, he would have to worry about that later. More pressing was the problem of finding the bloody nun. God be with the times when nuns lived in convents. Back then, finding her would have been easy. But these days they lived in their own little houses. Tidy sum that would cost in this locale too. These days they didn't even wear their nun's uniforms. It was cardigans and hairdos for nuns now.

Still, he wouldn't be put off the search. These were new times. But this was the new Gary. He was a man whose time had come. He could – he *would* – find the wimple in the haystack.

Turning on to Manor Street, he saw a poor unfortunate stumbling along. Joking Jesus, what kind of savages lived up here? This miserable wretch had obviously been tarred and feathered, and forced to dress in a hideous clown's outfit. Under a thatch of black furlike gack and white feathers, his little red eyes and ginger brows were etched with misery. Gary's heart felt fit to burst. There was always someone more down on their luck than you.

The victim threw himself at the bonnet of Gary's van, waving his arms and yelling wildly. From a distance came the wail of approaching police sirens.

'Are you all right there, fella?'

'You gotta help me, mon,' cried the prostrate creature. 'Please, bro – help me out.'

Gary Reynolds stepped out of his van, reached down and gently pulled the sobbing heap to his feet. Micky McManus gulped back his tears, steadied himself and looked into the eyes of his saviour.

A strange and magical thing happened then. As the two men gazed into each other's eyes, nature – or at least Stoneybatter – seemed to stand still. Pitterpatter went Gary's heart, patterpitter went lovestruck Micky's, the commingling of the heartbeats like beautiful music. Two hearts. Two gallants. Thrust together. Destined for togetherness until the very end.

'Get in the car,' said Gary, after what seemed an eternity. 'It's all going to be okay. I'm here now, and there ain't no one is ever gonna harm you again.' He'd heard that somewhere – the telly maybe? But it fitted and he meant it. So why not say it?

'Don't forget your seat belt,' he said softly as they sped down the street, around a corner and off in the direction of the Phoenix Park, just as the Gardaí arrived to claim the ministerial body.

Grainne O'Kelly sneaked a glance across the Incident Room at Pascal Greer. He was unshaven and rough and his uniform looked as though it had been slept in. If only all the force took their jobs as seriously, the country would be a fine place to live in, she thought.

How delicately he was holding the phone. His eyes were bloodshot, touchingly sad. But then again, why wouldn't they be? Paschal was a sensitive man; he had seen the worst of humankind yet could still feel emotion, still experience empathy, even with his level of uncanny expertise. Of course his sensitivity wasn't always appreciated. It had earned him the reputation of being a wuss. But who cared a damn for the insults and jeers of the cerebrally challenged end of the force? They were footsoldiers, plodders, penpushers and has-beens. One day Paschal Greer would show them all.

While Inspector O'Kelly was thinking these thoughts, Sergeant Greer was feeling bad. He could barely hear the assistant pathologist's voice down the telephone line for the ringing of a hangover in his aching ears. It seemed that almost every breath he took provoked a boilingly painful gag. Vague memories of the previous night haunted him. What had possessed him to go to bed with the minister? Surely he could have put up a bit more resistance? How could he have jeopardised everything, and so casually? He could easily be exposed as a fraud before nightfall, drummed out of the force with shame and mockery – quite possibly jailed for conspiracy to murder.

He listened to the halting report the distressed pathologist was giving him down the line. God, the poor chap was in a terrible state. 'Tell Inspector O'Kelly I need her,' he gasped, before hanging up with a sudden heart-rending sob.

'Ma'am' – Greer felt he had to address his superior formally, though in truth he wanted to shout out his love – 'they'd like to see you down at the morgue. That was Brendan Mulligan, one of the new assistants. He's the one who did the post-mortem. He sounds very upset.'

'Thank you, Sergeant. You're . . . doing a great job,' she said. 'I'd bring you with me on this one, but I think you should take a few hours off. Have a rest and freshen up. Maybe we can get together later and assess what we have here.'

Good Lord, she thought, bringing herself up sharply. What was she saying? What would he think she meant? Indeed, what *did* she mean?

'Case-wise,' she added limply, limping off on her

walking stick, a deep warm blush reddening her face.

Sergeant Greer watched her undulating gait. He was sick with longing for her to simply hold him and tell him that everything was going to be all right, that she was on his side, that she understood, that they would leave for South America in two hours' time.

He just wasn't sure about her tie-dyed light-blue suit.

'I got you these,' said Gary Reynolds, throwing bottles of hair dye and a packet of hair wax on to the bed he had shared for so many years with Madelene.

'Groovy, mon,' said his new lover.

Micky McManus was scrubbed clean of his previous persona. He felt a little sad at leaving behind his Rasta ways. But it had to be done.

He knew that Gary was down at heart too, he was just being noble enough to try and conceal it. His rescuer had found the whole Rasta thing exotic and pleasing; it had brought a strangeness to their love-making, an excitement.

'I was thinking you could dye your hair brown, and your eyebrows . . . and y'know . . .' Gary blushed a little. 'Whatever else.'

'Thanks,' said Micky. 'That's . . . really thoughtful.'

'I thought you could use the hair wax to make little tiny dreadlocks. With those and a pair of dark glasses, nobody'd be any the wiser about you. But you'll probably have to tone down the clothes a bit.'

They both sighed.

'I guess you can't have everything,' said Micky sombrely.

'No,' agreed Gary, lying on the bed beside him. He felt good, pleasured, deeply fulfilled. For once in his life he was *doing* something. Yes, the sex had been absolutely wonderful. But he had also found a soulmate in whom he could confide. He had told Micky McManus all his problems and Micky had listened, whereas Madelene had just fucked off.

They lay in contented silence for a while, and then Micky began to speak in the language of their love.

'Say, I been thinkin bout yo problem, Gazzamon,' he said, encouraged to continue by the big man's affectionate smile. 'An it seem to me dat I got de slooshan.'

'Yeah?'

'For real. Now you dig, Gazzamon, dat I gotta homeboy by name-a Dusty. An dis bro Dusty, he de *maan*.'

'The man?'

'Yeah. De dustbin man.'

'Oh. I see.'

'An what dis cat doan know bout refuse, it aint *worth* knowin. You dig?'

'I . . . do dig, yes.'

'Bitchin. So we goan pay him a visit, Gazzamon. We goan get down and dirty with Dusty. And righteous Dusty goan fix us up good. Cos ah got da complexion to make da connection.'

Gary collapsed in a fit of giggles. 'I fucking *love* the way you talk.'

Micky was delighted himself with how his patois had improved. Since he'd been rescued by Gary, his confidence, his self-esteem – even his abilities – had increased tenfold. Together they were invincible.

'You done me good, Gazzamon. Now it mah turn to do you.'

'I *dig*,' said Gary happily, rolling on to his side to hold his Micky.

* * *

Brendan Mulligan was inconsolable. His shoulders shook, his voice wobbled as he tried to put words to the death of Jacinta Kinch. Drying his tears, he attempted to begin again – but a splutter of emotion was all that came.

'I understand, Brendan,' said Inspector O'Kelly sympathetically. 'Just take your time. I know this can't be easy.'

'It's a terrible business. All these recent murders. We live in lawless and barbarian times. And poor Patsy Roberts still locked up in the Ranch.'

'Yes, she's been sectioned, temporarily. But I'm sure . . .'

'Poor woman.'

'I'm certain that in the fullness of time she'll be back to her old self again. And really she's in the best of hands. Dr Joyce out there does tremendous work.'

'Yes, I hear it's like a holiday camp. And full of celebrities having breakdowns. So I suppose she'll be in the best of company anyway.' He began to tremble again, fighting to hold back his tears.

'Brendan, please don't worry about Mrs Roberts. We have to try and act professionally – now more than ever.'

'Call me Buck,' he said, struggling for self-control. 'And don't worry about the way I'm going on. I just . . . can't believe the minister's dead.'

'It's a terrible shock.'

'Justice,' he muttered, shaking his head.

'I know,' said Grainne. 'The whole country is a bit stunned. She seemed so invincible. So full of life.'

He gave a sudden wrenching gulp and began to gnaw on the heel of his hand.

'And I know,' she added, delicately, after a pause, 'that you and she were – well, an item for a while.'

They both looked at the swollen cadaver on the slab, the sheet pulled back to reveal the formerly ministerial splendour, a large Havana cigar still clutched in the right hand.

'That's true,' he replied grimly. 'We were.' And then he gave a small disturbed titter. 'So it was all the more pleasure to *cut her up*. By Christ, that woman was *some fucking wagon*!'

He started to choke and splutter again. And now Grainne realised that actually he was laughing. Soon he was in a paroxysm of laughter, rocking back and forth on his heels. She thought she'd better not say anything about it. People have many different ways of expressing grief.

'So can you tell me, Brendan – er, Buck – what was the cause of death?'

He dried his eyes and managed to stop guffawing. 'To be honest, Inspector, she was in terrible shape. She could have gone at any minute. Her liver alone was so enlarged, it took two of us and a fireman to lift it out.'

He gestured to a huge yellow organ in a nearby stainless steel sink. Grainne managed to stifle a gawk.

'Her lungs were like two tar sponges. Again it took three of us.' He pointed across to a glass specimen jar labelled TOXIC in which the gruesome objects had been lodged.

'Her heart was in tatters, all of her arteries were clogged.' He paused for a moment, as if an idea had suddenly come to him. 'It was a surprise to find a heart, I suppose.'

'Now Buck . . .'

'We found some ginger pubes in the bed, indicating possible recent intimate congress with a person – or persons – of the red-haired persuasion. We'll be screening them for DNA, obviously. And by the way she was as pissed as a newt when she died.'

'But what exactly killed her?' pressed the inspector. 'Or to come to the point, was Mrs Kinch murdered?'

'Actually, it was natural causes,' he said, spluttering a bit and tittering again. 'More or less natural at any rate.'

'Please elaborate,' insisted O'Kelly. She was getting impatient now.

'Well,' said Mulligan, regaining his composure, 'she was poisoned by her own body, but in an unusual way.'

'Go on.'

He was frantically trying to restrain his mirth. 'Her body was so overworked and clogged up that it wasn't using, or able to use, all of its natural outlets for waste. And so some . . . gaseous material accumulated in the gut and festered, I suppose you could say. And whatever debauchery she was indulging in that night, the trapped substances were agitated all the more, and put an unbearable pressure on her internal organs.'

'So what are you telling me? What exactly did she die of?'

'In lay people's terms – a trapped fart,' he said, then he slid to the ground and bellowed with glee.

'Welcome to Gull City,' said the binman, grandly, as the birds squawked and shrieked around him.

He stood proud in a luminous orange romper suit, surveying his vile-smelling multicoloured heap. This was no ordinary dump. This was a dump that had won prizes. Top Dump, three years in a row, in Dublin Corporation's annual dump competition. Two more years and the trophy was his to keep. This was his world. This was his glory.

Dusty Conmee was lord of all he surveyed, including the two supplicants who now stood before him. Gary was in mustard, Micky in lime green. The former had had his hair slicked back very hard, the latter looked as though a little woolly hedgehog had fallen from the sky and landed on his head. They both wore wrap-around mirror shades.

'I've done some calculations,' announced Dusty with confidence. 'Given the date involved, and the location from where the item was collected, and the peculiarities and preferences of the garbageman concerned, I think we're dealing with C Section in the Eastern Quadrant, between the tenth and twelfth vectors, and on a 30 degree axis to the base. We're talking an area of twenty feet square, give or take six inches. Gentlemen, shall we?'

As they trudged off, Micky looked at Gary's gob-smacked face.

'I told you the man was an artist and a genius.'

Dr J.P. Joyce glanced across his desk at the gaunt, wide-eyed woman, and marvelled once again at how such long hair could stand on end.

'Good morning, Mrs Roberts, lovely to see you again.'

But a soft grunt was the only response. He rose with a sigh and went to the window. Patients were walking around in the grounds. There were times when he found his work deeply stressful and wished he was back in his native small town of Ballingarry. Psychiatry had been good to him, that much was true. And yes, he had a talent, he had helped many people. But sometimes he wondered if he had made the right choices. Literature had always been his first love. In college he and his friends had written poetry; some had continued to write later on, one was a noted literary critic. How he envied those friends at times like this. Living down the country in little cottages. Lately Dublin life had been getting him down. The city was becoming more dangerous, more violent. All these murders were bad for the place.

He went back to his desk and sat down.

'Now tell me – Patsy – what would you like to discuss today?'

'Dreams.'

'Excellent, excellent. Dreams, yes. Tread softly, and all that, as Mr Yeats would have it.'

'Yeats is dead,' said Patsy, simply.

'Indeed he is,' laughed the eminent doctor. 'And a good thing too, after all – because they buried him.'

Patsy Roberts began to rock to and fro. A sound gurgled in her throat and rose to a scream.

Grainne O'Kelly was glad of the traffic jam on College Green. It gave her some much-needed time to think.

She didn't know how she was going to phrase her interim report to the Assistant Commissioner. 'Trapped fart' wasn't exactly media-friendly. And if the tabloids ever got hold of the ginger pubes, so to speak, they would have the greatest fucking field day since the bonking bishop.

As though reading her thoughts, a newspaper vendor approached with an early edition of the *Evening Herald*. KINCH'S LAST CLINCH, screamed the front page headline.

The story inside was by Eddie Lambert, and purported to have been smuggled out of Harcourt Street Garda Station, where he was being held for questioning about Mrs Kinch's death. He promised gory first-hand details of a sordid drug-and-booze crawl through the pubs and clubs of Dublin, followed by a fully-fledged orgy (with tequila and cigars) involving participants 'from the highest levels of law and order in this country' and culminating in the 'execution-style' death of the Minister for Justice. He insisted he had taken photographs to prove his allegations but said the films had been forcibly extracted from him during an illegal strip-search.

A statement from the Garda Press Office said that Lambert's rolls of film had been confiscated by the authorities as a danger to the State. Grainne wondered if they would have been developed by now. If what Lambert alleged was true those images would be invaluable – a pictorial diary of the events leading to the minister's death.

The photo of Lambert over his article caught her eye. He looked as though he had ginger hair. All his hair was ginger, presumably. As soon as she got back to the station she would suggest the taking of a DNA sample from him.

She flicked on the radio and listened to the tributes which were flooding in for the late minister.

'A wonderful woman, a lady, and indeed, some might even say, a gentleman,' intoned the Taoiseach.

'A no-nonsense law enforcer, with a grip like iron,' said a senior civil servant.

'A large character in every way, always willing to give the leg up to the younger members of the force, be they male or female or indeed from the canine division,' said a Garda spokesperson.

The traffic slowly haemorrhaged into life. Even though Grainne was not looking forward to facing her superior officer, the prospect of returning to the station suddenly made her heart tingle.

She fidgeted slightly in her seat. The anticipation of seeing Paschal Greer was so exciting. Oh, she had tried to hide it, had tried to be discreet – after all, a police station is no place for romance. But each time their eyes met, each time they collided in a corridor, she felt a jolt of electricity rush up her spine. It was so intense that it sometimes frightened her. Could she dare hope that he felt the same way? Would he ever respond? Was he totally indifferent to her?

She thought of her boring, unreliable boyfriend; useless Paddy Dignam the bird fancier. In the beginning, she had found his ornithology sweet. But that hadn't lasted long. Grainne thought birds were lovely and all that – she just couldn't see the point of spending hours waiting for them to appear, only to disappear again in a flutter. She simply didn't have those precious hours to waste, not in her line of work.

She remembered a drunken conversation they'd once had, on the way home from the annual Twitchers' Ball. Paddy had turned to her in the taxi and murmured: 'You know, Grainne – *you're* a bird too.'

She had preened a little and asked: 'What kind?'

'An emu.'

'. . . Huh?'

'Oh yes,' he'd continued, 'a beautiful emu. Long legs, elegant neck, huge pretty eyes.' Then he'd sighed unhappily and added: 'But flightless. You must learn to fly, Grainne. Fly!'

The fucking dodo. She *would* fly. Into the arms of Greer if she could.

'Oh brave new world that has such creatures in it!' exclaimed Dusty Conmee, atop a mound of burst refuse sacks.

He shushed away some rats with a wave of his hand. They went off cheerfully to choose another pitch. He turned to look at his non-quadruped companions, who were stumbling awkwardly over the hills of steaming rubbish. They didn't look nearly as happy as the rats.

'This is it,' Dusty indicated. 'Let's get dug in.'

Gary looked miserably at Micky.

'Come on now, Gazzamon,' encouraged Micky. 'You know there ain't no other way.'

Micky wished he felt half as upbeat as he sounded. The smell and the filth were ghastly, unbelievable – worse, even, than his old Rathmines bedsit. He ripped at a bag gingerly. The strange things we do for love.

The trio worked in silence for a quarter of an hour, then Gary shouted: 'Over here. I think I've found it!'

He delved deeper into the reeking bag before suddenly leaping back in abject horror. '*Arghh* . . . Oh sweet Jesus!'

Micky and Dusty rushed to his side. They gaped into the bag with disgusted fascination.

'This is bad, isn't it?' said Micky after a pause.

'It could be a lot better,' Gary replied.

Dusty nodded in fervent agreement as the rats began to congregate behind him.

Grainne's pal Sinead, secretary to the Assistant Commissioner, was waiting on the steps outside the station.

'Just to fill you in,' Sinead said, 'he's looking for you, and he's in the foulest mood I've seen since I missed a period last March. That was a false alarm, but this isn't. That journalist's photographs are in, and he's not pleased with what's in them at all, at all.'

With an apprehensive heart, Grainne O'Kelly rapped on the AC's door and quickly entered when she was bade.

His face could only be described as thunderous.

'Sit down, Inspector,' he ordered. She did.

'Before we get to the meat and drink of the *bags* that has been made of these last weeks, you can fill me in on the pathologist's report – it may provide the light relief that I so badly need right now.'

Nervously Grainne cleared her throat. For some reason she raised her eyes to the portrait of Patrick Kavanagh behind the AC's desk. The poet seemed to be grinning back at her, as though enjoying her discomfiture.

'Well,' she began, haltingly, 'it's hard to know where to begin, sir.'

'Just *try,* would you, Inspector, I'm in no mood for suspense.'

'Well the main . . . thrust, as it were, of the report is that Mrs Kinch died of natural causes.'

'Thanks be to God for that at least,' he said darkly. 'For the record, what were the natural causes, so we can tart them up for a press release?'

This was the moment Grainne O'Kelly had been dreading.

'. . . Em,' she said. 'Well . . . that's just it.'

'For Christ's sake stop prevaricating and get on with it, O'Kelly. We haven't got all day. What did the mad old witch die of?'

'Constrained wind.'

'What?'

'She was poisoned by trapped gases in her duodenum, or thereabouts. In the middle of vigorous sexual intercourse with a red-haired person, probably male.'

The Assistant Commissioner's face went from grey to deathly pale.

'Do you mean to sit there and tell me that the Minister for Justice died of a trapped fart while riding the mickey off some . . . *fucking carrot-top*?'

'That would seem to be it, sir, yes. I think the pathologist's report will be a bit more technical in some respects. But that's about the height of it, yes.'

'Mother of the divine Jesus,' he said. 'Lovely hurling altogether.'

Grainne could think of nothing to say. She watched as the AC stared blindly around the room, a look of desperation on his weary face.

'Very well,' he sighed, 'as things could hardly be bleaker, I think it's time for us to take a view on these photos, don't you?'

Something in his eyes made Grainne very afraid, but the train of fate was rolling now, and there was no stopping fate on its tracks. He pulled a bundle of photographs from his drawer and slid them quickly across the desk to her.

In her time on the force Inspector Grainne O'Kelly

had seen some shocking things. But nothing she had ever seen had prepared her for this. Picture after picture of the dregs of humanity ripping it up in the night-clubs of Dublin – the images were even worse than Lambert had promised in his salacious article. She recognised some of the grotesquely drunken faces. Here was the minister with Lambert himself, looking as though they were sucking each other's lips off. But who was that attractive girl? And who was that black man? Her mind was racing as she turned to the last photo. Her heart seemed to putter and stop. A freezing sensation flowed through her body. A man's face could be clearly seen in profile, about to be subsumed into Jacinta Kinch's bosom, while her hand thrust its way down the front of his trousers. She recognised the face. She recognised the trousers. They belonged to the man she loved – Paschal Greer!

Horrified, she stood and ran from the office, only dimly aware of the AC's shouts.

She dashed down the corridor to the Incident Room.

On the noticeboard was a blown-up copy of the same vile photograph – but instead of the minister's face Grainne's own had been inserted. Men were standing around and laughing.

Greer came in and did a double take when he saw the picture. Then he seemed to notice Inspector O'Kelly.

'Grainne,' he cried out, in terrible anguish.

'You utter *bastard*,' she spat. 'You stupid, lying bastard!' Her heart felt as if it would burst with anger and sorrow.

'Grainne, please – listen to me,' he pleaded, large tears beginning to roll down his scarlet cheeks.

'There's nothing more to say, you've seen to that.'

Paschal Greer was all out of options. So he did what he should have done many weeks ago. He stepped forward, took Grainne O'Kelly in his arms and kissed her.

Now there was no more need for words.

Chapter Twelve: by Charlie O'Neill

Well, now. Flip it now. That's just the last straw, thought Sergeant Greer as Inspector O'Kelly punched him bang in the kisser just as he was about to slip the tongue in.

He met the wall like a sheep against a farmer's headboard.

Goodnight.

He wouldn't have minded but for a few delirious moments he'd thought it was all going to be okay. If the truth be known he had surprised himself. Kissing her like that! Holy Kamoley.

The kiss? Ah, lads. The way he grabbed her. In fact it was a bit awkward – his Weetabix watch had got stuck in her earring. But so fecking what? It was the impulsiveness of it all. Yeah, the passion.

It's amazing how the gammiest situations – those moments when things just can't get any worse – can turn instantly into the greatest. And then back again. The last thirteen seconds of his life had been a rollercoaster. Now as he lay semi-conscious on the police-blue linoleum floor he felt the rollercoaster might well be on the way down again, and a key structural bolt was about to shear.

For some reason he was imagining he was back in his childhood, tucked securely under a safe, warm blanket. Not being able to see just yet, he had no way of knowing that in his attempt to sit up he had thrust his head under the inspector's skirt. Though unable to open his rapidly mauving eyes, somehow he managed to get to his knees. Then he thought he heard his beloved Grainne yelp – actually it was more of a squawk than your common-or-garda scream.

It was then that Sergeant Paschal Greer realised what was going on, that he had, in a sense, gone undercover. And this was no bedroom farce we had here – no way. He could hear the sound of many police boots rushing into the Incident Room. Oh janey maney, he fleetingly thought: in other circumstances what I wouldn't give to snorkel through these damp rushes.

Mortified, he moved decisively forward to get out. Unfortunately Grainne moved in the same direction to get off. She moved back. So did he. It went on. They almost hit a rhythm. He tried to get up and clamber out.

From three different directions, twenty-two police witnesses including the Assistant Commissioner converged on the scene just as Greer's stubbled chin grazed her thigh wound. 'Jesus, Paschal!' she groaned. 'Get down! Get down!'

In fairness now, things did look a bit compromising.

Grinne looked at her astounded audience with characteristic composure. 'He was just coming to,' she casually explained as the pummelled face of Sergeant Paschal Greer emerged from under the hem of her skirt.

'Jeepers, I can't believe I went down that easy,' he offered.

The grapefruit light was fading fast and a clammy stink

hovered over the dump. Three men stood silhouetted against a horizon of mangled car wrecks and decomposing rubbish. Unable to move – not yet anyway – they stared gravely into the bag which Gary was holding half open.

Suddenly all three leapt. A family of rats scrambled forth from the bag, Mammy Rat scuttling up Gary's arm. Dropping the bag, he screamed and howled; then fell on his arse into a gully of garbage. The scream had a fairly dramatic effect on the topography.

The entire surface of the dump seemed to come alive. Seagulls, crows, pigeons and magpies rocketed skywards. Hundreds, maybe thousands, of rats scurried for cover. Even Dusty was a bit shook up.

The sensation of the rat running up his arm was one of the most shocking things Gary had ever experienced. But that was nothing – it was almost pleasant – compared to the sensation he was about to have. For the briefest moment after the landing, all seemed calm. Then the earth moved for Gary Reynolds.

Beneath his bulk he felt a medium-sized raiding party squirm and scutter and squidge and scramble. Others scooted across his legs, groin and chest. One nuzzled his neck – albeit with little affection – and another wet-nosed his armpit through his torn T-shirt. A little one ran on to his face, stopped dead, swivelled – and doubled back leaving two perfect brake marks on his cheek. Gary's weedy nostrils felt the whish of a damp tail. As he lay there, a giant barrier to a rodent refugee crisis, Gary Reynolds drew a deep breath, composed himself, gathered all his manly resolve. And then he panicked like fucking fuck.

Rule:
If you find yourself
lying in a seething, squealing bed
of terrified rats –
GET UP!

'Get up!' shouted Dusty. But the rule went unobserved. Gary didn't get up. He writhed and rolled and screeched and lashed out.

'Get up!' Micky roared. But Gary didn't get up. He stayed down. And he shat himself. And he started bawling.

'Get the fuck up!' Dusty tried a variation on the theme. Gary rolled over and tried but failed. He swallowed a mouthful of dump-soup with big bits.

By this stage his bulk and convulsions had killed at least nine rats, left several others disabled, still more with minor injuries and most of the remainder with low self-esteem. And as every dog on the street will know, a rat with low self-esteem is a dangerous rat.

By now there was a fair dose of the latter around, all staring in shock at the unfolding rodentocide. A counter-attack was quickly looming. Gary felt the strong and experienced hands of Dusty Conmee haul him quickly out of the hollow. He was speechless and shaking, covered in shite, fur and blood (and that, quite frankly, was just his own).

Micky McManus threw a car door at the rallying rodents and they scooted away for cover. He rushed over to Gary and hugged him. Mind you, when he got the smell, he backed off . . . but sensitively.

'Flip it, lads,' said Gary shakily, 'that's the most frightening thing that's ever happened to me.'

'You okay, Gaz?' Micky looked into his eyes.

'No. But I'm . . . I'm so glad you're here, Mick.'

'That was pretty traumatic, eh, Gaz?'

'I'm a disaster, Mick, I can't do anything right. I thought I was going to fucking die.'

'Yeah, Gaz, it was a close one. But you did fine, look at you. You survived it, Gaz. Nothing can stop you.'

'Mick, you're so good to me—'

'Ah for Jayzus sake will yis stop all that fuckin Mills and Boon wuss talk,' snapped Dusty. '*I'm* the one who saved your life anyway!'

Back in Gary's backyard, Gary and Micky opened the evil-smelling rubbish bag with great anxiety and rubber gloves. The stench hissed out in nearly visible clouds. The two lads backed away to regroup.

Micky was the first to step forward again. He administered a few running kicks to the bag to frighten any squatters who remained inside. But all had fled, no squeaking was heard – just a series of sodden sickening squelches. Closer went the boys and poked with sticks. Again no ratty lodgers were detected.

Gary and Micky moved closer still. The bag had ripped all down one side and was presenting its putrefied display of dregs, dross, decay and debris.

When he realised that this was indeed his own rubbish, Gary Reynolds was mightily glad to have left his previous life behind him. Blue bread, furry fondue, spotted spinach, pallid parsnips, chancy cheese, reeking rhubarb, slimy spuds, rank rabanadas.

If it is true that one should judge a person's character not by what he acquires but by what he discards then Gary Reynolds was in considerable trouble. Putrid prunes, rotting rouille, mouldy mackerel, manky milk, dodgy dumplings, retchy rissoles, awful offal and foul fowl. He had always held that Madelene was a seriously pretentious cook.

The brown envelope lay in the depths of the bag; sodden, marinading in pungent stinkjuice. Not that it really was brown any more. Gary managed to poke it out with a stick. The corners were either eaten or had rotted away. He picked up and opened the slippery package – syrupy pus wept from its wounded corners. The pages inside were drenched and infested, the edges of the bundle tattered, chewed and filthy. But miraculously, all the writing – or markings – seemed to be intact. Gary clasped the malodorous bundle to his ample bosom and pogoed around like a happy teenager.

'We could be lucky, Mick, we could just be lucky, lucky!'

'We'll have to dry 'em out, Gazzamon – make sure they're okay.'

'We'll do it tomorrow when it's fine. I've an idea,' said Gary as he ducked into his garden shed.

Incident Room, 9.25 a.m.

Inspector Grainne O'Kelly pheromones into the room. The idle chat fades and slowly dies.

Her audience of seven – uniformed and plainclothes – is male; Greer is among them, out of uniform, morose.

The inspector parks herself on the edge of a desk, her tight skirt losing the battle with her long taut legs. Six tongues involuntarily lick their owners' peeling lips. Greer stares at the floor.

'Okay, listen up. Time to get our asses in gear.'

She is pleased with this opener.

'This investigation – if you can flatter it with such a description – has been a fucking disaster right from the get-go. But that's going to change. From here on in. Anyone doesn't like it, there's the door.'

She rests a foot on the rim of a small plastic bin. The skirt, unable to cope, now ascends further. Fourteen eyes imagine they're working vice.

'Reynolds. Nestor. Dunphy. Roberts. Andrew Andrews. Jacinta Kinch. Somebody tell me something about them.'

Silence reigns in the Incident Room. Nervous gulps. Confused glances.

'Now listen up, schmuckos, and listen good. I know all of these deaths are somehow connected. Don't ask me how or why. I feel it. And we're under serious pressure from the top. Latest bulletin: new minister being appointed – probably a pitbull, self-righteous PD. The force's reputation is at an all-time low. Not helped by the sordid colour pictures in the Sundays. Thanks to our colleague, Sergeant Greer.'

'Grainne, please . . .'

'*Inspector*, to you.'

'Inspector, I . . .'

'Greer, you're grounded – for the duration of this investigation you will be as good as handcuffed to that desk.'

Everyone stares at Greer. He sinks even further into his seat.

'So, boys. Are we getting the picture? We've no leads, no capable witnesses, no shred of evidence apart from one DHL invoice – sweet-fanny-all as a matter of fact!'

Seven heads bob in tempo with her every move.

‘So it’s back to fundamentals. Dullard and Durak, you’re on round-the-clock stake-out. Bloom and Blixen’s gaff. Till further notice. They so much as pick their noses, you get back to me.

‘Deludey, you’re on house-to-house – neighbours, deliveries, postman, meter readers – you raise anything, I mean anything – I’m the first to know.

‘Dolt, take the DHL invoice and do some police work. I want to know what was shipped, to who and why. You don’t find out, you don’t bother coming back.

‘Dowdy, you’re on the minister’s last sordid evening – why that house, who was there, where are they now? Start with Greer over there, then Lambert. And find that weirdo black guy in the photos. There’s a younger woman too, good-looking. Find her.

‘Dunder, you start with the first murder. Talk to friends, neighbours of Reynolds. There’s family – a son and daughter – ask them to come in. Skeletons? Inheritance? Baggage? The works.

‘Okay. That’s it. Any of you find yourself at a loose end, you’re filling out dog licences with Sergeant Greer.’

Somebody chuckles. When she glances up she sees that Greer is gone. Maybe she’s been too hard on him. But no. If he can’t take the dressing-down he deserves he’s not going to hack it for long in the force.

‘We’ll have a case meeting first thing every day, 9.15 a.m. I want daily reports on each assignment. If I don’t see progress – new evidence, a firm lead, a witness, something solid – in the next twenty-four hours, I’m going to shaft you so hard you won’t walk straight for a year.’

The men look at each other. What a promise. Soft sighs of desire are suppressed.

'Okay. That's all, folks. Hit the bricks.'

Officers Deludey, Dullard, Durak, Dowdy, Dunder and Dolt get up and begin to file slowly out of the room.

'And lads . . .' adds Grainne with a kind of simpering concern.

They all look back.

'*Bí cúramach* out there.'

It's a turning point, thought Sergeant Greer. On a voyage of no return. Or something like that.

His public humiliation by the woman he loved had sent him spiralling into self-loathing. But now he was coming out of that. Anger was what he felt right now. Anger at himself but also at her. Okay, he had fucked up – the party with the minister and all that – but he hadn't meant to betray Grainne. He wasn't even sure that he had actually *had*.

He understood that she had to give him a hard time in front of the others. But it still hurt, he couldn't deny it. The lads were only rookies after all – whereas Greer was a freshly baked muffin of a sergeant. Taken off the streets and confined to barracks.

Mortifying. And yet in its own way quite exciting. God she was forceful. So full of passion.

He had allowed himself to become deflected from his goal – to solve the case and win his Grainne. Winning her love now seemed impossible, but at least he might still win her respect.

Greer tried to assess his situation. In some ways being tied to the desk might actually suit him. In the last few weeks he had come to realise that his strengths were not those of the front-line officer. No, he was more of your thinking cop, your methodical, assiduous shape-of-the-case strategist. Check the facts. Check the paperwork. Check each shred of even minor evidence. If it isn't evidence, check it again; check it until it *becomes* evidence.

He left his desk and went purposefully down the corridor. This was a turning point all right.

Now he was in the evidence lock-up, looking through the cardboard box-file labelled *Reynolds Murder*. Every case was unique but this one was a bit more unique than most. He had no idea of exactly what he was looking for but he looked all the same, sorting, sifting. Case report files. Jason Dunphy's confession. The forensic report from the crime scene at the caravan.

When he opened the crime-scene folder some photos fell out. They were close-up pictures of Tommy Reynolds's body, taken from many different angles.

The poor man. What a way to go. Greer looked slowly through the cold, hard images. Then he noticed something odd. What was that? In the picture of Reynolds's right foot? He raised the photo and squinted to make out the detail.

The corner of a crumpled piece of paper was protruding about an inch above the hem of the dead man's sock. Was it – it seemed to be – a £10 note?

Greer rummaged through the box. Among the statements, maps and diagrams he found a £10 note in a plastic evidence bag. He took it out. Looked at it closely. James Joyce's face seemed to stare at him mockingly.

He couldn't tell what made him do it, but some inclination he didn't understand made Garda Sergeant Paschal Greer slip that banknote into his pocket.

Sure, they had won their court case, but Bloom and Blixen were not happy chancers. Matter of fact, they were mad as hell. And though they saw no immediate likelihood of being fingered again, for the first time in their crooked careers they were starting to feel that things were a little out of control. More worryingly, they didn't quite know what to do about it.

Mrs Bloom sat in the backyard, a changed woman. She had lost her faith in inhumanity, had even stopped recording the take-offs and landings in her notebook. If only people kept their promises, she thought; if only there was a bit more decency in the world. Once upon a time there was honour among crooks. But those days were clearly gone for ever. Crooks these days were downright dishonest.

Tommy Reynolds, for example – in a way this was all his fault. If only he had produced the goods he'd promised, things would have turned out fine and dandy. But he hadn't. Despite all the chances they'd given him, he'd let them down, time and again. Not only did he not keep his side of the bargain, he didn't even give back the seed-money they'd advanced him. Yes, it was counterfeit. But morally that didn't matter. It was the principle of the thing, after all.

As for Roberts and Nestor – what a pair of eejits. What a bags they had made by shooting poor old Tommy, when all she had wanted was to give him a fright. It wasn't right to shoot a man with a heart condition. Beat him stupid, okay, but there's no need for violence. In the old days you could *rely* on your bent policemen to do what they were told and follow simple rules. But nobody respected authority any more.

Look where it had all led. Poor old Nestor. Nobody liked cop-killing, least of all Mrs Bloom. When that happens, the climate changes. Police do their job harder when one of their own is cut down. Well, that's only natural. But in that kind of atmosphere it's virtually impossible for a woman to do a dishonest day's work. O yes.

Even their court victory had a down side. Up until then they had managed to prowl and raid from the cover of the anonymous undergrowth of suburbia. Suddenly, in court, they were out in the open. Exposed for the whole world to see. Only this morning two reporters had phoned. And the milkman had left a note with his delivery – 'Saw your pic in the paper. Didn't know I had celebs on my run!'

Now they were being cased, around the clock. The van was so obvious that it had to be the police. You'd think they could at least *try* to be inconspicuous. But no, the van was painted pink with three big aerials and a constant crackle of walkie-talkies from the back.

The attention didn't annoy her so much as the timing. Well, she'd always known that one day it would come. That's why she and Mrs Blixen had been working with Dymphna. For years they'd been planning that one day she would succeed them. Why, they'd been about to 'make' her when all this unpleasantness had broken out – about to promote her to being 'a goodgirl'.

They hadn't got around to letting her know that she was to be the next godmother of serious crime. They'd wanted it to come as a surprise; it was always nice to give a young person a break. In the meantime they'd been helping her, shaping her, loving her – moulding her in their own image. It could have been a seamless takeover. But then Tommy Reynolds had spoiled it all.

'Bad, bad timing.'

She had said it out loud.

I must be under pressure, she thought.

Now she was genuinely worried about Dymphna. And a little confused by her sudden disappearance. The girl had vanished into thin air. They had read in the *Evening Herald* about the infamous house party with the minister and had been startled to recognise their own dear girl in the photographs. What on earth had Dymphna done? What an unlikely collection of people to have in her home. A policeman, a journalist and the Minister for Justice, not to mention a former Taoiseach. A sweet-natured girl like Dymphna Morkan could get into trouble in company like that.

Perhaps she had been doing a little freelancing? Getting the minister on-side? Courting a stooge in the press? Yes, she was a good and resourceful girl. But she had clearly fallen in with a bad crowd. Why hadn't she come to them for help since then? Maybe she knew the house was being watched. By now, of course, the telephone would be tapped. But surely she could have figured out a way to get in touch. The milkman would have delivered a message discreetly. Maybe something terrible had happened. Maybe she was lying dead in a rubbish skip somewhere.

Oh Lord. Young people today.

But there were other things to worry about too. With the cops leaning on them, business was bad. And no real wonder, when you thought about it. Mrs Bloom felt they had let their standards slip. But what could you do? You couldn't get the staff. In the old days they had only ever worked with the very highest calibre of low-life criminal psycho scum. But those happy days had faded now. Given the ropy cast of losers, fatheads and glorified gombeens with whom they'd had dealings in the last few weeks, she wouldn't be at all surprised if the Garda investigation turned up a crucial clue which would lead directly to their door; or worse – to their offshore bank accounts.

Gloomy Mrs Bloom closed her nightblue notebook, not even hearing the landing approach of SLA 173 from Schiphol (originating in Colombo, Sri Lanka). She put on her coat, nodded to Mrs Blixen to follow and walked out into the street.

'So,' she called, in the direction of the van. 'What price are the Friesian polly heifers getting these days, Garda Durak?'

Garda Durak tried his best to smile back nonchalantly but a gnawing sense of fear made his crooked mouth twitch.

Meanwhile, at the rear of the van, Mrs Blixen was affixing something to the window.

'You won't get away with this, you know,' said Mrs Bloom, as Mrs Blixen slipped back into the house.

'How's that now, love?' asked Garda Durak.

'We're watching you,' said Mrs Bloom. 'Twenty-four hours a day. We know your every move.'

She smiled and walked on towards the corner of the street. Garda Dullard looked at Garda Durak.

'It's a trap,' said Dullard. 'They're trying to lure us away from the house. You follow her on foot. I'll keep an eye on things here.'

Durak hopped out and began to shadow Mrs Bloom. His mind was full of all sorts of thoughts and so he failed to notice the sticker on the back window of the van, saying, in red letters, on a very black background: *Paedophile Society of Ireland – Day Trip.*

Mrs Bloom slipped into McCarthy's pub; she went

through the lounge bar and into the back corridor where she inserted a coin in the public telephone and quickly dialled a number.

'Hello? Eddie Lambert? It's Pauline Bloom here . . . Remember that little favour you owe me, love?'

Four hours after the end of his shift, Paschal Greer folded and pocketed the 'case map' he'd been working on. He switched off his computer – well, he couldn't find the switch so actually he unplugged it – and left the office to go for a walk. Nobody bade him goodbye but he didn't mind. He wanted solitude. He needed to think.

As he walked into town – cutting across Montague Lane on to Camden Street – he felt an overwhelming craving for sweets. Proper sweets. Sweets from a jar. He stepped into one of his favourite premises.

Kavanagh's Sweet Shop on Aungier Street was a perfectly preserved country-style shop which held out cheekily in the city centre against all the bland trendy stores and new hotels around it.

'The usual, Paschal?' Mr Kavanagh asked.

'Yeah I spose.'

Whistling, Mr Kavanagh filled a bag and handed it over. Paschal had three Licorice Allsorts in his mouth before he'd even paid.

'What's this, Paschal – what's this at all?'

'Hngh?' replied Paschal, his jaw packed.

'God now, that's awful altogether.' Mr Kavanagh playfully clicked his tongue. 'And you a policeman, Paschal. Are you not ashamed?'

'How do you mean?'

'Well this £10 note. It's a fake you're after giving me.'

'. . . Is it?'

'Course it is, Paschal. Sure look at it, can't you?'

Sergeant Greer approached the counter. 'It looks real enough to me,' he said.

Mr Kavanagh shook his head and smiled. His fingertip tap-tap-tapped on the banknote.

'See him? James Joyce?'

'What about him?'

'Well on a real tenner, Paschal – he isn't wearing a bow-tie. Look.'

Mr Kavanagh fumbled in the greasy till, finally producing a genuine ten-punt note. What he had said was absolutely correct. The face of Joyce was identical on both notes. But on the true legal tender he was *wearing a necktie.*

'But . . . that's Tommy Reynolds's tenner. The one from the file. I'm sorry, Mr K. I must have given it to you by accident.'

Mr Kavanagh nodded. 'You see a good few of them around these days. You'd want to have eyes in the back of your head, so you would. Blooming terrible the things they get up to.'

Sergeant Paschal Greer felt his heart whomp. He had just stumbled on his first major lead.

The Assistant Commissioner's doorbell rang at 10.20 p.m. He ignored it and settled back in his armchair. The buzzer sounded again, more insistently this time. He gave a soft curse under his breath.

'Tessa?' he called.

He was watching *NYPD Blue*, his favourite programme. At least it had complexity, moral ambiguity. It had quite cathartic plot lines, well-defined characters

– not like most of the sordid rubbish that nightly filled the television screen. He hated interruptions to *NYPD Blue*. The bell rang a third time but he didn't budge.

'Get that, Tessa, will you?' he yelled, with the practised presumption of thirty years of marriage.

In the kitchen his wife placed the AC's black shoes on the newspaper beside the polish. She shuffled to the hall, turned on the outside light and without opening the triple-locked door called out: 'Who is it?'

No one answered.

'Who's there, please?'

No response was offered.

She eased back the curtain and checked outside. Rain was falling. There was nobody in sight.

'Top Cat?' she shouted in to her husband. 'Sorry to bother you, lovie, but there doesn't seem to be anyone out here. It's strange.'

'Okay, Bunnykins. Sipowitz is about to go back on the wagon. I'll be there in two secs.'

'I'm frightened, Cuthbert. Can't you come out now?'

Sighing, he got up and went into the hall. Since this inexplicable spate of Garda murders his wife had been even more nervous than usual. Maybe she was right to be. These were dangerous and unpredictable times. Sinead had often said that he had to keep an eye out. A man in his position would have many powerful enemies. And a man who had both a wife and a mistress had two good reasons to keep himself alive. Sinead could be very cutting sometimes.

'Now,' he smiled, opening the front door. 'There's nothing to be worried about, after all. Is there?'

'I suppose not.'

'Ah! Look.' An A4 envelope with his name on it was

lying on the step. 'It was only a courier. Most probably papers from work.'

'All right, then. Would you like a sandwich, Top Cat?'

'Yes, little Bunnykins. That would be lovely.'

Tessa went back into the kitchen as he picked up the envelope. He thought he heard a car drive off as he tore it open and peeked inside.

He felt the blood drain from his face.

He stared in terror at the photographs of himself and Sinead. They were naked except for the shaving foam and the hurleys.

> YOU WILL SEND THE ENCLOSED MEMO TO ALL YOUR OFFICERS TOMORROW – OR YOU WILL GO THE WAY OF KINCH

The hall seemed to swim before his shocked eyes.

Outside in the night, Eddie Lambert put his foot down.

A smelly, smoky, seedy bar like this was just what Grainne O'Kelly needed. It suited her mood, she felt at home here. Whiskey was a thug to her tongue but a warm friend on the way down. An edgy piano themed her off-key life.

Earlier in the evening, back at headquarters, Garda Dunder had called in a report to the effect that he had managed to interview young Gary Reynolds, who was claiming to have been legally bequeathed by his father the first half of the now famous last novel of Joyce. His story had checked out with Gertie MacDowell, Tommy's, and now Gary's, legal adviser; though she hadn't been in a position to comment on the document's authenticity, nor to say how such a potentially valuable item had ever come into Tommy's possession. For his part, Gary didn't know either. But he wanted what was rightfully his.

Dunder said the manuscript had been badly damaged in some kind of flood, adding that for some reason there was a godawful smell off it. Its pages had apparently been hung out to dry on a number of clotheslines in Gary's backyard. A friend – a chap called Micky – was helping him dry it. Such a casual arrangement had made Grainne laugh. She'd ordered that Gary be given police protection. It was possible – maybe even likely – that he would turn out to be a target too.

'And see if you can get a photo of the father,' she said.

'Why'd'you want that, boss?'

'For the press campaign. Build up a profile – who knew him, who saw him, what were his movements?'

'Okay, I'll try.'

'Bike it over to me quick. I'm leaving for Kinch's funeral in an hour.'

Grainne looked around. She liked this bar. An odd thought made her smile – she never would have found it if she hadn't been participating in the funeral of the dear departed minister. As she followed the cortège through the small neat suburbs which ornament the first slopes of the Dublin mountains, she had stalled her car for perhaps a minute and then driven on a half-mile or so, only to come upon the aftermath of the crash – or, more accurately, of several crashes.

In the chaos she managed to piece together that a driving instructor had swerved to avoid a Corporation worker who had fallen asleep propped against his shovel in the middle of the road. That swerve had caused the hearse carrying Minister Kinch's coffin to brake too sharply – which in turn caused a pile-up of nineteen state BMWs, Mercs, Rovers, Saabs and Volvos. The hearse skidded and flipped across the road, propelling the coffin out of the back window and on to a prop truck for a Garry Hynes production of *Dracula* at the Gaiety Theatre.

When the debris had finally been cleared Grainne O'Kelly had felt in need of a drink. She had noticed a bar across the road. To hell with the funeral, she thought to herself. She really wanted a break from death.

Now in Colonel Knowledge's, on her fifth whiskey, she found herself reflecting on the events of the day. Things were going better. She had asserted herself with the team. She had an instinct that the case was beginning to crack open. Paschal Greer came into her mind. She wondered how he was, if he was okay? She felt a stab of yearning deep in her heart. What a shame that it hadn't worked out. How could he have been as unreliable as all the others?

Well, there were more important matters on which to concentrate now. She examined the photo which Dunder had got from Gary Reynolds. It had been found at the scene of Tommy's murder but it was too old to be of much use for the media campaign. It showed Reynolds in his twenties, his wife beside him and a couple of kids. The family looked innocent and happy but there was something unsettling about the picture. The date on the back was very strange: 'June 1948' in Reynolds's handwriting. Why would he have put that date on it? The clothes in the picture were definitely seventies. The car was from the 1970s too. The most likely explanation was that Tommy had gone gaga at some point. But it was still strange. She couldn't explain it – but it almost *did* feel as though it was that old. It wasn't the image, it was something else. The *paper* on which the picture was printed felt ancient. She decided she would drop the photo down to the lab the next morning, see what a chemical analysis might turn up.

But let tomorrow look after itself, she thought. Grainne O'Kelly was enjoying herself now. Slowly relaxing. Sipping her drink. The whiskey lit a golden glow in her insides, warming a desire she hadn't felt for a while. Oh my Paschal. What a chance we missed. The piano music seemed as intoxicated as she was. She stretched slowly, arching her back as she liberated her hair to kiss its way across her shoulders.

Grainne O'Kelly felt magnetised by the music. She found herself walking towards the piano corner, a slow sexy sashaying stride. Frankly, the music wasn't even that great. Was it just that she was a little drunk? Well, if she was, she didn't care. It was out of tune, out of tempo, out of date and certainly out of place. But there was something about it. A haunting honesty. A loneliness she connected with. A kind of bog sleaze.

Then she heard the voice. A familiar voice.

My dream last night
The station's blue light
You ran naked, smiled and fell on me.

It couldn't be, she thought, her excitement rising.

We worked undercover
Cop lover to lover
A first-degree sexual felony.

Jesus, she thought. It was Paschal Greer!

And – what's more – he could sing too. It was definitely him, through the subtle clouds of smoochy smoke. Her own Paschal. Her own secret love. But he didn't look a bit like himself. The cigarillo. The Falmers jeans. The Nobber Slashers Hurling Team polo-shirt. The cream slip-ons. The skilful fingers tantalising the ivories.

Assaulted my wound
Battered my hope
You took my love to the cleaner's
My heart is in jail
And I'll never make bail
But I'm missing your misdemeanours.

The song cut straight to her loins and seemed to harmonise with the bluesy croon of her now dangerous desire. She slid lithely on to the piano stool beside him, sparks of static exploding around her curves. Shocked, he turned to her, his lovely voice faltering. Clearly he had been drinking heavily. Then somehow he managed to retain his composure. He continued, staring into her full, firm, heaving . . . eyes.

Laundered my heart
Fenced my hope
They warned me just to scoff at her

Grainne couldn't stop her finger caressing middle C.

You know what I'm needing
Oh pull me for speeding
My most arresting officer

They fell into each other's arms and began to kiss.

'You're a talented man,' she whispered provocatively.

'Grainne . . . I mean Inspector . . . I didn't expect to find . . . you look so lovely, janey malaney . . . I dug up an interesting piece of evidence on the case . . .'

'Paschal, the only evidence I want to dig up tonight is in your Falmers.' He blushed bright pink. 'Sorry – I'm a bit drunk,' she continued. 'But I know what I'm doing. Tomorrow we'll deal with work. Tonight I want to play. Maybe in the cold light of morning this will be one horrible sordid mistake. But right now I want your caks for grilled rashers.'

'But Grainne—'

'I want to play, Paschal.'

'Fine. I can handle that. I want to play too.'

'I mean *really* play, Paschal.'

'Fair enough so, Grainne. I'll just go and do my wee-wees.'

Paschal Greer came back from his widdle a changed man. In the back of the taxi he almost stopped Grainne O'Kelly's heart when he brushed the inside of her arm and stroked her lovely lips with a fingertip as light and hot as magic. Taking her in his arms in one deft movement he seemed to gaze deep into the core of her soul, his calm craving eyes demanding love and greed from hers, his mouth kissing her neck and shoulders with hot and horny breath.

You could nearly say now that things were moving along fairly handy.

By the time they got inside Grainne's apartment, the situation was getting a bit primitive. When Greer whipped out his police-siren light both their natives became definitely restless. The purple-blue glow flashed around the room, picking out two prowling, lecherous animals.

'Sergeant Greer?' said Grainne in a velvety whisper.

'What?'

'I want you. Now.'

'Work away so.'

She fingerwalked down the front of his Falmers.

'Jesus, Paschal, but you're a big boy.'

'That's . . . my ah . . . truncheon, Grainne.'

'Oh shite, sorry – so it is . . .'

He guided her hand with his.

'This is my . . . y'know,' he said.

Her eyes opened wide. Her hand double-checked.

'Oh Paschal.'

'Oh Grainne.'

'O yes.'

'O yes.'

They kissed – long, caring and carnal. Greer had the horn of a Polish pole vaulter.

'So, Grainne, what's your favourite position?'

'Commissioner,' she said as she lifted him on to the mantelpiece.

Later that night as they rode the range (an Aga) for the fifth time, using wide Sellotape, an eight-inch G-clamp, a jar of lemon curd and the toner cartridge for a photocopier, Grainne came up with her fourteenth theory.

'I've got it!' she said as she repeatedly flicked the cartridge.

'Over a bit,' said Greer.

'It must be because we're both from the country; similar cultural backgrounds, y'know? Oh, Paschal – *tighten the clamp, Paschal.*'

'Maybe,' he groaned. 'Okay, pump the toner, baby! But wait a second – you're from Dublin, aren't you?'

'I'm not, my little Paschal lamb, I only let them think I am. They wanted more Dubs in the force, y'know. Tighter, Paschal, now – *whoargh*.'

'That's gas. Oh Jesus, Grainne – *tone me harder*!'

'So you see,' said Grainne '– one more good turn, oh Jesus, thank you! – you're from Nobber. I'm from Muff – a match made in bog heaven. Okay. Now, Paschal, the Sellotape! *Now!*'

'You're sure you want this?'

'Does Padre Pio cheat at hide-and-seek? Of course I want it! *Now!*'

'Right so! Let that toner tone!'

'Oh yes!' said Grainne, dribbling delirium.

'Oh y-y-y-yes!' said Paschal. Just dribbling.

'Bog feckin heaven!' Grainne cried out, collapsing in ecstasy on the melted lemon curd.

Dowdy woke Dunder beside him in the unmarked Opel. He was feeling nervous, very jumpy. Only yesterday two of his colleagues, on watch in a van outside the Bloom–Blixen residence, had suffered an inexplicable and terrible beating from a gang of angry local parents.

'Denis!' he hissed.

'Derek? . . . What is it?'

'We've got company. Look.'

A nun carrying an ISPCC collection bucket and what looked like an umbrella walked up to the door of 18 Copse Parade and rang the bell. The officers watched as Gary Reynolds opened the door. He and the nun smiled and chatted for a few moments. Then the bigboy seemed to invite her inside, pausing briefly to offer a casual wave to Dowdy and Dunder – as if to say 'Everything's okay, lads.'

'What do we do now?' said Dunder anxiously.

'We wait and see,' said Dowdy. 'If there's anything suspicious we move in. But let's face it, it's only a nun.'

'Spose so,' said Dunder. 'Let me know.' He slid down in the seat and closed his eyes. Dowdy waited for a few minutes.

'I'll call it in anyway, just to be on the safe side. Will I?'

But Denis Dunder was dozing again.

Chapter Thirteen: by Donal O'Kelly

Sinead Eglinton couldn't believe her eyes. She read and re-read the single stark page the Assistant Commissioner had slammed down on her desk.

He'd spat in Irish: '*Déan é sin! Go tobann!*'

She tried to say something – what's wrong with you, Cuth? Or why are you suddenly talking in Irish? Or why are your eyeballs that funny shade of purple? But she didn't get the chance to say anything at all.

He glared at her like Frankenstein's monster when things were gone from bad to worse and the flaming torches were coming up the hill. She found herself picturing their most recent tryst. He'd been the simple-grin Frankenstein back then, the stupid gobshite. O yes! Bouncing up and down with his blubber rising and falling and his floppy bits flicking and flapping. She'd had to shut her eyes. Jesus, even the memory made her shudder.

But now he was giving her the other Frankenstein look. The look that said: 'Oh, how cheerfully I could kill you.' Men. For God's sake. How quickly they changed. They'd put years on you when they got in a mood like that. In Cuthbert's case there was the age factor of course. At that age men went wonky inside: hormones and genes and weird psychosexual impulses shaking around with all the predictability of a nuclear cocktail mixed in a leaky bucket.

The chain reaction was in progress now. White face. Purple eyeballs. Swollen knuckles. Irreversible meltdown. Spouting gibberish in Irish.

'*Na habair! Na habair focal! Dun do chlab!*'

Spit flew all over Sinead, the offending page and the desk. His mouth was like a showerhead in a Midlands B&B. He turned on his heel, tripped over his shoelace and hurtled angrily out of her office.

She sat very still, looking blankly at the page.

URGENT: MEMO

To the acting Minister for Justice and all officers of the Garda Siochána

Inspector Grainne O'Kelly has been removed from Operation RANK and transferred to Allihies, County Cork, with immediate effect. Sergeant Paschal Greer is promoted to Inspector and will be heading up the inquiry as from today.

She felt herself begin to boil with rage.

Operation *RANK*!

She fumed. The baldy twister! She herself had come up with that name. She'd suggested it to him only the other day – in the middle of one of their afternoon sessions. God in Heaven, it would have to stop. His big red face and his flapping cheeks. Blowing like a bellows. His eyes as big as dinner plates. Reynolds, Roberts, Andrews, Nestor, Kinch. Operation R.A.N.K for short, she'd said.

Now he'd stolen her suggestion and was passing it

off as his own. Bloody men. They were all the same. Behind every successful man there was a woman who was fool enough to give him everything he knew.

She felt like going into his office and lifting his baldy head by the few hairs on the back of it and slapping it into one of his beloved sculptures again and again and again.

But what good would that do? She was only upsetting herself. He wouldn't even be worth the effort. And anyway, there was someone else who needed her support now. She looked again at the memo. Poor Grainne.

Grainne O'Kelly heard a loud, shrill sound fill Harcourt Street Police Station. It took a few moments to realise it was coming from her mouth.

Two words from the memo seemed to burn into her brain. 'Removed' was one. 'Allihies' was the other.

Three generations of O'Kellys proud members of the force, and now this bitter and undeserved shame. Priests were defrocked and lawyers disbarred. But when a garda was Allihied there was no coming back.

There was a third word on the page that her anger was preventing her from actually managing to say out loud.

'Grr . . . *Grrrr* . . .'

'That's enough now, Graw,' Sinead said gently. 'His day will come, never fear.'

'How could he do it to me? After what happened between us?'

'Come now, pet, pull yourself together. Let's go out and do some girltalk.'

'But . . . what about my *investigation*? All my work?'

'I know. It's difficult. But these things happen.'

'... Grrr ... Grrrrr ... GreeeeeeeeeeR!'

As he sauntered up Harcourt Street towards the station, Paschal Greer was grinning from lug to lug. Holy Kamoley, he couldn't believe it! An inspector already – he was zooming up the ranks. The little town of Nobber would be so proud. And so would his beloved Grainne.

Now they were equal – both inspectors. They'd have babies who'd grow up to be inspectors too. Higher and higher they'd go, ever upwards – he and Grainne ascending together, a little division of baby Greers stepping up the rungs of life's ladder behind them. Paschal was getting dizzy at the prospect.

He wondered if she would mind at all that he was taking over her investigation. But he was sure she wouldn't, not when she thought about it. Grainne was a generous and selfless soul, she would regard his promotion as marvellous news. The extra money would come in very handy – doubtless they would have to start saving for a house soon. Yes, he was certain she would see the bigger picture. After all, Allihies needed crimestoppers too.

He sprinted up the steps of the station, up the stairs and into his new office.

He took the drawers out of Grainne's desk and left them in a neat stack on the floor beside the photocopier. They'd have a wild celebration tonight, he thought, as he slid his own drawers into the slots so recently hers.

It was a pity that none of the lads was around. But they'd all been ordered out on a round-up of asylum-rejects who needed encouragement to board a charter flight to a former nuclear test-zone in Siberia. He'd overheard the station sergeant on the phone last night ordering up extra truncheons, gaffer tape and paddy-wagons.

Oh well. He was all on his own. Still – might as well make a start.

The pretty nun stood smiling and nodding, collection box in one hand and gun in the other. Micky sat on the sofa, nervously watching. What remained of his hair was an intriguing mixture of yellow, purple and green clumps – anything except ginger. A combination of stress-induced alopecia and the entire Joke Shop stock of hair-dye had left him looking like a half-plucked parrot.

'What do you really want?' asked Gary Reynolds.

'Would the Kinchkiller mind if we had a word alone?'

Micky's eyes flashed terror for a second.

'Bollocks. It was a trapped fart she died of,' he snapped. 'Don't you ever read the papers?'

'But who *released* that fart? It would have stayed happy enough, moseying around inside her for the rest of her natural. Except *you* had to go and *prove* something to the human race – you dumb macho pseudo-Rasta prick!'

'Now, now, sister, calm yourself,' said Gary. But he had to admit he was quite impressed.

'Are you going to let her talk to me like that, Gazzamon?'

Gary nodded towards the door. 'Upstairs. Go.'

Micky rose from the couch with his mouth in a pout. 'Is this your idea of a supportive relationship? If it is – it sucks, man!'

He stormed from the room and up the stairs.

'Anyway,' he shouted down, 'it was the stupid copper did the damage to Kinch, not me. What I did was nothing new. It was *him* who was doing the weirdy stuff.'

He slammed the bedroom door very hard. A moment later they heard him throw himself on the bed.

Silence settled on the living room for a time. Then Gary spoke:

'Dymphna Morkan. Right?'

'Blixen and Bloom once gave me orders to kill you, Gary Reynolds.'

'For my half of the book?'

She nodded. 'Of course.'

'How'd they know I have it?'

'They didn't as such. But they knew you'd be getting it one day.'

'They did?'

She laughed. 'Your father told them. Nice man, your father. But he talked too much.'

'So who's got the other half?'

'Use your brain, can't you?'

'Bloom and Blixen?'

'Think again, Bigboy.'

'Not . . . you?'

She grinned.

'How many pages?'

'Three hundred, Gary. Same as you. Together we have the whole thing between us.'

'Prove it.'

'I'll show you mine if you show me yours.'

'Okay. You first, though.'

She gestured towards her ISPCC collection-bucket. 'Open it,' she said.

'You open it.'

'For fuck's sake . . . Do you think I'd announce that I had orders to kill you and then just . . . kill you? With some kind of collection-bucket bomb?'

'You might.'

Dymphna sighed and opened the lid. She tilted the box towards Gary Reynolds. Three hundred pages of scrawled incomprehensible brilliance lay like a fat buff corpse in its collection-bucket coffin.

'How did my dad get his hands on this?'

Dymphna gave a soft laugh. 'You like stories, Gary?'

'This one have a happy ending?'

'Tell me,' she said, screwing her eyes closed. 'O tell me a tale . . . by the loothering waters . . . of night.'

'. . . Huh?'

She opened her eyes and peered at him. 'Imagine it's night.'

'Okay.' He shrugged.

'You're in Zurich. It's the winter of 1940. You're a simple woman from the arsehole of Ireland.'

'Yeah?'

'And your simple heart has led you to take pity on a half-blind Irish writer with a chin as sharp as my umbrella. His name is James Joyce. A truly great man. Like many great people, a little bit touched. He's not well at all. He has terrible ulcers, constant pain. He spends his days wandering the streets of Zurich, muttering and doodling and scrawling in his notebooks. Covering the pages in strange letters and symbols that mean fuck all to anyone who manages to sneak a glimpse.'

'Go on.'

'On a dark moonless night – New Year's Eve, 1940 –

poor Joyce knocks faintly on your humble door. "Missus," he goes, "I'm not long for this world, and you've been kind to Nora and me." The woman just figures he's drunk again. But he presses a bundle of papers into her hand. "God knows it isn't much – just a piece of my work. I was planning to turn it into a sort of novel. It's inspired by the passing of poor old Yeats; he was kind to me too, in my youth especially. But time, you know – I feel it running out. Maybe we all do on New Year's Eve." Well the woman tries to refuse. But he won't take no. "After I'm gone you never know. They might come in – you know, handy. Maybe. For something. I couldn't say. Perhaps at least they'd be a little keepsake – of a friend who wished he had a better way to thank you for your kindness."'

'He leaves and you throw the meaningless papers on the couch. You don't know it yet – but in a fortnight he'll be dead. Next morning your niece Evelyn is leaving to return to Ireland. She's looking for something to read on the journey. For a joke you give her the crazy notebooks. "Here," you say. "A little light reading by a chap from Dublin."'

'Jesus Christ,' breathed Gary Reynolds.

'Many years later Evelyn's daughter Patricia finds a bundle of old papers in the bottom of a drawer. She asks her mother to tell her the story behind them.'

'But . . . not the Patricia *I'm* thinking of?'

Dymphna nodded. 'That's how James Joyce's last novel fell into the possession of the late Patricia Purefoy – the same poor warm-hearted screwed-up Patricia that your father hooked up with in the caravan up the mountains.'

'Holy fuck.'

'One day, Patricia shows your da the notebooks. He sees the potential straight away. Starts working on a very clever plan.'

'What was it?' asked Gary.

'Your father comes to Mrs Bloom. She's big into the counterfeit cash racket at the time. He's invented some kind of chemical solution for artificially ageing paper – a forger's dream. He says it can make brand-new paper register as a hundred years old. Or whatever age you want it to be. Fool every known scientific test in the world.'

'But I don't understand. If he had the original . . .?'

'You really don't get the scam, Gary, do you?'

He looked at her dumbly and shook his head.

'Mrs Bloom had moved into the antiquarian books market as a cover. The money was good but nothing major. Your da offered her a way to make the biggest killing of her career. We'd be talking private Caribbean islands here. Just one thing he had to do.'

'Which was?'

'Borrow seed-money from Bloom to bankroll the first experiment – to forge the first of what was going to be many copies of James Joyce's only unpublished novel. He needed highly expensive inks, very rare dyes. And he needed time – which money could buy him.'

'Jesus.'

'They were going to use her contacts in the States and Sri Lanka to release a copy on to the market every six months or so; keep going until the scam was discovered. And by then of course they'd be billionaires. Living it up some place far away.'

'So what happened?'

'Dunno. Something must have gone wrong with the formula.'

Gary sat quiet and still for a moment. An ache of grief for his father's sad demise came over him.

'The first copy was never delivered. To be honest I don't think it was ever even made. That's why – you know – what happened to your da happened.'

'And the original?'

She shrugged. 'You have three hundred pages. And I have three hundred pages. Which brings us neatly to the obvious question.'

'Which is?'

'Which is – you feel like doing some business, Gary?'

'I don't know. I need time to think.'

'Where are they?'

'Where's what?'

'Your three hundred pages.'

'Upstairs.'

'Upstairs? You mean where Micky is?'

'I know a spot. Further up in the mountains,' Sinead said to Grainne as she cranked her fifteen-year-old Toyota into gear.

Grainne just nodded.

'Don't worry, pet. Men are just . . . wankers.'

'Look . . . I think I'd like to be alone,' Grainne said.

'But I can't leave you by yourself. Not up here.'

'I want you to, honest. I need to think.'

A bus was coming down the lane towards them.

'You take the car,' said Sinead. 'I'll catch this.'

'Don't be silly.'

'*You* don't be stubborn. Now take the keys.'

Sinead jumped out of the car and ran for the bus.

* * *

The open bedroom window and the knotted sheets told their own story. The parrot had flown. Micky was gone. And so were Gary's carefully dried-out pages.

He hung his head and sobbed as he stood at the window. And then he heard a sound behind him.

He turned.

Dymphna was aiming her gun at his chest.

'Give me one good reason,' she said, 'why I shouldn't blow you away.'

'Em . . .' Gary hated these compulsory questions. He looked at the ceiling. He looked at the floor.

'One good reason . . .' he repeated, playing for time.

'Now I've told you my story you might go to the cops. I can't allow that to happen, Gary. So I'll give you five seconds to think of a reason. After that – I'm afraid it's goodnight.'

Gary gulped.

'Five.' She stepped closer. 'Four.' Closer still. 'Three.' The mouth of the gun moved to his neck. 'Two . . .'

And then it came to him. A sudden burst of revelation.

'Dymphna!' he roared.

'Cut the bullshit.'

'I have the formula!'

'What formula?'

'The paper-ageing formula!'

'Oh, yeah. Sure you do.'

'No, honest – I really do. Professor Durrus in Trinity told me it was skin cream! My sister Margaret found it in a milk bottle up at my da's shack. I'll bet my . . . I'll bet my . . .' The gun hovered. 'I'll bet my bollocks it's the paper-ageing formula – it's written on that jotter page.'

'What jotter page?'

'The one stuck to the kitchen wall downstairs.'

Cre-aakk!

Paschal Greer looked up from his desk. The distant part of the office was in darkness.

'Grainne . . .?' he said hopefully.

The word gusted gently down the room. It was difficult to see in the shadows, but the person who had entered seemed to raise an arm and point at him.

'Grainne? . . . Love? Is that you, pet?'

A hollow female laugh came back.

The hazy vision began to glide towards him through the jumble of filing cabinets, partitions and desks. Slowly it took on a shimmering green aura. His memory bank overflowed. His brain was awash with a torrent of dread. He stared at the approaching apparition. And now, as she came into the ghostly beam of his Anglepoise, he could see she was wearing . . . nothing – absolutely nothing except a sky-blue nylon Guiney's sheet that kept falling away from her and flowing around her, revealing and covering and revealing again the tremulous terrifying titanic torso he had last seen on that godawful night in Stoneybatter.

Swathed in the billowing Guiney's sheet she leaned down to kiss him, her dreadfully memorable breasts swinging before him. '*Don't look, Paschal*' echoed in his head from some far-off place. But, yet again, he found he couldn't obey. *Oh, Paschal. You rascal!*

Shuddering, flailing, he awoke at his desk. His heart was thundering, his face drenched with sweat.

He had the strangest feeling that his Grainne was in danger.

* * *

The wind threw a handful of dust and dead leaves in her face. She looked at Tommy Reynolds's old caravan, still swathed in crime-scene tape. Behind her, the moon shone down on the ruined cottage.

Grainne O'Kelly took a deep breath and made for the door.

Chapter Fourteen: by Gerard Stembridge

Gary Reynolds had decided to linger on in bed. It seemed like the safest course at this stage. Lying on in the morning was a great thing, everyone knew that. And doing nothing was definitely better than doing something which, as far as Gary was concerned, clearly only led to trouble.

Stretched on his back he recalled the smell of toilet blocks with a certain sense of peaceful happiness. Was it only three weeks ago that things had seemed so simple? Riding along in his van, 2FM in his ears, disinfectant in his nose. Where would he eat lunch? Hot food or sandwiches? Carvery or a lunch special with tea, bread and butter? That was all he'd had to worry about then. From the vantage point of his current state it seemed to Gary that such a life not only had its good points – in truth it had been almost blissful.

Was it all gone for ever, he wondered? Was the toilet-block business as fucked as his love life? He hadn't made any deliveries in so long now. Not since his father was murdered, really. His customers had been leaving threatening phone messages; most had announced they were taking their business elsewhere. Gary understood. They had no option. But somehow he couldn't get it together to call them back, offer explanations, resume business.

The truth was, he had become obsessed. Maybe he

had even gone a bit mad. Curling up tighter now under the duvet, deliciously warm, sensually snug, he told himself that none of this hassle was really his fault. Like his father getting murdered, say – what had that to do with him? That was the start. It could have been the end. If only Gary hadn't *done* something. If only he'd had the sense to let things lie.

A mid-morning second sleep was attempting to flow through him. If only he could relax . . . close his mind down . . . let nothing in, just pleasant sounds and smells . . . and the jessamine and geraniums and cactuses and Glasnevin as a boy yes and she kissed me under the cemetery wall yes and—

Eeuuugghhh! . . . fucking . . . *fucking rats!*

The memory shrieked him awake as it had done for a few nights now. That little rat running across his face – that was definitely the worst thing of all. Out of all the nasty things that had happened these last few weeks that little baby rat was definitely . . . Jesus. And it had been his own fault, he knew that. He could have just not bothered going to the dump. He could have given up. He could have done nothing. Doing something only meant that something else would turn out crap.

Gary was fully awake now, his head buzzing. What was it exactly that was making him *do* things? He had never in his life felt those urges before, but for the last couple of weeks it was do-do-do, do one bloody thing and then do another. And everything he had done had only made things worse, until now his life was one big mess. He was afraid to open a newspaper in the morning, petrified at the thought of what awful new event would be splashed in bold across the front page.

Okay, so he very rarely picked up a newspaper anyway. But that wasn't the point. He was still afraid. And yet at the same time here he was still doing things, still making everything worse, being really scared, having to *deal* with things all the time, even right up to last night – if it wasn't multiple murders it was rats or James Joyce or being left by an ungrateful pseudo-Rastafarian. Holy God. It was a bit of a spread.

Last night was something he *especially* didn't want to think about. But no matter how he arranged himself in the bed, no matter how he drew the duvet up around his ears, he couldn't find a way back to that lovely dozy state he had managed to drift into a few minutes before. It was gone for good now – replaced by last night.

He tried to be positive. There were *good* bits about last night. The boy-Garda and girl-Garda kissing – that was nice. The shouting that went on before the kissing was awful; but then, suddenly, they seemed to calm down. And she had just pulled him towards her and kissed him and held him. And he, the boy-Garda, had started crying.

Gary had never seen a Garda crying before. Of course he wasn't in uniform, so he didn't look like a Garda crying. If Gary hadn't overheard that his name was Inspector Greer, then it would have looked like any ordinary grown-up crying. But he did overhear. And it made a difference. The other Inspector's name was Grainne. She looked lovely at that moment, caressing him and soothing him.

There was a thing to ponder now. If Gary hadn't done something, after Dymphna had left (no doubt to report to Blixen and Bloom), if he hadn't decided late in the night that he'd had enough, that he was going to drive in to Garda headquarters right now and demand to see Inspector O'Kelly, and tell her (or someone) everything he knew and get it all off his chest – if he hadn't decided to *do* that thing, then he wouldn't have arrived at her office door, or heard the voices shouting inside, or stopped outside for a bit of a listen, or eased the door open just a tiny bit to see who was there. He would never have been witness to that tender moment between the two law-enforcement officers.

At first, mind you, there was little enough tenderness. O'Kelly and Greer were at it like angry cats.

'No right. You had no *right*.'

'And you, Grainne? What did you think you were doing?'

'My job, Sergeant Greer.'

'Inspector to you.'

'My job, *Inspector*. Though I'm better at my job than you'll ever be.'

'You're just jealous.'

'You're weak and insecure.'

'You're a wagon.'

'You're a coward.'

'Take that back, Grainne!'

'I won't.'

'You feckin will.'

'Not a chance.'

'If your friend Sinead hadn't raised the alarm—'

'I was fine.'

'Only because I arrived in time.'

'Yes. In time to get in my way.'

'I came as fast as I could, Grainne—'

'I was on to something and you screwed it up.'

'Broke speed limits, red lights and all . . .'

Gary had already decided it was time to go, forget the whole confession thing, leave them at it. But then:

'I discovered something *important* in that caravan. A major clue.'

'What was it, then? If you're so smart.'

'The grease in the roasting dish. I had a lick of it.'

'And what were you doing licking filthy old grease?'

'I had the munchies – will you listen to me? It's not normal grease. It has a chemical kind of taste.'

'So what?'

'It's a clue, isn't it? We must get it and test it first thing tomorrow. Find out what it is.'

'You're talking rubbish, Grainne.'

'I'd know already if you hadn't made me drop it in the dark, you imbecile. And dragged me out of the place.'

'I rescued you from doing permanent damage to yourself, choking on your own vomit or something—'

'You interrupted me in the course of my duties.'

'And you know why I did it?'

'You disrupted a crime scene, you moron. You mullah!'

'I did it *because I love you, Grainne.*'

Gary in his bed, sweating a little now as his body and the duvet swapped warmth generously, felt the tiniest erection as he thought back to the scene that ensued. And he wondered why he couldn't have left it at that. He should have just gone quietly home and let the romance of the memory sustain him. Why couldn't he do even that simple thing?

In fact, he nearly did. He so nearly did. He didn't interrupt Inspectors O'Kelly and Greer. He did slip out of Garda headquarters. And he did manage to get into his van. It was already pointing in the right direction for home. He oh-so-very nearly went home. The key was in the ignition waiting to be turned. But then he found himself thinking:

What was that grease doing there in the first place? His father had always been strictly vegetarian.

Gary had panicked as he'd slowly realised what was happening to him. He was having what he dreaded most – inspired thoughts. He fought them back bravely. He tried to escape them.

Lying in bed now, he panicked again, his cautious erection wilting and dying as he remembered the unconvincing answers he had managed to come up with: his father must have rejected vegetarianism in the last few years; he had recently entertained some meat-eating friends and, being a polite host, had cooked them a chicken; the grease had been left by a previous tenant and his father had never bothered to clean the oven – no, no, NO!

The truth was that Gary knew exactly what the grease was for.

Now he sat up in bed and looked around; a selection of different kinds of paper was scattered over the red crested carpet. Hotel letterhead. A page torn from yesterday's *Evening Herald*. Brochures for medieval banquets at Bunratty Castle. Late last night the papers had looked clean and new. Now they were faded, wrinkled, discoloured – they appeared and felt as though they were a hundred years old.

Gary Reynolds had made that happen. He didn't know exactly how just yet – but he knew that what had happened was all down to him.

Again he let his mind drift back to the previous night. As though watching a film he saw himself clamber into his van and turn it in the direction of the Wicklow mountains.

The clock on the dashboard flashing 2 a.m. The brightly lit Stillorgan dual carriageway almost deserted. Passing through Foxrock in a mood of grim determination. A squad car overtaking him in the fast lane just as he came to the Silver Tassie pub – he'd watched it speed ahead towards the Shankill roundabout. Even the squad car didn't scare him; it only served as ample reminder of how little time he had before O'Kelly and Greer remembered their professional duties and started out for his father's caravan. Pushing the speed limit on the final stretch of motorway. Turning off near Avoca Handweavers. The wild exhilaration. The mad buzz.

Then the winding roads growing smaller and darker. Dublin began to seem so far away. That awful sense of being alone. Not the cheerful solitude of truckin' along motorways in broad reassuring daylight, sucking down the fumes of scented disinfectant and warbling along to the hits of the day; not the relaxing and faintly tumescent solipsism of a stolen morning in bed; but that solitary state where you are never alone – where jostling fears crowd your brain, offering for your terrified consideration unhappy accidents, tragic collisions, lethal attacks, the ghoul in the darkness.

Gary didn't want to go there. Even though he was now within a mile of his father's caravan, suddenly he just didn't want to go there.

He stopped the van. Breathing quickly. Fearfully listening to the sounds of the night. God oh God, if only Micky was here. He stepped out on to the cold black road, lit up a cigarette, looked around. Nothing was moving. All seemed still. His troubled heart began to calm. But then he happened to glance quickly over his shoulder. And what he saw made the blood freeze in his veins.

It was one of those things. He hadn't seen the headlights and then the very moment he spotted them they were turned out. There had been no sound of a car.

Maybe Gary had imagined it. He knew it was really easy to do that when you were on edge. If he had been with other people they might have persuaded him that he was seeing things, that it was just nerves, and he would have agreed. But Gary was all alone and he knew he had seen something, the way you always know when you are alone and you see something. The bit inside him that knew things knew this for sure.

Quietly he clambered back into the van. Closed his door. Tried to think.

As though possessed of a will of its own, his hand reached out and turned the ignition key. Before he had any real idea of what he was doing, he was roaring and bouncing along the dark road again, his heart thundering against his ribcage. He seemed to be going to the caravan after all. Sweating with terror, he glanced in his mirror. He could see no headlights behind. But he knew with horrified certainty that he was still being followed. There was nothing in the world he was more sure about.

A plan, a plan. He had to make a plan. 'Who am I fucking fooling? I can't make a plan. I'll go in, grab the dish of grease from the oven, run out and drive away again as fast as I can. Is that a plan?' He didn't have time to answer his own question because suddenly he could see the black shadow of the caravan looming up at him out of the darkness. He skidded to a stop, brakes squealing, ran for the caravan, pulled open the oven door.

There was no dish of grease inside.

Of course not. Typical. How could there be? How could even the smallest thing *ever* work out for Gary Reynolds? Naturally there was no grease. Why did he ever think there *would* be? The fates had written in his Book of Life that if he ever opened an oven door to look for a dish of grease there would *be* no grease, because Gary Reynolds was a fat unlovable fuck, doomed to remain forever thus, unable to understand or control anything in his life and that was . . . that was . . . *the dish of grease on the floor*! Dancing around in frustration he had managed to step in it. Of course! Where Inspector O'Kelly had dropped it!

He grabbed it, cantered back to the van and roared away. Maybe everything was going to plan after all. He threw back his head and gave a hearty laugh.

He had been going for less than a minute when he rounded a bend and saw two parked cars.

The first was a big old tank of a sixties saloon with three shadowy figures seated inside. Two of the occupants were of indeterminate sex, the third, in the back, was definitely female. Dymphna, Blixen and Bloom perhaps? He didn't intend stopping to find out – mainly because Inspector Paschal Greer was standing at the window and questioning the driver while Inspector Grainne O'Kelly stood close by, alert by the door of the unmarked Garda Opel Kadett.

All five heads turned to look at him as he flashed

past, ducking and revving and lurching onward. His time had run out, he knew that now. He would have to make a dash for it.

Anywhere but Dublin, he managed to think. There they can track me down like a dog. Head for the open spaces, Gary. Don't do anything predictable now.

For the next few hours he rode around the Wicklow hills, finding the odd main road and losing it again, once veering by accident on to a floodlit bypass then swerving back off as quickly as possible into the darker and shadowy byways. He roared through one-street towns, hardly noticing their names. Only occasionally did he recognise a pub or little café to which his toilet-block business had led him in happier times. The Nighttown Arms. Penelope's Plaice. The Hades Hotel. Sirens Nightclub. But everywhere was closed and shuttered up – no refuge or hideyhole could he find from his pursuers.

Yes, he was sure they were back there somewhere. They were too clever to let themselves be seen – both the cops and the others, whoever they were. They had their pursuit technique down to a T. Stealth and sneakiness. Silence and cunning. Exiled from Dublin and lost in the night, Gary knew that none of these dismal desperado towns with their wide thoroughfares and closed-down carparks could offer him shelter, even if they were so inclined, which from past experience might not be the case. He was a man alone. But fuck 'em! Who needed them?

He drove on.

It began to rain but he didn't let that slow him down. Forward he sat, close to the wheel, watchful, attentive, staring through the wipers. The rain cleared.

The moon came out. The empty roads glistened in the beam of his headlights. Still he drove, weak with tiredness, unable to tell if he was in Carlow or Tipperary or Kilkenny or Laois – or any of those counties for that matter. All he knew was that he was still free. Still free but not safe. In the game, O yes, but not holding many cards.

Finally city lights appeared in the distance. A shout of joy burst from his breast. There would be back-streets and alleyways in which he might hide. He drove on, hope flowering in his heart. You could always lose yourself in a strange city, he thought. So Gary Reynolds decided to get lost.

As things turned out, getting lost wasn't hard for him. He squinted and craned for clues as he zigzagged through the empty streets. Turn left – William Street. Left again – High Street. Another right brought him down a small grimy lane which had no name that Gary could see. Right again. Gerald Griffin Street. Jesus, thought Gary, why the full-name treatment for him? I mean you never hear Daniel O'Connell Street, do you?

He passed through the junction at Gerald Griffin's far end, U-turned, took another right and sped on to Wicklow Street. Then left down the street named for someone called Thomas. He was sure he must have lost his pursuers by now – he himself was dizzy with the twist-and-turn of it all – but still he didn't know where he might end up. A left turn led him to Little Catherine Street. Was it Catherine who was little or was it the street? Surely, he thought, there had to be somewhere – anywhere to rest his head for a while. Right on Cecil Street. Nothing there. Finally, on the next corner, he saw a little sign that might have been manufactured in heaven itself. It informed him that he could stay at the Royal George Hotel for only £35, breakfast included, and, best of all, with off-street parking.

'We're closed, residents only,' snapped the night porter through the glass door. Gary was clutching a quantity of paper items and a Spar bag containing a tin of old grease, but somehow he managed to wave some money. 'I want a room,' he pleaded.

Cautiously the porter opened the door.

'You want a room? What are you doing looking for a room at this hour?'

'I've been driving for hours. I'm too tired to go on. I need some sleep.'

'All right so, but the bar's still closed. Resident or no resident. You understand me?'

'Not to worry. I'm only fit for sleep anyway.'

'I always lock up at four. If you'da been here twenty minutes ago now I'd have been able to fix you up with a little something all right, but at this stage you know, in fairness . . .'

'It's fine, I don't need a drink.'

'Right so. Once that's understood.'

'It is.'

'It's just you know, sometimes fellas do be so mad for more that they'll check into a hotel just so they can avail of the residents' drinking privileges, you see what I'm saying?'

'Of course I do. But . . .'

'So I thought maybe, you know, with you turning up at half-past four, that was your wheeze, your little number, you know – that you were after falling out of Ithaca, or Club Circe with no woman but a tongue on you for more pints like some of the other scum, oh please, Mr MacDhuireas, let us in. All that crack.'

'Honest to God, I just need a bed.'

'Oh I can see that all right. I'm not saying you don't. I'm not saying anything at all of that kind. It's just I see all sorts turning up at the door here.'

'I can imagine.'

'Well, I suppose I could let you have a pint. But no more, mind. And not a word to anyone, all right?'

'I really don't want a pint, thank you.'

'A whiskey then maybe. Or a little gin and tonic.'

'Honestly I just need my bed.'

'A cocktail so. That's my last offer.'

In this manner of minutes, seeming hours ticked by. But Gary did make use of some of the check-in ordeal to pick up some tourist brochures from a rack on the counter, for, despite the hour, the tension and the pain of the drive, despite even the endless drone of the porter's drinking soliloquy, somehow – incredibly – Gary's brain was now forming a plan.

'Grease is the word,' he had softly snickered, as he knelt on the floor of the hotel room at 5.30 a.m. 'It's got groove, it's got feeling,' he'd lightly lilted, dunking a glossy brochure for Bunratty Castle into the gluey viscous liquid that he felt must surely be his father's sacred elixir. The grease seeped into the paper. He let it soak for what seemed like an adequate time before gently lifting it out, shaking off the excess syrupy gloop and holding it delicately up to the light.

He brought the sodden brochure across the room to the sink. Nothing magical seemed to be happening. Maybe he'd let it soak for too long? Perhaps not nearly long enough? He waited and watched. Its appearance didn't change. Sighing, he reached into his jacket and pulled out the old school photograph he had found in the van just moments before scurrying into the hotel.

He dunked the photo in the gluey bath but this time only for the briefest instant before whipping it out and placing it on the washstand. Again, nothing happened, the photo remained unchanged except for its coating of pungent slime. He cursed aloud and began panicking again, dipping more and more papers, faster and faster. Now in a frenzy of wild experimentation he started to try out different possibilities and approaches, every combination of grease and paper his exhausted mind could come up with.

He tried lightly dipping just one side of a Lotus-Eaters Chinese Take-Away menu, leaving the other side completely dry. Dipping, removing, dipping again, dunking, drying, merely moistening, splashing, flicking, carefully coating, applying the grease with a toothbrush from the bathroom, scraping it back off with a spoon from the tea-tray. Surely to God it would only be reasonable to expect just *one* of the methods to work. But after an hour of soaking and swirling nothing at all had really changed, expect that an ugly black pool had formed on the carpet beneath the sink.

Through the window he saw that the dawn was rising now. Only by a massive effort of will had he managed to keep going all night long. And for what, in the end? It had all come to nothing. He gaped about the messy room, at the soggy oily mushes of paper that had once been brochures, snaps and stationery. Gary Reynolds could have cried.

Despair broke over him, a black wave. To have come so close and then meet defeat. The solution was here – right here in this room; not to be able to see it was just too much to take. All his new-found energy, his drive, his *commitment* were bubbling away down the plughole with the useless dirty grease.

He would burn the evidence. Destroy the whole lot. Forget the dream of ever taking control – just go back to being a sad little loser. Micky had been right to leave him after all. Everyone in his life had always left him.

Bitterly he grabbed his soaked class photo and brought it over to the wastepaper bin. He flicked on his lighter, applied the flame, ready to drop it just as soon as it caught. But strange – it didn't seem keen to burn. He moved the lighter a little closer. Now the flame was licking the very centre of the photograph, but still the paper remained unaffected.

No. Not quite unaffected. It curled a little at one edge, but elegantly, and rather beautifully. The flame gave off a strange purple glow. A whisper-soft hiss could be heard from the paper. Gary Reynolds's eyes widened. Was he imagining this? Surely he was. He stared again. Blinked twice. Shook his head.

A slow but definite transformation seemed to be unfolding. It was like watching a Donabate sunset or a cake rising in the oven – you knew it was happening but from moment to moment it was hard to actually observe the change. Still he told himself his eyes were playing tricks. Too much tiredness, too much stress. And yet – *and yet* – as the minutes ticked past and he tried to keep his hands from shaking, the picture took on an antique sepia-tinted tone, the paper began to shrivel and corrugate, tiny hints of crinkles breaking out on its surface, until the photograph of the class of 1981 came to look like something you'd find in a Victorian attic.

Heat.

Jesus!

That was all it needed.

'*Daaad!*' Gary Reynolds howled. '*You did it, Dad . . . I love you, Tommy.*'

The application of heat to the grease; to the compound, the solution – whatever you wanted to call it – that was the key to unlocking the magic! Well he knew he hadn't got it all perfectly right. There was probably loads of stuff about temperatures and conditions, relative distances, different kinds of paper – he knew nothing about that but right now he didn't care. The details could wait for another day.

The family photo he had found, dated 1948. Surely this must be the explanation for the strange date! Tommy must have used his mystical potion to age it. Gary could see it all now. If you analysed the paper on which that photo was printed, it *would* be from 1948.

He had broken through. He had cracked the code. Now he knew how his father did it. And now he, Gary Reynolds, had awesome power. Fake first editions? That was small fry. Profitable, yes, but a glorified party trick compared to the mind-boggling potential this stuff truly had. Oh, if they wanted fakes they could have them. He'd give 'em priceless fakes till they begged him to stop. But with something like this he could literally rewrite history. He wondered if there might be a living in that.

Wildly enthusiastic, he tested his discovery; applied the humble flame of his lighter to all the other bits of sodden paper. As the alchemy worked again and again, Gary began hearing triumphant music in his head but gradually the martial trumpeting faded and was replaced by an annoying but rather persistent problem.

The manuscript.

How was he going to get hold of it?

Okay, so he'd cracked the secret of the paper-ageing process – but others now had the priceless text.

Bugger.

There's always bloody something.

He knew right then that he hadn't a clue how to get it back. He still hadn't a clue as he finally succumbed to sleep. As he pulled the duvet over himself and closed his weary eyes, his final thought was that when he woke up tomorrow morning – at least, later the same morning – he still wouldn't have a clue.

And now it was later the same morning. Actually, to be precise, it was early afternoon. And Gary had been right – he *didn't* have a clue. But he had something else. He had a secret.

Good. Yes. A valuable secret. That's a very nice thing to have. Something to have in my father's memory. Cool. Yes. Something that people will happily kill for. Or torture me for. Or track me down to the ends of the earth for. Hunting me. Jesus! Horrible! How did *that* happen? *What will I do?*

He thought he should probably get out of bed.

This he did, and quickly dressed, trying to settle himself with the comforting thought that at least he had managed to shake off his pursuers, had fled to a city where no one would think of looking for him, a city where it was easy to be anonymous. He opened the curtains to a sunny Limerick day.

What's there to do in Limerick? he wondered, as he gazed down on O'Connell Street so busy and bustling – so busy, in fact, that he didn't pick out the watchful little eyes in the coffee shop across the way.

But they saw Gary. O yes.

Chapter Fifteen: Frank McCourt

'In confidence, Doonan,' said Dr Jim Joyce.

'Of course,' said Professor Doonan Durrus discreetly.

'Strictest confidence, Doonan?'

'On my mother's head.'

'I know that what I am about to do is as serious as breaking the seal of the confessional – but someone else has to know and you're the man.'

'My lips are sealed, Jim. Fire away.'

'These are desperate times in Dublin. The Celtic Tiger prowls the streets of Dodge City – if you catch my drift.'

'Lord, indeed I do. Murder, violence, fornication. I've never seen the likes of it.'

'But what I'm going to tell you, Doonan, will shock you. Will we have another drink?'

'We will, Jim.'

Professor Durrus found a space between two Germans at the Horseshoe Bar and brought the large whiskies back to the table in the corner. His old friend looked troubled and weary. A memory came back of their college days. Jim had been the most promising poet in the student writing group but had surprised them all by opting for psychiatry in the end. That was a pity, Doonan Durrus sometimes thought; it hadn't brought him very much happiness. His old friend lowered his eyes now and spoke in a whisper.

'These murders,' said Dr Joyce, 'they're all connected: Reynolds, Roberts, Nestor, Andrews – and the suicide of young Jason Dunphy. Not to mention the, er, passing of the late Mrs Kinch. There is skulduggery in high places and a depravity you'd find only in the old night-town of *Ulysses*.'

'Tsk, task,' said Professor Durrus.

'I will tell you all this so that we can save Dublin. There is, for instance, the case of Patsy Roberts – now my patient – and the late Andrew Andrews. You've heard of the man I mean?'

'You mean he that was shot by some . . . pseudo-Rastafarian, Micky McManus?'

'That's just what I'm getting at, Doonan. It wasn't Micky McManus at all. That's what Mrs Roberts said to the police, I know; but that, I am afraid, was not the truth.'

'So who . . .?'

'It was Eamon Dunphy.'

'Good Lord!'

'No, not that one – another by that name, avenging the suicide of his son, Jason. The poor lad whom Andrews drove to his death.'

'Mother o'God.'

They had a few more whiskies and Dr Jim Joyce, breaking the code of the shrink, told the professor of the life of Patsy Roberts, of her years with corrupt Joseph now pushing up daisies, of her hatred of her mother, Mrs Pauline Bloom, of her sordid affair with Superintendent Andrew Andrews.

'Jesus,' said the professor.

But the talk of whips and clamps was not what had startled him. Rather it was the mention his good friend made of the rumours of a lost James Joyce manuscript, six hundred pages given by the master to a goodly washerwoman who had taken care of him, and he in his dotage.

'And where . . . would that manuscript be now, Jim? Do you know?'

'It would be valuable, wouldn't it, Doonan?'

''Twould, indeed. Priceless.'

'Hmm. This is . . . something we might want to talk about, isn't it, Doonan?'

'Crucial, Jim, crucial.'

'I have information, Doonan, and more coming from Patsy. You'll have guessed by now that she is my source on the subject.'

'It's funny your mentioning it,' Professor Durrus said. 'I had a visit a while back from someone who claimed she had it.'

Dr Joyce looked startled. 'The manuscript?'

'Mm. Half of it anyway.'

'Good Lord. You did?'

'Oh yes, Jim. I most certainly did. I've been thinking about the whole matter. Long and hard.'

'I . . . have to confess that I have too.'

'You know, if a person got his hands on something like that, Jim – he might never have to work again.'

'Yes. I know.'

'Makes you think, doesn't it?'

'I wonder if she'll ever come back. Your visitor.'

'Oh I'd bet on it.'

'Why so sure?'

Professor Durrus peered into his glass and chuckled softly. 'A great thing about the study of literature,' he said. 'It gives you an insight into psychiatry.'

* * *

'Professor Durrus?'

'Ah. My dear. Hello.'

'Are you busy?'

'You were here before in the matter of a manuscript. You had three hundred pages of James Joyce's last work, didn't you?'

'Yes, I did. I do still.'

'Three hundred valuable pages, numbered 300 to 600; which would be absolutely priceless if you could find the first three hundred, eh?'

'Well, yes.'

'Come in, my dear. No, leave the door open. There might be talk.'

'Talk? What kind of talk?'

'Trinity Professor Behind Closed Doors With Gorgeous Woman. You know the kind of tittle-tattle that goes on in this town.'

'I'm not that kind of girl, Professor.'

'Ah yes. The little innocent. The holy nun.'

'I'm not sure I understand what you mean.'

'Surely you don't think – Dymphna, isn't it? – surely you don't think that after the headlines, one murder after another, the rumours that swirled, the visits to my office of your delectable disguised self and that tub of lard, Gary Reynolds, that I couldn't guess what was going on under my nose and the nose of every breathing creature in Dublin? I *am* a professor, after all.'

'I . . .'

'Americans sidle up to me in the courtyards below. Oh, Durrus, what's this we hear about a lost Joyce manuscript? And if the Yanks know about it and you,

Bloom, Blixen and Gary Reynolds know about it – then the whole bloody world knows about it or so it would seem.'

'But . . . Bloom and Blixen . . . how do you . . .?'

'My dear, if you want to know something in Dublin you don't have to hire a private detective. There's always a little snake like Eddie Lambert or a man beside you in a bar who will spill his guts for a small whiskey. You tell anyone something in confidence in this town and you might as well be yelping out the window. That's why there's no real underworld in Dublin – no *omertà* if you will. Everyone blathers. Everyone in Dublin is writing a fucking memoir. Thank God Limerick has been mercifully spared.'

'You're from Limerick?'

'From Limerick, yes, and resented by the jackeen academic gang up here – UCD and Trinity, one as bad as the other. But who better to get the overall view, the *gestalt* if you will, than a Limerickman?'

'Well I wasn't saying . . .'

'Don't get me going – just *don't* get me going about the sniping we've had to tolerate down the years. Say you're from Limerick and faces are made. Am I sensitive? You bet your lovely arse I'm sensitive. But things are changing, my darling Dymph. I'm in the driver's seat, on the pig's back. The world is mine now, I have it in the palm of my hand, by the short hairs, by the little ginger pubes. If you will.'

'Ginger pubes?'

'Micky McManus? The phoney Rastafarian? Come come, don't pretend you don't know him. Oh, he and I fell into chat one happy day recently as he plied his pitiful busk on Grafton Street, now in mufti. Badly drunk he was and stoned. When he heard I was a Joyceman he had some interesting beans to spill. Especially when I promised him a one-way ticket to Jamaica and a bong for his troubles.'

'You know that loser?'

'From my vantage point at Trinity – objective, disinterested – I know everyone in dear dirty Dublin, my dear.'

'And when I came here before, you already knew about the book?'

'From the academics, the literati, there are interesting rumours. From the media a pattern of headlines and stories. If you have half a mind you know something is up. You sit back and watch. You sally forth and listen in the pubs. You make enquiries, discreet and otherwise. And why?'

'Why?'

'Because there's a manuscript out there, a billion-dollar set of scrawls. Six hundred pages of Joyce's sideways passage into lunacy. They could be blank, for all I know. But even if they were they would still be priceless. All he had to do was raise his hand over them, blow his nose in them, wipe the sweat from his brow or the leavings from his arse. *Anything*. All things Joycean are sacred now. The American universities are panting for the bits and pieces, the left-over scraps of Irish life. And you're here for something aren't you?'

'Oh, Professor . . .'

'Call me Doonan. That's what my friends do.'

'There was something you were going to tell me about Micky.'

'Ah, yes. The little caper between you and Gary the Tub. He told me all about it.'

'Oh, Doonan, I have so much to tell, so much to offer, and I know you can help me.'

'Do sit here, Dymphna.'

'On your lap, Doonan?'

'You won't find anything more comfortable because, Dymphna, I do desire you.'

'Do you, Doonan?'

'I do, Dymphna.'

'Well, do it, Doonan.'

'No, dear Dymph, remove no clothing. I want our relationship to begin on a pure and musical note. Stand on this chair. Keep your clothes on. Don't be afraid. Turn your back to me so that I can hold your hips. Yes yes o yes. Bend over if you would. I am now placing my nose between your glorious buttocks and humming.'

'Hmmmmmmmmmmmmmmmmmm.'

'Do you like that, Dymphna?'

'Oh, Doonan, do it again. I am trembling like a tuning fork.'

'In my hands, my darling, and with my nose in your sweet cleft, you are a tuning fork. Humumumumumu mumumumumum . . .'

'Oh, Doonan, I'll die, I'll die, oh, oh, yes, indeed, yes.'

'Verily, Dymphna, humumumumumumumumumu mumu . . .'

'Doonan, Doonan, kiss me, disrobe me, do me.'

'Not now, my darling. Not with the door open. People passing will think I'm reciting from *Finnegans Wake*.'

'Oh. Oh. My dearest Doonan.'

'They don't know that wommmen around the world from Bethlehemmm to Mmmadagascar clammour for my hummm. They plead with their mmmen to hummm them but it mmmanifestly fails. Only I, the hummmer, have the secret mmmagic and mmmusic, the proper mmmajestic pitch of the orgasmic hummmm, the level, the volummme, the key, flat or sharp, that requires adjustmmment according to climmmate, geography, the last mmmeal consummmed and the religion of the hummmee. Besides, I think we should consummmate our mmmarvellous relationship in Limmmerick, city of my dreammms, hommme of my forefathers and fore-mmmmothers, city of the Broken Treaty, formmmerly the holiest city in Ireland and the British Isles but now gone to hell commmpletely with the dint of the coveting and various feeble attemmmpts at the hummmm. But winds of change are blowin' and Limmmerick will be Home of the Hummmmmum-umumumumm.'

'Ah! Doonan, don't stop please.'

'Enough, my love. Enough for now. Descend from the chair and let us proceed quickly Shannonwise from where my uncle, jolly night porter at the Royal George Hotel, informs me that our tub of lard is ensconced on the premises, making a mess for the maid with the paper he's trying to burn in his room. You are wondering why I'm so hostile to Gary Reynolds, plump loinfruit of the late Tommy? The fat one came here and, when I mentioned you, the nun, he showed his greed. And I made him pay dearly, with my little plan. He will pay again unless my mood mellows between here and Limerick. But before we take another step, Dymphna my dearest, tell me one thing: are we in this together? With Joyce manuscripts, magic chemicals and restorative creams there are millions to be made. There are stray pages to be regained of course: Eamon Dunphy has one; Fat Gary has the other. There has to be trust between you and me. There has to be love.'

'Oh, Doonan, after that hum I'm yours for ever.'

'Let us seal it with a kiss. *Dúṇ an doras* there, darling, lest there be gossip among the hoi polloi.'

Micky?

What animal instinct prompted him to make his way to the old bedsit, the scene of the crime, so to speak, where Sergeant Joe Roberts took away his ghettoblaster to make up for unpaid rent, depriving misfortunate Mixer of his only comfort, propelling him into a life of crime when all he wanted was the simplicity of the Rastafarian way, the reggae raggamuffining, the odd spiffing spliff? Why, he wondered, as he dodged through the streets with 299 pages of James Joyce under his oxter, why can't people just leave people alone?

Micky had little notion of the value or character of the smeared, stinking pages he carried. He knew only that people like Gary and bogus Sister Dymphna would go to great lengths to get their hands on the package. He knew also that his loyalties lay with Gary for with Gary he had lain and never was there such a lay. Thinking of the great fat pink body enfolding his own triggered a hum primordial. Like a dog he sniffed at the memory of Garyscent: ratsting; dumpmusk; lemon-whiff of pubjacks; traces of Madelene herself, bitchwife, who had darkened the life of the fairfat Gazzamon. Now – *now at last* – Micky knew.

He knew the love that lay too deep for language, that love that passeth understanding, the love, God help us, that dare not speak its etcetera. And Micky, liberated from stick of master and sermon of priest, knew that what he hefted under his arm was for him and for Gary the key to the future. From the dim memory of drink and drugs he recalled a whispered conversation with a man from Trinity, a man promising hot sizzly heaven beyond in Jamaica if Micky could but deliver what he now transported in the malodorous envelope. But the Knowledge from the College, what was his name? Oh, yes, Doonan Durrus. Said buttie would have to dig deeper into the professorial pocket. *Two* fares to Kingston would Micky be requiring and guaranteed lifelong in-the-bank incomes for himself and his Gary. O there they'd be lolling in the surf, the whiteness of them, dipping in the caress of the cool Caribbean and relaxing on the boiling sands of beach with the bong, the beer and the hourly bonk.

And how was Micky to know, avoiding the front door and climbing up the back wall of the bedsit house, that Eamon Dunphy – no, not that one – now occupied his old room and lay there on the bed weeping over his poor hanged boy but thinking at the same time of Patsy Roberts and how gorgeous and sexy she looked when she shot Andrew Andrews in the head?

How was Micky supposed to know all this? They don't print signs on walls for ersatz Rastafarians about to climb through their old bedroom windows advising: Please Keep Out, Killer Sleeping. Not that Eamon was really a killer in the technical sense: he didn't pull the trigger. Patsy Roberts, now brooding all agloom in the loony bin, did.

Micky hardly had his head in the window when he felt the muzzle of a gun in his ear. He wanted to say: sorry, wrong window, wrong house, but he was being pulled in by what remained of his hair and told to shut the fuck up or his brains would be in the garden with the aspidistra. Under other circumstances he might have asked what an aspidistra was but the gun was being jammed into his ear in a most hostile way. How was he to know this was the toy gun of the late Jason? How, indeed, was Micky supposed to know anything?

'Don't look at me, you little fag, or I'll blow your face away.'

'Oh. Sorry. Just visiting, mon.'

'Don't "mon" me, you ginger-tufted reprobate. What are you, a fucking Romanian or something?'

'No no, mon. I mean, *man* – sorry. Irish. Dublin. Bred and buttered, ha ha.'

'What's that under your arm?'

'Oh, paper. You know. Just paper . . . for wiping.'

'Let me see.'

Eamon Dunphy pulled out a few sheets and studied them. 'Shit,' he said. 'This is the same scrawl and scribble I have on *my* sheet. Where did you get this, you prickle-headed gouger?'

'Oh, I ah, I ah . . . just came back from the dump. Like to collect old paper. Never enough paper in the lavatories of Dublin. Carry me own, mon.'

'I *told* you, don't mon me. You a pansy?'

'Wha'?'

'A fairy. A faggot.'

'No, no. I'm no batty-boy. Love me mother. Great devotion to Our Lady of Knock.'

'That doesn't mean you're not a faggot. Half the people climbing holy mountains are faggots looking for forgiveness and redemption.'

'I . . . I didn't know that.'

'Now you do, you stubble-scalped gurrier. You can never tell what you'll learn when you climb through a window.'

Micky had gleaned from the movies that keeping on talking was often an effective means of defusing dangerous situations. You got the chap with the gun to think of something else – maybe lose his concentration – so you could jump him, administer a vigorous battering and flee into the night. But such an approach was all very well in the movies. Faced with an armed and non-fictional psychotic, another tack would have to be tried.

He wondered if he should try to get the chap's pity. Present himself as just another underdog wounded by society. Then try and give him a kicking as soon as he turned his back.

'This useta be *my* room, yeh know? Useta be happy here with me music and that. Kicked out because I couldn't pay the rent. That bleedin' Roberts took me ghettoblaster. Desperate, I was. Tried to get it back. Broke into his gaff. Shite move. His missus was there. Mott called Patsy.'

The nutter turned and glared at him. '*What?*'

'. . . What what?'

'You said Patsy?'

'Well . . . Yeah.'

'Patsy? Last name?'

'Well, yknow.' Micky shrugged. 'Roberts, like.'

'Shit, shit, shit. That's how I *found* this fucking place.'

Micky gulped. 'Yer . . . not makin' sense, pal.'

'The address was scrawled on the back of the page she gave me. She said I'd make a fortune with this . . . formula she had for a new drug. And like a sap I believed her. She thought I was going to kill her. And what was the formula? You want to know?'

'Well . . . not really.'

'It wasn't a formula at all. It was a home-made map of the bloody Zurich underground! With the names of the stations written in pig Latin. That's what this Dutch chemist told me and he sitting there in front of me all blushing and embarrassed. Because that's one thing about the Dutch – they know their pig Latin. And in among all the bloody pig Latin, dirty, filthy rantings to some woman called Nora. Vile repulsive stuff you wouldn't show to a hoor! That wagon Roberts told me it was a formula that would make me rich. And when the Dutch fella tried to mix it all up, do you know what it came out as?'

'No.'

'Water, that's what! Muck-flavoured water!'

A few nights after the visit to Tommy Reynolds's caravan Paschal noticed something different about his beloved. 'Do you know what 'tis?' he said softly. 'There's a glow to you, pet. I never seen the likes of it before. You were always gorgeous but now you're gorgeouser than ever. Look at yourself in the mirror there.'

He'd never grow weary of her naked body, the hair cropped to her neck in proper cop fashion, the long white slimness of her glorious back, the buttocks, sweet suffering Jesus, each one an occasion of mortal sin, not that he gave a curse about sin or even its opposite, the state of grace, not when he was gazing on the sweetness of the line that separated one side of her arse from the other, a line that travelled down and under to a heavenly place where only he, by Christ, would ever venture for if he ever found another interfering with that sacred territory he'd tear their head off and shove it down their neck because what he was gazing on now was his for ever, the loveliest arse north or south of the border or even among the farflung diaspora with the little purple birthmark in the shape of the shamrock and the legs which were made to wrap around his own hips and thighs or to sling over his shoulders when the humour was on the two of them.

'God,' she said suddenly. 'I had a freckle here and a little spot there and they're gone now, love. I wonder was it that basin of grease I fell into at that shack. My skin looks like a baby's lately.'

She turned to him and the glory of her frontally left him silently speechless. 'Whatever was in that grease must have done me some good.' She laughed gently. 'Maybe it's some kind of an anti-ageing thing. That's what Mr Reynolds used to work at, you know. Back when he had a proper job.'

'I love your nipples,' he said. 'The way they stand up in the chill.'

'Never mind my nipples. I have an idea.'

'So do I.'

'Not that. Hurry up, petal, and put on your clothes and we'll take a spin back to his old caravan. See if there's more of his potion lying about. For the crack, eh?'

'The way they bulge a little under your blouse sometimes. It's lovely.'

She smiled. 'Get up this minute or I'm leaving you here.'

He got up but it was hard for him to put on his trousers with the tremendous hardness that was upon him. He asked her if she could help him in this matter and she threw a jug of cold water over his stiffness so that he slid into his clothes no bother.

'That wasn't fair,' he said, but he knew it was pointless, realising now in his own culchie way that nothing in the world can compete with a woman's vanity, not sex, fame, power, money, nor even the promise of paradise itself. If a woman can find a way of removing a spot from her face she'll gnaw her own leg off, never mind sacrifice husband, children and family. He followed her to the car and sat in anxiety while she drove like a fiend through the streets of Dublin.

But when they reached the caravan and found all the grease gone, the language out of her mouth so shocked peaceful Paschal that he wondered if this was the same Grainne who had fondled him and murmured to him of rose-covered cottages and babies and legs of lamb with peas and mashed potatoes that would be waiting for him when he came home from his job as Detective Superintendent, which of course was inevitable when you saw how rapidly he had risen in the ranks. Was this the same Grainne, standing there spewing out four-letter words in fantastical profusion, enhancing these with frequent muthafuckas, who would suckle their babies and coo and cuddle?

Ah well. If you were a police officer you were bound to absorb the juicy language of the streets and if she wanted to go on like that now and then, where was the harm in words after all, and couldn't he simply humour her for a time while rejoicing in the nice nipple bulges in her blouse?

She prowled the caravan, whimpering out of her: 'There must be some left. There must be some left.'

Then slipping and sliding she let out a little scream. 'This is it! There's a big splodge of it here on the floor. Oh, God.' And next thing he knew she was down on the knees and rubbing some of it on to her face. 'Here,' she said. 'I'll prove it to you.' Off with her skirt and her panties after it. She turned her back and peeped over her shoulder. 'Here,' she said. 'Rub some on my shamrock and you'll see it disappear. Go on.'

'Ah, no,' he pleaded. 'I love your shamrock.'

'Damn it. Do it.'

'But you were given that shamrock for a reason, Grainne.'

'Fuck the reason and spare me your mulchie philosophy. Smear it!'

He did smear the dear little trefoil and of course it disappeared.

'God above. It's gone,' he told her. 'This is like going to Lourdes or Lough Derg.'

She turned to him, her eyes glistening, her face clear of any sign of age, any blemish or wen or freckle or pimple or wrinkle or spot or stain. There was nothing on her face but her face itself, nothing but the skin with which she was figuratively born – and she glowed. Unbuttoning her blouse she moved quickly towards him, stopping to run her hand in the grease on the floor. 'Undress,' she said; and when he did, she took the length of him and rubbed it with unguent till it rose slowly at an angle of ninety degrees and expanded in length till it seemed ready to accommodate the Tricolour, the Union Jack and Old Glory himself.

She drew him to the floor and when he entered her whispered: 'We'll stay here for ever. Let it be our honeymoon cottage. We'll buy it.'

'Can't,' he said. 'It's still a crime scene.'

'We could talk to what's-his-name, Cuthbert, the Assistant Commissioner. He'll take it off the list. Sinead will help. We'll find out who owns it.'

'Oh, I know who owns it. Bloom and Blixen.'

She laughed. 'Is that true?'

'Course. Reynolds signed the land over to them, I meant to tell you. I only found out when I looked at the deeds. They own every caravan between here and Oola.'

'Where is Oola?'

'Lovely little town between Limerick and Tipperary. If we're ever transferred down the country we'll ask for Oola.'

Eamon Dunphy collapsed in a rage on the bed. 'Wouldn't any man do what *I* did, Micky? Kill the killer of his own son.'

'Er . . . Course he would, Mister. Can I go now please?'

Dunphy kept the gun trained on him. 'But not here, oh no. Not in dear dirty Dublin. Makes a man bitter. Gives him the pip. You can dander up to the North and kill everything that moves but down here they'll hang you for doing the natural thing.'

It was just at that moment that a terrible racket began to sound from the landing outside. It would have been clear to any person of average intelligence and was even clear to Micky McManus that a number of quite possibly burly neophyte Templemore-trained gardaí were banging on the door in hopes of an arrest. 'Open up bejasus or we'll knock the door down.' Micky recognised the indigenous accents of Cork, Kerry and Mayo and since talk with their likes would probably be unhelpful he grabbed the weapon from Mr Dunphy's hand, sprang back out the window and fell amidst the aspidistra with three hundred pages of the Daedalus-begetter still stuffed down the front of his trousers.

Where was Gary Reynolds when a boy needed him?

'No problem, Sinead,' said the Assistant Commissioner. 'If that's what they want – a miserable caravan on the edge of nowhere – they can have it. All they have to do is arrest those Bloom and Blixen bitches and I'll give them every caravan from here to Oola.'

'Where's Oola?' said Sinead.

'Lovely hamlet between Limerick and Tipperary. They're known for the flannel sheets they give you. Very warming in chilly times.'

'I'd love that,' Sinead responded dreamily. She was already looking around for a younger man; someone who wouldn't see scratching his arse or belching as foreplay.

Inspector Pascal Greer had to sit in the car while Inspector Grainne O'Kelly arrested Mrs Bloom and Mrs Blixen. He was trying to conceal an erection which had refused to subside ever since being anointed with the papery potion. 'Don't worry,' said Grainne. 'Give grease a chance.'

Mrs Bloom and Mrs Blixen thought it highly amusing that they should be arrested again after the farce of their previous trial when all they'd had to do was bribe the judge. M'lud didn't find it quite so amusing. Having discovered that his payola was almost all counterfeit, he had sworn revenge and vowed on his own honour that next time proper and terrible justice would be done. Unless of course another payment was offered, triple the previous one, with the notes guaranteed for authenticity by certified accountants.

Through Wicklow and Carlow, Kilkenny and Tipperary, twisting and turning and doubling back – but Gary Reynolds knew in the depths of his heart that he would never shake off the black BMW. In such an assumption he was proved to be correct. Mrs Bloom and Mrs Blixen had seen to that. As long as you had the technology you didn't even have to be a good driver – and Eddie Lambert was anything but. All he had to do was place a microscopic device on Gary's van and follow the bleepedy-beep over hill and dale, by valley and mountain, by hamlet and stream, and usually back to the streets of Limerick.

Another miniature device planted in Gary's shoe allowed the king of the gossip columns to keep track of his quarry from Jury's Hotel across the river. 'Oh, the wonders of modern technology,' said Eddie to his pillow, though he wondered what the hell Gary was up to tonight; the shoe-implantment had been going beep beep beep for many hours and was now coming between the ginger scribe and his much-needed beauty sleep.

Why couldn't the fat bastard go to bed like a human and stop walking around the room going beep beep beep? He'd call the Royal George, that's what he'd do. He did do this and asked for Gary's room, subsequently telling its flabby inmate: 'For Christ's sake, I'm in the next room, a weary traveller trying to sleep. Would you ever stop walking up and down, you sad walrus.'

Gary told him: 'Fuck off', but Eddie merely dozed

off, amazed as always at the easy way the Irish have with language. After a while the beeping slowed down and the Titian-head tabloider knew it was safe to sleep. Except – except – what if the fatboy had had *a change of shoes*? But no. That was daft. Reynolds wasn't the type. He'd wear the same shoes till they fell off his feet, the great big incapable hippo-arsed gimp.

Next day weary Eddie went to the coffee shop across the street from the Royal George. But Lord love a dick – what the hell was this? Assistant Commissioner Cuthbert Staines and his assistant Sinead were present, chatting away with Professor Doonan Durrus and Ms Dymphna Morkan.

Did somebody drop a bomb on Dublin?

They saw him, oh, they did. And just when he wanted to ring Bloom and Blixen.

'Don't bother,' said the professor, reading his mind. 'They're in jail.'

But, as he spoke, in strode Bloom and Blixen followed by Micky McManus and Eamon Dunphy, Jason's father, not the other one. The professor, being a Limerickman and, therefore, a gentleman, jumped to his feet to offer a chair to one of the ladies. The Assistant Commissioner, usually a lout, followed suit. Mrs Bloom gave the professor a flirtatious little smile and Dymphna shot her a look of pure hatred. Mrs Blixen waggled her bosom at Cuthbert Staines. He grinned and gave Sinead a guilty look but she shrugged. Before too long, she was contentedly thinking, you'll be reduced to fingering yourself, you miserable lump.

'How . . . how . . .?' said Eddie Lambert.

'Every man has his price,' said Mrs Blixen. Mrs Bloom added smilingly: '*You* should know that, Eddie.'

'Oh, mon, oh, mon,' cried Micky in excitement, 'there's *Gary*. Yo, Gazzamon – over here, Homie!'

Gary came over and sat at the table.

'Now,' said the professor. 'We're reasonable people. If we have our differences, then we're here to settle them. The situation couldn't possibly be any more simple. Everyone wants something and it's usually what someone else has. I want Dymphna and Dymphna, I hope, wants me. Dymphna wants something that Micky has and Micky wants something that Dymphna has. Gary wants Micky and Micky wants Gary. Cuthbert here wants to be the Commissioner and the ladies Bloom and Blixen have arranged for that – though he, in return, has to consider what *they* want and what they want is control of Dublin and various counties to the east of us, not excluding the Isle of Man where many a happy pound idles and earns interest. Oh – the AC will also release Sinead from his clutches.'

'Ah, here now,' said the Assistant Commissioner, but the professor continued, insistent, his voice riding over him. 'Mr Dunphy wants the world to stop hounding him over a little understandable bloodshed and the ladies have taken care of that matter too. Young Eddie Lambert, who is here among us, has paid off his debt to the self-same ladies and is free to go back forthwith to his tabloid existence. Silence may be the best policy, Eddie.'

Lambert got up and looked around. 'You want a roid back to Dublin, babe?' he said to Sinead. 'I got me a beamer parked outsoid.' She rose quickly from her chair and left alongside him.

'In a moment,' the professor continued, 'Inspector Grainne O'Kelly will be here with her intended. What they want is each other and, strangely enough, the caravan once occupied by Tommy Reynolds. Ah! Look! Here they are. Here are the inspectors – and now we can proceed with our summit meeting. No, not here in Limerick but a few miles down the road in Oola, where there is peace and quiet and flannel sheets for those of us with the thin blood. Into the cars and let us meet in the mellow bar of the Hotel Oola. Ooh la la.

Off they went and adjourned to Oola.

Drink was taken and there was rowdiness.

'I am asking ye for the last time,' said the professor, lapsing into the antique *ye* so beloved of Limerickmen, 'to observe the proprieties. Ye are in the County Limerick now and it might be advisable to leave yeer jackeen ways behind ye.'

The inspectors, country people, took exception and pointed out they were not jackeens. The professor took this under advisement. 'Could we now move on?' he pleaded.

It was agreed that the inspectors, in return for laying off the sisters Bloom and Blixen, would take possession of the Reynolds caravan and environs in perpetuity. Glasses were raised to their marital bliss.

It was resolved that Eamon Dunphy's Dutch chemist would be immediately engaged to analyse the miraculous grease, and the one-page formula for its production held by Gary, with a view to future large-scale production, all profits to be shared among this group here present. Eamon himself would act as liaison with the Dutch chemist for they can't always be trusted, those lowlander pharmacists.

Gary Reynolds suggested that while Grainne had had a happy experience with the grease or ointment – his own had been different. The shoe he was wearing when he stepped into the grease had aged and wrinkled and was ready to fall off his foot. Upon subjecting it to closer scrutiny he had found a little thing like an electronic chip and he wondered – only wondered, mind you, no disrespect intended – if anyone here present had anything to do with that.

'It was for you own safety, love,' Mrs Bloom told him. 'Look at what happened to your poor father.'

Whereupon Gary reared up in high dudgeon. 'And that's another thing I want to bring up. *What* happened to my poor father?'

'Now, now,' said the professor mildly. 'No point in pursuing that. What's done is done and can't be undone. Your poor father wasn't a well man for some time, Gary. In truth he died of a heart attack, God rest him. He is gone above to his eternal reward and must be looking down on us now, smiling with the knowledge that what he left us in that baking tin is about to bring us a vast fortune.'

'Not with them bad bitches ready to rob us blind,' said Gary.

It was easy to see from the exchange of looks at the party that Gary's time on this planet would be more limited than necessary if he didn't curb his language and remarkably pronto; that Micky who loved him might soon be bereaved, perhaps driven into the arms of Madelene for a lifetime of joyless heterosexuality and listening to Daniel O'Donnell rather than Niggaz With Attitude. For each member of the assembly there was writing on the wall, the writing scrawled there by Bloom and Blixen, who were being closely and admonishingly watched by the professor and his bride-to-be.

'And now,' said the professor. 'Only one thing remains.

The matter of the manuscript known as *Yeats Is Dead!*'

Gary and Micky gave innocent glances as if to say, *We* don't have it.

But no use. There were too many fine minds in the room, all bent on profit.

'Dymphna has in her possession pages 300 to 600,' said the professor.

There was a silence.

'Various universities in Texas are vying for the manuscript – the complete manuscript, I mean. Austin is competing with Dallas which is competing with Houston which is offering millions, yes I said millions, with shares in oil wells and condominiums – or more accurately condominia – on glamorous Caribbean islands, first-class travel guaranteed.'

Micky shifted in his seat. Gary glared at him. Grainne said, 'Micky, come outside with me a minute.'

In the bright Oola moonlight she drew out his freckled schlong and rubbed it with the grease, the ointment from heaven, and as she stroked and caressed and massaged him he moaned, 'Ooooh, mon, ooh, me got the ting, take me to Jamaica, oooh, Gary, oooh, oooh.'

Inside they heard him and knew Grainne was doing God's work, that all would be well, that the pages would soon be reunited into one hefty unreadable manuscript which would challenge the decoding talents of hundreds of professors for hundreds of years – though Professor Doonan Durrus would not be among them.

Soon he would be retiring from Trinity College. Now that he had found love it was time to change his life. He had it in mind to make several large charitable donations. A Mrs Patsy Roberts would be receiving a substantial cheque. Soon, he knew, she would be fully restored to mental health. There were many other causes he and Dymphna wished to support, but one in particular was especially dear to his heart – a friend, a good man, who wanted to give up his job and write poetry. Professor Durrus would make sure that Dr Jim Joyce was able to do that soon.

He sat back in his chair and pondered his own happiness. He and Dymphna had already made a side-deal to secure a few jars of the ointment from the baking tin in Gary's little room at the Royal George Hotel.

But then, up and down the table and all around, side-deals of many descriptions were being struck. What would always keep this group united, in Dublin or the Caribbean or anywhere in the world, was the knowledge that everyone else was up to something. That, in the end, was a great comfort.

Especially when you knew, as Professor Durrus did, that James Joyce had never written anything called *Yeats Is Dead!*

He raised a silent glass to his old friend Tommy Reynolds. The greatest joker he had ever known.

The Writers

Roddy Doyle is the author of six widely acclaimed novels, *The Commitments*, *The Snapper*, *The Van*, *Paddy Clarke Ha Ha Ha*, *The Woman Who Walked Into Doors* and *A Star Called Henry*. He won the Booker Prize in 1993 for *Paddy Clarke Ha Ha Ha*. He wrote the script for the feature film *When Brendan Met Trudy*, which premiered in 2001.

Conor McPherson's plays include *The Good Thief*, *This Lime Tree Bower*, *St Nicholas*, *The Weir* and *Port Authority*. He won the 1997 Meyer Whitworth Award and the 1996 George Devine Award, a Guinness Ingenuity award in 1996 and the Stewart Parker Award in 1995. He also wrote *I Went Down* which won the Screen-writing Award at the San Sebastian Festival in 1997. His acclaimed film *Saltwater* was released in 2000.

Gene Kerrigan has written six non-fiction bestsellers including *Hard Cases, Another Country* and *This Great Little Nation* (with Pat Brennan). He was born in Dublin, where he writes for the *Sunday Independent*, often about political scandals and miscarriages of justice. He has been voted Irish Journalist of the Year on two occasions.

Gina Moxley's first play *Danti Dan* was produced at the Project Arts Centre, Dublin, in 1995. Following a national tour it transferred to the Hampstead Theatre, London. *Dog House* was commissioned by the Royal National Theatre, London. *Toupees and Snaredrums* (in collaboration with David Bolger) premiered on the Abbey Theatre's Peacock stage in 1998. Gina won the Stewart Parker Award in 1996. She is currently writing a play for the Royal Court Theatre, London.

Marian Keyes began writing short stories in 1993. Her first novel, *Watermelon*, was published in 1996 and immediately became a huge international bestseller, as did her subsequent novels *Lucy Sullivan Is Getting Married*, *Rachel's Holiday*, *Last Chance Saloon* and *Sushi for Beginners*.

Anthony Cronin is one of Ireland's most distinguished men of letters. His books include fiction (*The Life of Reily*), criticism (*A Question of Modernity*) and a classic memoir of Dublin literary life (*Dead as Doornails*). He has also published many volumes of poetry, and acclaimed biographies of Flann O'Brien and Samuel Beckett.

Owen O'Neill is a writer, actor and stand-up comedian who has performed all over the world. He wrote and starred in *Shooting to Stardom*, which won the Irish Short Film Award at the 1994 Cork Film Festival. Owen's one man show, *It's A Bit Like This*, was short-listed for the 1994 Perrier Award at the Edinburgh Festival, and in 1998 he won the LWT writing award for his one-man play *Off My Face*.

Hugo Hamilton was born in Dublin of Irish/German parentage. His books include the acclaimed novels

Surrogate City, The Last Shot, The Love Test, Sad Bastard and *Headbanger*. In 1992 he was awarded the Rooney Prize for Irish Literature. His latest novel, *Sucking Diesel*, will be published in Autumn 2001.

Joseph O'Connor's debut novel *Cowboys And Indians* was shortlisted for the Whitbread Prize. Among his subsequent works are the novels *Desperadoes, The Salesman* and *Inishowen*, the short story collection *True Believers*, the stage play *Red Roses and Petrol* and the anthology of comic journalism *The Secret World of the Irish Male*. His work has won many prizes, including the Macaulay Fellowship of the Irish Arts Council and the Miramax Ireland Screenwriting Award.

Tom Humphries is an award-winning sportswriter with the *Irish Times*. He has written three bestselling non-fiction books: *The Legend of Jack Charlton, Green Fields: Gaelic Sport in Ireland* and *Sonia O'Sullivan: Running To Stand Still*. His journalism has been published in Ireland, Britain and the United States and he has been voted Irish Sportswriter of the Year on three occasions.

Pauline McLynn shot to fame playing the inimitable Mrs Doyle in *Father Ted* and has since appeared in Alan Parker's film adaptation of *Angela's Ashes* and the comedy *Dark Ages*. Her first novel, *Something for the Weekend*, was published in 2000 and became a bestseller. Her second novel, *Better than a Rest*, has just been published.

Charlie O'Neill won the Stewart Parker Award for his acclaimed first play *Rosie and Starwars*. His most recent play, *Hupnouse*, was produced by Barabbas Theatre in

Dublin and received ecstatic reviews. He is now developing a screenplay with Rough Magic Films.

Donal O'Kelly is an actor and playwright. His solo plays, *Catalpa* and *Bat the Father, Rabbit the Son* have travelled the world to high acclaim. Other plays include *Judas of the Gallarus*, *Asylum! Asylum!*, *Farawayan*, *Trickledown Town* and *Hughie on the Wires*. In 1999 he was awarded the Irish-American Cultural Institute Butler Literary Award.

Gerard Stembridge is a playwright and filmmaker. His theatre plays include *Lovechild*, *The Girls of Summer* and *The Gay Detective*. His radio writing includes the satirical series *Scrap Saturday* and the BBC play *Daisy the Cow Who Talked*. For television he wrote and directed *The Truth About Claire* and *Black Day At Blackrock*. His screenplays are *Nora* (co-written with Pat Murphy) and *Ordinary Decent Criminal*, while he wrote and directed two other films, *Guiltrip* and *About Adam*.

Frank McCourt taught for thirty years in various New York high schools and city colleges. His volumes of memoirs *Angela's Ashes* and *'Tis* were bestsellers all over the world, the former selling four million copies and winning the Pulitzer Prize. His play, *The Irish And How They Got That Way*, has been produced in New York, Boston, Chicago and Melbourne, Australia. He lives in New York.

The Team

The editor and authors would like to sincerely thank our two Project Directors: John Sutton, who managed all business aspects of *Yeats is Dead!*, and whose tenacity, managerial skills and hard work were essential in bringing it from idea to reality, and Sean Love of Amnesty International's Irish section for his unwavering dedication, encouragement and commitment. Many thanks are also owed to our Project Managers: Ann Sheridan, who co-ordinated the effort with boundless efficiency, good humour and coolness under pressure, and Phill McCaughey whose patience and infectious enthusiasm were as invaluable as her organisational ingenuity. Throughout the four-year gestation of *Yeats is Dead!* administrative support and project management were provided by Public Communications Centre, Dublin: enormous thanks are due to all the staff.

Everyone involved in originating, writing and developing *Yeats is Dead!* would like to thank Ania Corless at David Higham Associates, who agreed to come on board as the book's Foreign Rights agent, and Liz Sich and Melody Odusanya of Colman Getty PR who managed the media aspects of publication. Finally we want to express warmest thanks to Dan Franklin, his assistant Jason Arthur, and everyone at Random House for publishing our book with such energy, care and skill.

Support Amnesty International

Individual supporters of Amnesty International can have a tremendous impact on Human Rights. When Amnesty members heard that Nigerian editor Chris Anyanwu had been sentenced to fifteen years in prison for her beliefs they began to campaign for her release. She was freed after three years.

Later she wrote: 'It is impossible to paint an accurate picture of my reactions as I sat in that tiny cell, the floor carpeted with cards and envelopes, generated through Amnesty's efforts. . . I knew that I was not alone – but all these cards are little drops of water that combine to create an avalanche of pressure.'

By buying this book, you have already helped to promote the cause of Human Rights. You have contributed to the ongoing day-to-day fight against the imprisonment of prisoners of conscience and the use of torture and execution. Your support has made a real difference – but we can all easily do more. Amnesty gets results because of its supporters. The more supporters it has, the more people can be helped. Please see below for how you can support your country's section of Amnesty International.

With many thanks,

Joe O'Connor

Joe O'Connor, Editor, *Yeats Is Dead!*

If you are not a member of Amnesty you can join now, simply by contacting the relevant Amnesty office listed opposite. If there is no number listed for your country please contact the International Secretariat. Thank you again for your support.